Murder Under the Hammer

Colin Holcombe

Chapter One

The outside temperature was just 12 degrees as Thomas Carter made his way along Oxley Street to his little Opticians business. It was a little cool for early June but he knew that as soon as he was inside his little optician's shop, his valued assistant Cathleen would have a steaming hot cup of black coffee for him.

Thomas had left his old life in Bristol, England, behind him, when his marriage to Charlotte had broken down. He'd felt he needed a completely new start in life and had moved half way around the world to Campbelltown, Sydney, Australia in 1998.

His little optician's business was doing well enough, but the mortgage on his house, combined with a not unsubstantial business loan, was keeping him working, even though he longed to retire. His wish for retirement wasn't because he no longer enjoyed his work, he did, and it wasn't because he was old, quite the contrary in fact, he was only fifty years of age, but on moving to Australia he had discover a love of both sailing and scuba diving. If he was able to retire now, he would have a lot more time to enjoy his recently discovered interests.

Entering his place of business, his assistant greeted him with her usual cheery smile as he walked through the door, "Good morning Mr Carter," she said, in the broad Irish accent that endeared her to his customers and that he supposed she would now, never lose. In fact, he did sometimes wonder whether her accent was now practised and put on, rather than still natural.

"I see your first appointment's not until ten, so I'll get you your coffee," Cathleen continued, "it's a little nippy this morning, don't you think?"

"Thank you, Cathleen, that would be lovely, did you get a paper on your way in this morning?"

"You know I did, I'll bring it to you with your coffee."

Both Thomas and Cathleen like to keep up with what was happening in the world, and as Cathleen always bought a morning paper on her way into work, Thomas had got into the habit of reading Cathleen's paper, rather than buying his own. Sitting at his desk at the back of the shop, he looked at his diary to see what the day had in store while he waited for Cathleen and his coffee to appear. Eventually Cathleen emerged from the small kitchenette that was just behind his desk and asked, as she always did, "Would you like to read my paper then while you enjoy your coffee?"

"Is there anything interesting in the paper today?" he enquired.

"Not really, just the usual rubbish really, although you'll no doubt be pleased to hear your cricket team is doing well in England....there's an interesting article about pollution in the world's oceans....and, oh! and there's a story about some lucky person in

England...Bristol actually...isn't that where you're from originally?"

"Yes that's right, I was born in Bristol," answered Thomas, his interest aroused, "how has this person been lucky?"

"Well, they just put a bronze sculpture up for auction, and would you believe it!...it fetched over three million English pounds, now I'd call that pretty lucky, wouldn't you?"

"I would indeed, that does seem an extraordinary amount of money, what was the sculpture of for goodness sake?"

"It's of an African slave, it says here...a female slave kneeling on the ground with her hands raised," Cathleen continued, "her chains are broken apart and apparently that's to symbolise her freedom and the end of the slave trade, but I have to say that she doesn't look all that happy to me, if I'd just been released from slavery I think I'd be up on me feet doing a jig, wouldn't you?"

The hair on the back of Thomas's neck stood on end, and rising from his chair he entered the little kitchenette, "Is there a picture of this sculpture," he almost demanded, making Cathleen jump and almost spill boiling water as she poured out the coffee, "can I see it?"

Cathleen was more than a little shocked by Thomas's abrupt manner and quickly put down the kettle she was holding to pass him the paper, "There it is," she said pointing, "top right of the arts page."

Thomas took the paper from her and stared at the picture of the bronze as if he'd seen a ghost.

"Is everything all right Mr Carter?" she asked, a little confused by his reaction, "Do you want to sit down, are you ill or something, you've gone quite pale."

Thomas read the article that accompanied the picture.

"Exciting find. A bronze sculpture depicting a female African slave in a kneeling posture with her hands raised and spread wide, and her shackles broken, was sold in Bristol, England last Friday 25th May.

Made and signed by Irish sculptor, John Edward Carew (1785–1868) who moved to London in 1809, it was commissioned by abolitionist, William Wilberforce that same year to commemorate the passing of The Slave Trade Act of 1807.

It went under the hammer for a record £3,200,000. The price realised exceeded all expectations and was a new record price for a piece by that artist. The exceptional price obtained for the piece was put down to its historical importance.

In 1787 William Wilberforce came into contact with Thomas Clarkson and a group of anti-slave-trade activists, including Granville Sharp, Hannah More, and Charles Middleton. They persuaded Wilberforce to take on the cause of abolition and he soon became one of the leading English abolitionists. He headed the parliamentary campaign against the British slave trade for twenty years until the passage of the Slave Trade Act of 1807." The bronze is believed to have been purchased by an American museum."

Carter appeared deep in thought for a moment and the two of them stood perfectly still, as if acting out some strange Victorian stage tableau. Then Thomas announced to his bewildered assistant, "Cathleen.....I need you to call Dianne in to cover my appointments for a few days....I have to go to England for a while...I'll be relying on you to keep things going here until I get back."

Shocked, Cathleen replied, "I'll do what I can of course Mr Carter, but when will you be going?"

"Right away, I'm sorry to dump you in it like this Cathleen, but you know the business inside out, I know you can cope. Apologise to everyone for me, will you?"

"But this is really short notice Thomas....why do you have to go to England so suddenly?....and how long will you be gone?"

Carter began walking towards the door with Cathleen's paper still in hand, "I'm not sure how long for, I'm sorry, but a few days at least, I'll ring you from England when I know more," and with that he was out of the door and gone, leaving an extremely bemused Cathleen staring out of the window after him.

"Well there's a fine kettle of fish," she muttered to herself

****

Four days after Thomas Carter's unexpected departure from Australia and his return to Bristol, a car

9

pulled into the kerb and parked in a space overlooking one of Bristol's favourite beauty spots, The Sea Walls, overlooking the Avon Gorge. The driver of the car looked around and listened for tell-tale signs that anyone else was about. The actions that he was about to engage in, had by their very nature, to be clandestine. Although he didn't expect anyone else to be at this location at two-thirty in the morning, he was nervous and had to constantly check that he was alone.

As he got out of his vehicle, he could feel himself trembling and he had to steady himself against the car for a moment before proceeding. The cloud cover that had been present for most of the day meant that the night was warm, and, more importantly for his purpose, dark. All was as quiet as expected.

During the day, this beauty spot above the Avon Gorge would have been teaming with visitors, joggers and sight-seers, all anxious for a view of Brunel's magnificent Clifton Suspension Bridge that spans the Avon Gorge some 245 feet above the river Avon. At night, there could always be the odd stray insomniac, unable to stay in bed, or a car with a courting couple inside, hoping, as he was, that they were the only ones about, but it was he thought, a bit late, even for young love to be out and about.

Without properly shutting the car door, afraid of the noise it would make, he walked across to the cliff edge. It was protected by a low wall some two-foot-high that was surmounted with Victorian iron railings. The railings consisted of decorative turned uprights every six foot or so, with two horizontal bars joining then together. Horrible, unsightly, twenty-first century wire mesh, had been added at the back to stop the very young, or the very stupid, from climbing between the bars.

With a fresh look about he placed one foot on top of the low wall and grabbing hold of the top rail he pulled himself up so that he could peer over the edge.

He looked out into the darkness where the best part of three hundred feet below him were the twinkling street lights of the Portway, a busy main road that follows the meanderings of the river. The other side of the river, the Leigh Woods side, was in almost complete darkness, illuminated only slightly when the moonlight found a gap in the clouds. On that side, the steep sides of the gorge rise up from railway line and old towpath that snake their way along the riverbank. The part of the gorge where he now stood was at almost its steepest part, and he thought, ideal for his purpose.

This was it then, he couldn't put it off any longer, with a final look around he returned to his car and opened the boot. Seeing the dead body staring back at him with lifeless eyes made him wonder, not for the first time that night, whether he was actually up to the task that lay before him. He would have to bear the weight, not just of the body, but of the guilt of his actions as well.

Although he was a big man and kept fit and the body was that of a short slight man it had nevertheless been an effort getting the body into the car boot by

11

himself. Lifting it up and over the wall and railings would be even more of a task, and might still prove to be beyond him.

Leaning forward into the boot, his hands still trembling, he caught hold of the top half of the body and pulled it towards him. Then, crouching down low, he lifted the two arms and the head over his right shoulder. Straightening up, and at the same time manoeuvring the body so that its waist was balanced over his shoulder he stood up, at the same time wrapping an arm around the corpse's legs to prevent it slipping.

Again, he looked nervously around before proceeding towards the railings for a second time. Supporting the weight of the body on his shoulder whilst standing still was relatively easy for a man of his build, but walking with it was something else, however, after a supreme effort he found himself standing before the railings once more. Grasping hold of the top rail with his left hand and holding the body in place with his right, he placed his right foot on the top of the wall for the second time that night and attempted to pull himself aloft.

He almost lost his grip and tumbled backwards. In the end he had to let go of his victim's legs and trusting that having both arms raised would keep the body draped over his shoulder, he took hold of the top rail with both hands this time. Hauling himself up in this manner also proved an impossible task. He realised that he had approached the problem in entirely the wrong way, there was simply no way he could get the body over the top of the railings on his own like this, not with the body over his shoulder anyway.

He allowed the body to slip off his shoulder but with some difficulty he kept it upright wedged between the railings and his own body. He then managed, with some considerable effort, to turn it so that it was facing out towards the cliff face. The top rail was just chest height, so he was able, again with a little difficulty, to drape the arms of his victim over the top, grasp the body in a bear-hug just below its hips and heave upwards. He felt great relief when the top part of the body slumped forward over the top rail, as he was then able to grasp the lower part of the legs and tip them up and over as well.

The relief he felt as the body disappeared from sight was immeasurable. He turned and slumped back, resting his buttocks against the low wall while he recovered some composure and got his breath back. He held one hand out flat in front of himself and watched it shaking uncontrollably.

He actually began to feel sorry for himself, how had he ever got himself into such a mess....well....greed, that was how it had all started, but how was it now going to end?

After a couple of minutes recovery time interspersed with guilt and self-doubt, he again turned and hoisted himself into a standing position atop the wall, peering over the edge for any sign of the body.

There was none, not even when the moonlight made its infrequent appearance, and quite what he would have done about it if there had been, he neither knew nor cared, his task was complete. All he had to do now was live the rest of his life with the knowledge that he had taken someone else's.

He was just beginning to feel that his heart had some chance of returning to a normal beat, when he heard footsteps. Panicking slightly, he turned to look in the direction he had heard them. A young courting couple were strolling towards him arm in arm. He cursed his luck, but thankfully, they appeared oblivious to their surroundings.

They were quite close when they appeared to notice him for the first time and they just stopped and stared. It occurred to him that, seeing him standing on top of the wall as he was at this time of night, they might think that he was contemplating suicide and about to jump.

"It's all right," he called to them in as calm a voice as he could muster, "I'm not thinking of jumping or anything. I'm just trying to get some air to clear my head, it's a lovely night, isn't it?"

The couple said nothing, and although they briefly looked in his direction they appeared somewhat indifferent to him, only having eyes for each other, and as they resumed their walk he wondered if their reaction to his presence would have been any different if he had been about to jump.

He found himself wondering how long they had been approaching before he heard them and whether they had seen him with the body, but everything about their manner suggested not.

Still somewhat anxious he returned to his car. The presence of the couple had been unfortunate but there was nothing he could do about it, so he got back into his car and after a few deep breaths to calm his nerves, he drove away. He was ready for some sleep now, secretly disposing of a body had proved exhausting. He had already cleared up the mess back at his office so apart from giving the car boot a good valet and disposing of the clothes he was wearing, everything was taken care of. He slowly began to relax a little more.

On the journey back, although physically he was feeling more relaxed, his mind was in turmoil and he kept replaying the events of the day, wondering if any of them would cause him nightmares.

****

Ian Cable had been a bird watcher all his life, ever since his dad had first pointed to a kestrel hovering over a field when he was just seven years of age. He had always found the Clifton Suspension Bridge a good vantage point and was there today because peregrine falcons had been spotted on the Clifton side. Standing as he was, on the Leigh Woods side of the bridge, he trained his binoculars onto the cliff face below that part of the Downs known as The Sea Walls. He had travelled to some exotic locations around the world in the pursuit of his hobby, but being here at the Avon Gorge could compare favourably with any of them in his book.

The peregrine falcons, however, appeared to disagree with him, and had so far failed to put in an appearance. He was beginning to think that the information he'd been given was wrong and that he was wasting his time.

Just to the right of his present search area, about forty feet or so from the top of the cliff, there was an outcrop of vegetation and there was something about it that made him zoom in. On closer inspection, what he'd at first thought was just a strip of old material that must have been blowing in the wind and been snagged by the bushes, now looked like the sleeve of a jacket! Not only that! Just above it to the left was what, for all the world, looked like a trouser leg. Focusing in again there could be no doubt about it, a shoeless foot protruded from the end!

Was this some kind of student prank? he wondered, if it was, it was very convincing. He refocused his binoculars for a third time there could be no question at all now, there was a man's body caught up in the outcrop of vegetation, and there was no sign of movement coming from it. With his heart now racing he took out his mobile phone and dialled 999.

****

Inspector Paul Manley hated driving, and would normally prefer to be driven by Constable June Kelly, who had worked with him now for over three years. June was a good driver, having completed the advanced driving course with flying colours. Standing five foot seven with short, light brown hair she stood out as an attractive, smartly dressed woman, she was also, in Pauls mind, a clever detective, good company and an asset to the team.

June viewed Paul in a similar way, at six foot one with slightly wavy brown hair and trim physique most women regarded him as good looking. She'd become close to Paul and his wife Margaret over the years and viewed Paul as her mentor and Margaret as a friend.

Today, Paul was picking up his new car, a chrome blue Ford Mondeo, and he had a decision to make, he was one of only a handful of detective inspectors who regularly use their own cars for work, but now that he had a bright shiny new Mondeo, he was re-thinking it and considering using a police owned vehicle instead, he had a week to make up his mind.

The showroom assistant had just officially handed the vehicle over and June had just naturally slipped into the driver's seat.

Paul stood beside the driver's door and said, "Out...I'll drive."

"But you never drive Guv."

"Well today's different June, I've got a new toy and I want to play with it, if that's alright with you, so out."

June reluctantly exited the car just as Paul's mobile rang and after listening for a moment he said, "Come on, get in, we've got a call."

Paul slid in behind the wheel and drove off with June in the passenger seat, "Where are we going Guv?" she asked.

"The Sea Walls, sounds as if they have found a jumper up there."

"I don't remember ever seeing you in a jumper Guv?" asked June grinning.

Inspector Paul Manley, and June Kelly arrived at the scene, at the same time as Detective Sergeant Reg Evans, another valued member of Paul's team and at fifty-one the most experienced. They could see that a large area of The Sea Walls and surrounding Downs had already been cordoned off and that a team from cliff rescue were in the process of stowing away their equipment, having already recovered a body from the cliff face.

The Sea Walls is a popular place for visitors to Bristol. It's a good spot to get a panoramic view of the Avon Gorge and the Clifton Suspension Bridge. A semi-circular road separates the wide paved viewing area from one of the larger flat areas of The Downs, an area of over 400 acres owned partly by Bristol City Council and partly by The Society of Merchant Venturers.

As Paul and his colleagues pulled in, they could see that a body had been retrieved and was now laid on a groundsheet on the grass opposite the viewing area and that police officers were erecting a white tent around it to protect it from the elements and ward off prying eyes. Standing by the body was Doctor Dorothy Lansbury, a new appointment to the forensic team, and alongside her was a young uniformed constable who Paul didn't recognise and looked just a little uneasy.

Constable John Davis turned his attention to Paul and the others as they approached and introduced himself, "Constable Davis Sir. I was the first on the scene."

"I'm Inspector Manley and this is Sergeant Evans and Constable Kelly," said Paul in response, "what exactly has happened here constable."

"A bird watcher, Sir, that's him over there," replied Davis, pointing at a man in blue jeans and a brown gilet with both a camera and a pair of binoculars hanging around his neck and who was taking a keen interest in proceedings. "Ian Cable his name is Sir. He was using binoculars from the Leigh Woods side of the bridge and spotted the body about forty feet down from the top caught in an outcrop of vegetation and he called 999. Emergency services called us and the cliff recue boys who have just retrieved the body. Cliff rescue are equipped with helmet cams Sir and I asked them to record as much detail of the site as they could before moving the body. I'm not sure if that will be of any help at all, Sir?"

"No, I'm not sure if it will be any help either constable." said Paul, "but it was a good call, well done."

"Thank you, Sir."

Doctor Lansbury strolled over and joined the group, "Paul, Reg. June, I take it you're not here for the view?"

"That's right," said June, before Paul had a chance to reply, "although I have just spotted an ice-cream van over there," she said pointing.

"Yes, I saw that too." replied Lansbury, "I could just fancy an ice-cream myself."

"Shall we try and concentrate on the job in hand June, Doctor, we're not on holiday here," said Paul, trying to sound firm but not really succeeding, "Reg can get you both an ice-cream after we've finished here," he announced.

Reg looked slightly irked, "Me.... Why is it always me that buys the ice-creams?"

"Because you're one of the best Reg," said June, grinning from ear to ear.

Reg. wandered over to have a closer look at the body as Paul asked, "What can you tell us Doctor, I assume it's a suicide."

"I think you assume wrong Paul. Most jumpers choose to go off the bridge rather than the cliffs," Doctor Lansbury could see that Paul was about to ask why and pre-empted his question, "it makes for a more

20

predictable outcome, you see. This chap also has a substantial injury to the back of his head, that I think is too massive to have been sustained in the relatively short fall he had. I think the unfortunate chap was walloped over the head with something round and heavy."

"Walloped?" queried Paul.

"Well struck then, if you prefer, I just happen to like the word walloped, I use it whenever the opportunity arises."

"If it is a word?" queried Paul "you don't think it could have been caused by hitting his head on a rock in the fall?"

"No, I don't think the body would have gained enough momentum to have caused that amount of damage, he didn't actually fall all that far before getting caught up. Whatever it was that walloped him, there was considerable force behind it, which would suggest to me that it was wielded by someone. I should be able to tell you more after I've had a better look at him back at the ranch."

"Ranch?"

Doctor Lansbury smiled, "Really Paul, are you going to question every word I choose to use? For your information, if strangers ask me what I do for a living, I always tell them I work on a ranch, ranch is another word I like….and I think it sounds better than telling them I cut up dead people."

Paul stared at her and mulled over her answer before replying, "OK, good call. Any identification on the body?"

Constable Davis, who had been somewhat bemused by the casual nature of the conversation between obviously experienced professionals, handed Paul a wallet, "This was in his pocket Sir, along with a handkerchief and a hotel room key, you know, one of those plastic credit card looking things. It looks as if he was staying at The Clifton Gorge Hotel at least that's the name on the key. The man's name is, or rather was, Thomas Carter, and there's an Australian driving licence in that name in the wallet. But that was all Sir there were no car keys."

"Well, if he was staying at a hotel he's either on holiday or here on business," replied Paul, "either way he may have come by train and been getting around by taxi." He then turned to Reg who had returned from the tent that was now fully erected, "Reg, our rancher here says our man was murdered, or at least she believes he was, walloped over the head before he went over the cliff. Now, if that's the case, there's just a chance it could have happened here. So get SOCO up here would you, this could be a crime scene that we've all been trampling over."

"Our rancher Guv?"

"It's a long story Reg... Get some help up here to take over from you when you've sorted things out here. June can drive me over to The Clifton Gorge Hotel and we'll have a look at our victim's room...oh! hang on, I suppose there's always a chance that could be our murder scene, if it turns out not to be here, so better get someone from SOCO to meet June and I there as well."

"Will do Guv." said Reg looking over at Doctor Lansbury for an explanation of rancher which was unforthcoming.

****

The journey to, The Clifton Gorge Hotel, was less than three miles and when June and Paul pulled up outside, June said, "Thanks for letting me drive the new car, Guv, it's lovely."

"Yeh, well I got in the wrong door out of habit, that was all, I'll be driving back after we've finished here."

After negotiating the revolving doors, the pair went straight to the reception desk, behind which a man and a woman were deep in conversation. When they saw them approaching, the man turned away and entered the small office behind the desk and the young woman smiled at them, as if seeing them was the highlight of her day.

"Good morning, welcome to The Clifton Gorge Hotel, my name is Sam, how may I help you?"

Showing his warrant card to her Paul said, "Well Sam, I have reason to believe you have a Thomas Carter staying here?"

"After scrutinising Paul's warrant card as if it had been written in miniature the receptionist checked the computer on her desk, "Yes that's right inspector, he's staying in room 104 on the first floor, is there a problem? if so, I should call the manager."

"Mr Carter has been involved in an incident I'm afraid, and we'll need access to his room, and nobody else should go in there until we give the all clear. And I think you should inform your manager Sam, we may need the room for a while. Can you tell me, how long was Mr Carter booked in for?"

The receptionist, who now seemed a little flustered, checked the register again, "Until Monday, inspector, that's June 23rd. But I don't think I should let you have access to his room just because he's been injured or something."

"Well I'm afraid Mr Carter's injuries have proved fatal, Sam, and we are investigating the circumstances of his death, so we will need access. When did he book in?" The receptionist looked even more shocked now, but checking the computer again before replying "That was on Monday the 11th June."

"Who booked him in?"

"I did."

"Did he say why he was here? Was it for business or pleasure, do you know?"

"I asked him if he was on holiday, and he said he had some business to sort out and that he was going to visit some old friends while he was here."

"Did he say who these old friends were." asked Paul, just as June caught his arm and indicated that two officers from SOCO had just walked in.

June beckoned the men from SOCO over as the receptionist concluded, "No, he didn't say, but I did ring a taxi firm for him a couple of times. This is their card," The receptionist handed Paul one of a pile of business cards from Clifton Taxis that were in a neat little pile on a silver salver on the desk.

Thanking her, Paul turned to the two new arrivals who simply introduced themselves as Ben and Chris.

"Hi guys, it's room 104 on the first floor I want you to look at, here's the key," said Paul, handing the taller of the two men the key-card he had been given from the victims pocket, "It could be a crime scene, and we don't know, if it was or not. I need you to check it out, so that we can get in and search it without messing up a potential murder scene. Let me know as soon as your sure, one way or the other."

"OK Sir," acknowledge Ben, who seemed to be the more senior of the two, "are we looking for anything in particular?"

"Any sign of a struggle or blood of course, a murder weapon maybe, which we believe was a heavy round object of some sort, but that's all we have at the moment, I just need to know if you think there could have been a struggle or a murder in there. We'll wait in the lounge to hear from you."

The two men strode off in the direction of the stairs carrying four metal cases and a large rucksack between them. Paul and June meanwhile, ordered coffee and sat in the lounge waiting for the all clear on Carter's room and going over what they had gleaned so far.

"What are your thoughts Guv, do you think our man could have been killed here?"

"I think it's rather unlikely June. Whoever killed him would have had their work cut out to get the body out of the hotel unseen but I want to be absolutely sure before we search his room."

"What about up at the Sea Wall?"

"No, I don't think he was killed there either. It's most likely he met his killer during the day and it's far too busy up there for it not to have been witnessed. Now, if we assume the body was dumped late at night, we need to find out if anybody saw anything, even if it was just a car parked there or someone hanging around and looking suspicious. When we get back to the station I want you to arrange for an appeal in the papers and local radio and get some notices printed to be displayed around the Sea Walls and surrounding area, you know the sort of thing....Did you see anyone acting suspiciously....blah blah."

As things turned out, Paul and June didn't have long to wait before Chris and Ben returned after conducting their examination of Carter's room, so they both downed the last of their coffee and stood up to greet them, "Anything at all?" asked Paul expectantly.

"No Inspector," said Ben, there is nothing at all to suggest that anything out of the ordinary took place in room 104 recently, no sign of any blood at all, either in the bedroom or the bathroom, nothing knocked over, nothing broken, nothing out of place at all."

"Thank you," said Paul as the men returned the key card to him and left. He and June then made their way up to the room via the stairs.

"Have you got something against lifts, Guv?" asked June.

"Not feeling a little out of condition are you June?"

"No! why, do you think I look out of condition, Guv?" asked June, checking herself in the large ornate mirror on the landing as they went past.

"No, I'm just getting the lay of the land, June, we'll come back down in the lift, that way we don't miss anything."

"That's what I thought we were doing Guv."

Once inside the room, June walked straight across to the far side, passed the foot of the double bed and opened the small suitcase that rested on the luggage rack beside the window, "He travelled light Guv," she remarked "all the way from Australia with just this small case, I would have had trouble getting my smalls and makeup in here. Have you found anything, Guv?"

"There's an address book on the bedside table that could be useful in tracking down the old friends he was supposed to be seeing," Paul replied, as he flicked through the book, "it's got both English and Australian addresses and numbers in it, so we'll take that with us."

Paul turned and looked up from the address book in his hand, when a man knocked and entered the room. Dressed it what looked like an expensive suit the new arrival introduced himself, "Hello, I'm George Neil, the Hotel Manager, he stated with authority, "is all this going to take very long?"

Paul held out his hand and the two men shook, "I'm Inspector Manley and this is Constable Kelly," said Paul, introducing himself, "I'm sorry if our investigation interferes in any way Mr Neil, but we will need this room sealed for a while."

"Really, well that is rather inconvenient Inspector, I should like to get the room re-booked as soon as possible."

"Do you know if Mr Carter pre-paid for his room Mr Neil, or is the money still owing, because as I understand from your receptionist, Sam, the man was booked in until the 23rd, it's only the 15th today."

"Well that's as maybe Inspector, but I don't understand why you need the room at all, I understand from my receptionist that Mr Carter has been involved in a fatal accident, and tragic as that is...."

"The word I actually used was incident, not accident Mr Neil, we're treating Mr Carter's death as suspicious until we know otherwise."

"Oh my god! Well yes, in that case, I'm sorry, that must have come across as very uncaring of me. I will seal the room for you of course but I'd prefer to put a notice on it to say not to enter because it's being cleaned or something, rather than have that horrible yellow tape of yours put across the door, if that's alright. It could be very off-putting for our other guests. I'll leave you to it then Inspector, unless there's something else I can help you with?"

"Is there a safe in the room?" asked Paul.

"Yes, there's one in every room Inspector, it's in here, I'll show you."

The manager slid open the end door of the triple wardrobe to reveal a column of shelves in which was incorporated a small safe, "Would you like me to open it for you Inspector?"

"Please."

After punching a four-digit code into the keypad on the side, the manager opened the safe door and repeated, "I'll leave you to it now," and handing Paul a business card, continued, "if there's any other way I can be of assistance, my number is on there Inspector."

"Thank you, but that's all for now, you will inform all your staff that the room is out of bounds until further notice?"

"Yes of course."

Just as the hotel manager was about to exit the door he stopped and appeared suddenly concerned, "This isn't connected to anything involving....you know...Russian nerve agents or anything is it?...I mean..."

"No, no, nothing like that I can assure you, there is no risk to your staff or guests."

"Thank you, Inspector, you probably think I'm being a little paranoid, but after all that Salisbury, Novichok business, you just don't know what to expect, do you."

"No, I quite understand," said Paul, "you can't be too careful these days. I'll let you know as soon as we've finished with the room."

After the manager had left, Paul removed and examined the contents of the small safe. Inside he found four hundred and twenty pounds in notes, a passport in the name of Thomas A. Carter, the picture in which confirmed that the body was definitely that of Thomas Carter, some travel documents, including a ticket for a return flight from Heathrow to Sydney Australia and a newspaper cutting from an Australian newspaper, The Sydney Morning Herald.

"What have you got there, Guv," asked June.

"Passport, travel papers and a newspaper clipping from an Australian paper dated 31st May this year, listen to this, it reads."

"Exciting find. A bronze sculpture depicting a female African slave in a kneeling posture with her hands raised and spread wide, and her shackles broken, was sold in Bristol, England last Friday 25th May.

Made and signed by Irish sculptor, John Edward Carew (1785–1868) who moved to London in 1809, it was commissioned by abolitionist, William Wilberforce that same year to commemorate the passing of The Slave Trade Act of 1807.

It went under the hammer for a record £3,200,000. The price realised exceeded all expectations and was a new record price for a piece by that artist. The exceptional price obtained for the piece was put down to its historical importance.

In 1787 William Wilberforce came into contact with Thomas Clarkson and a group of anti-slave-trade activists, including Granville Sharp, Hannah More, and Charles Middleton. They persuaded Wilberforce to take on the cause of abolition and he soon became one of the leading English abolitionists. He headed the parliamentary campaign against the British slave trade for twenty years until the passage of the Slave Trade Act of 1807." The bronze is believed to have been purchased by an American museum."

"What do you make of it, Guv? The article must have meant something to our victim, or else why would he keep in in the safe with his important documents?"

"I have no idea June, but like you say, he must have thought it important. It refers to recent events that have taken place locally as well, so I wonder if it has

31

something to do with the reason he came here? Come on June let's get back and see what the rest of the team think about it all, we'll get someone else to finish up here"

"OK Guv. I certainly can't see anything else of any significance."

As they were leaving the room the manager returned with a type written notice that he taped to the door,

NO ADMITTANCE. ROOM CLOSED FOR
MAINTENANCE.

"There you are Inspector, that should do the job, without alarming guests."

Chapter Two

The room were Paul and his team work is a large rectangular area containing nine desks, only seven of which are in permanent use. His team hadn't changed worked since Paul was made an Inspector three years earlier, and in which time they have cleared up three high profile murder cases.

At one end of the room is a separate sub-office, partitioned off from the rest of the room by glass topped panels. This separate area serves as Paul's office and contains just the one desk, and although fitted with a door, the door is seldom closed. Paul preferred not to have barriers between the team and himself and could often be found working at one of the free desks in the main room, so as to feel more a part of the team, rather than its boss.

As he stood before the room's three crime-boards, the team looked on attentively.

"So far, we have a victim by the name of Thomas A. Carter," Paul began, "coming to England from Australia to see old friends and sort a few things out, what things we don't know, they could have been business or personal. Has anyone found out any more about him?"

John Campbell was the first to speak up, "I've now rung most of the numbers in the victim's address book,

Guv. although I'm having trouble locating a certain Peter Newbridge. I've left messages for him, but he hasn't got back to me as yet, and his wife says she has no idea where he is. Our victim's full name was Thomas Alexander Carter, and he was born here in Bristol in 1968. He married a Charlotte Clarke in 1988 and moved to Australia in 2006 after he and Charlotte divorced. He was an only child and both parents are dead. He has a few old friends in this area, but I've spoken to them and they all say they've not heard from him since he came home briefly, to sort out his mother's estate when she died in May 2017."

"That's good John, what about his contacts in Australia?"

"Yes, I've also spoken to a few of those, as well as the local police, but he seems to have been a bit of a loner, he never re-married and he lived on his own. An optician by trade, he ran a small optician's in Oxley Street, Campbelltown, Sydney. Now I've spoken to his assistant and receptionist, an Irish woman by the sound of her, and she said his trip to England took everybody by surprise, she had to cancel an awful lot of his appointments and his sudden departure has left a lot of his customers very angry, Guv. One thing of interest though, she did say that he seemed to make his decision to come to England just after reading that article about the bronze sculpture being sold for so much money."

"Well, that's interesting, it certainly looks to me as if our priority has to be finding out exactly what it was that brought our victim home, and whether the sale of this bronze sculpture had anything to do with it."

"Your friend Richard Drake is an antique dealer, Guv. He'll probably know which auction house sold the bronze and who might have been interested in it," commented Dereck Price, one of the more senior constables on the team.

"You're right Derrick, I intend to ring him right now in fact, and if he knows the auction house that sold the bronze June and I will go there straight away. In the meantime, see if you can locate his ex-wife, Charlotte, I'd like to know why their marriage broke down," said Paul, and then turning to constable Phillip Strange, "Phillip, contact the taxi firm that the hotel receptionist called for him, see if you can trace his movements since he arrived in England. Reg can you organise a more thorough search of his hotel room, June and I left when we had the contents of the safe, but there may well be more to find."

"OK Guv, are we looking for anything in particular?" asked Reg

"I've no idea what you'll be looking for Reg, but something else that sheds any light on his reason for coming here would be a step in the right direction. He had a reason for coming and we need to know whether it had anything to do with the bronze or not."

Entering his little office that was located at the far end of the main room Paul sat at his desk and rang his good friend Richard Drake, who also happens to be his wife Margaret's employer.

"Richard, it's Paul." He began as he heard the phone picked up.

"Hi Paul," came the reply, "are you ringing me from work? only I didn't recognise the number. Is it me or Margaret you want to speak to?"

"I am ringing from work Richard, yes, and it is you I want to speak to, I was hoping you could help me with something that's just come up. Do you know anything about the bronze sculpture of an African slave that was sold recently for some eye-watering amount of money?"

"You're talking about the William Wilberforce piece I presume? Over three million pounds it fetched, I wish my clients would spend that sort of money on bronzes."

"That's the bronze I'm talking about alright, anything you can tell me about it would be useful, where it was sold for a start? and who sold it? that sort of thing."

"Well it was sold, out at Winchester Auction Rooms, in Chipping Sodbury, but I have no idea who sold it, in fact I think it was an anonymous vendor. I'm afraid I can't tell you any more than that. I had no idea the thing even existed until I saw the announcement of the sale, I went to the auction myself because there were a couple of other things I was interested in, it caused quite a stir in the saleroom I can tell you."

"You weren't tempted to bid on the bronze yourself then? I know you have a liking for bronzes."

"Well it would have been nice to bid on something like that, and I admit I was tempted, but I was too afraid it might get knocked down to me and I would have to try and explain to Elizabeth why I had spent a couple of million pounds that we don't have."

Paul laughed, "Yes, I'd have to admit, I'd liked to have heard you trying to explain that to Liz. Where exactly in Chipping Sodbury is Winchester auction rooms? I can't place it."

"Well it's just outside Chipping Sodbury I think, I'm not exactly sure where the boundary is, but if you follow the Badminton Road, the A432, up through Yate and just past the Chipping Sodbury turning, you've got the caravan showrooms on your left, do you know it?"

"I know the caravan place you're on about."

"Well it's just past there on the same side of the road. It's a big farmhouse and converted barn. You can't see the buildings from the road, but there's a big signboard outside that is hard to miss. It used to be Winchester farm years ago, a family business, but the farm was losing money and the family started up the auction business selling farm good and agricultural equipment. Now they have a general sale every three or four weeks and an antiques sale three or four times a year."

"Is it still owned by the family?"

"Yeh, John Winchester runs the whole thing now his parents are both dead, and I believe his wife died as well a few years back, or maybe they split up, I can't remember,"

"Were you surprised when the bronze turned up for sale there?"

"I was a bit, an important find like that you would expect to go to one of the big London auction houses, but perhaps the vendor was local and didn't want to travel to London, who can say, maybe he'd sold stuff there before and was pleased with the service, who knows?"

"Thanks Richard, that's been really helpful," said Paul, preparing to hang up.

"Hang on....aren't you going to tell me what this is all about?"

"Not right now Richard, but Margaret and I are seeing you and Liz on the weekend I believe, and I might know a little more myself by then. Anyway, I have to go now, I've got an auctioneer to interview."

Paul hung up the phone and threw his car keys to June out of habit again as he exited this office. "Come on June, let's go and visit an auction, have you ever been to one?"

"No Guv have you?"

"I went to a car auction once, but I never bought anything, I was only eighteen, and I felt a bit intimidated bidding against all the dealers."

"Intimidated...you Guv, I find that a bit hard to believe."

In the car, June followed Paul's directions as they drove to Winchester Auction Rooms. Just as Richard had said, a large sign announced the location with an arrow confirming the location of the entrance.

As they turned into the grounds, past the big sign that Richard had mentioned they saw another, much smaller signpost, indicating that the main carpark was straight on but that the main offices and auction room were to the right. June turned right and they pulled up outside an impressive Victorian house. Slightly further on in the same direction they could see a large converted barn with a sign over the large triple doors that identified it as the "Main Auction Room."

Inside the front door of what seemed to be more of a Manor house than a Farmhouse, one of the front rooms had been incorporated into the entrance hall to make an impressive lobby. Both Paul and June were impressed. The wall to their left had been given over, museum style, to the history of the farm. There were early photographs mounted on the wall, along with small artefacts from its days as a working farm and then more recent photographs showing the main saleroom packed with people on an auction day. In front of the wall were two square, free-standing display cabinets filled with articles that were to be included in their next antique auction.

"Can I help you?" the receptionist behind the counter to their right enquired, "do you have an item for valuation?"

"No, we're police," said Paul, showing the woman his warrant card, "we'd like to speak to the owner, and that's a Mr Winchester I understand?"

"Oh! yes of course, I'll ring him and let him know you're here, can I enquire what its concerning."

"I just have a few questions about a lot that was sold here, nothing to worry about."

The receptionist, a woman who appeared to be in her mid-thirties, picked up the phone to her left, "John, there are two police officers here and they'd like to speak to you about something that we sold, shall I send them up?"

After replacing the phone, and with what Paul thought looked like a worried expression on her face, she said, "Mr Winchester's office is up the stairs and to the right, it has his name on the door so you can't mistake it."

When they reached the top of the stairs, John Winchester was standing in the open doorway of his office to greet them.

"Hello, John Winchester," he announced rather loudly, "what can I do to assist the police? We haven't been inadvertently selling stolen goods or anything, I hope?

"No, it's nothing like that" said Paul, "at least as far as we know. We just need a word about a particular item you sold recently."

Winchester escorted them into his office and with introductions out of the way, he sat behind an imposing mahogany desk and motioned for them to sit before it.

Winchester's office was a large room that looked as if it belonged in a stately home. There were oil paintings and gilt mirrors on the walls and the furniture was every bit as impressive.

"That's a very imposing desk," said Paul, admiring the heavily carved moulding around the top and the gold embossed leather writing surface, and thinking he was beginning to both think and sound like his friend Richard.

"Yes, it is rather splendid isn't it," replied Winchester, "far too good for in here actually, I really should get around to selling it on. Now what can I do to assist the police? I'm sure you're not here to talk about Chippendale desks."

"No that's right," said Paul as he removed a photograph of Thomas Carter from his inside coat pocket and handed it to John Winchester, "I'm sorry," he cautioned, "it's a post mortem picture I'm afraid, but I'd like to know if you recognise this man, have you ever seen him before?"

Winchester took hold of the picture and studied it, perhaps for a little longer than was necessary, "No, I don't recognise him at all Inspector, should I?"

"The other reason we are here is concerning the Wilberforce bronze you sold recently, could you tell me who the vendor was, and why they decided to sell it here rather than in London?"

"Good lord! Why on earth would you want to know that Inspector?"

"It's just something that's come up in the course of our enquiries."

"Inquiries into what, Inspector?"

"It would be helpful if you'd just answer my question."

"Well I'm afraid I can't help you with that Inspector, I don't know who the vendor was myself, he or she wanted to remain anonymous."

"How did they contact you?"

"Through an agent, a third party."

"Well then, if you could just let us have the name of the agent."

"Look Inspector, I'm not trying to be awkward, but that information is confidential, I'm sorry."

Paul was annoyed, and didn't care if it showed, "I wasn't aware that auctioneers have the same privileged information status as lawyers, doctors and priests," replied Paul, sounding somewhat irked, "in fact, I'm sure they don't, so I really must insist."

"And I'm afraid I must stick to my guns Inspector; the vendor must have his reasons for wanting to be anonymous. If you can show me that knowing the identity of the previous owner of the bronze will solve whatever case you're working on, then I may reconsider my position. Can you do that Inspector?"

"No, not at the moment, but this isn't the end of the matter, if I have to get a court order to examine your papers I will, but surely I don't have to do that? I'm sure you don't want to interfere with our enquiries."

"Look, Inspector, the last thing I want to do is have a falling out with the police, give me a little time and I'll get back to you Inspector, but I'm not inclined to break a confidence just like that, not without good reason."

"I'll give you until tomorrow morning to reconsider your stance on the matter, after that I shall apply for a court order, and that will be to go through all your paperwork," said Paul, realising that Winchester was not going to budge.

Paul had been looking around the office with interest, and now took a different tack, "As I've been sitting here, I couldn't help but notice your collection of African artefacts over there in the corner," he continued, pointing, "is that a particular interest of yours?"

The items Paul had pointed out were a couple of African shields, made from wood and animal skins, they were mounted on the wall to the left of the door they had entered by. Behind the shields, mounted crosswise on the wall like the swords in a medieval castle, were some lethal looking spears. On the floor in front of the display was an elephant's foot that had been made into stick stand, and in which were stood several more spears, two small bows, and what looked like a long wooden stick surmounted with a wooden ball. Paul rose from his seat and walked over to them for a better look.

"Weapons of all sorts interest me Inspector," answered Winchester, "at home I have a modest collection of swords and one or two firearms, all perfectly legal I can assure you."

"Yes, I'm sure they are, it wouldn't make any sense for a man in your position to take the risk of owning anything illegal, but this is a curious thing," stated Paul, lifting the wooden stick to examine it, "I assume it's a club of some sort, it looks deadly."

"It called a "Knobkierie" Inspector, and yes, it is a club, and deadly, it's from southern Africa.

Paul examined the club closely before returning it to the rather macabre stick stand, "Well thank you for your time anyway Mr Winchester," said Paul, as he replaced the African club in the stand, "I think that's all for now, but we will be in touch again I'm sure, please don't make me bring a court order with me." And as a passing shot, "Do you still live here at the old farm house?"

"No, I moved out long ago, when I got married. Mum and Dad were still here then. I now have a house in Leigh Woods, The Oaks. It's too big for me of course."

"And you live there with your wife and family?"

"No Inspector I live alone, my wife left soon after we were married and I've seen no reason to repeat my mistake. We never had children, so I tend to rattle around in the place a bit."

"I'm sorry."

"Don't be Inspector, I can assure you I have a very active and interesting life, and running this place keeps me pretty busy."

As Paul and June got back into the car June asked, "Why the interest in the African stuff Guv? Are you thinking that, what did he call it, a knobkierie, could be our murder weapon? Why would an auctioneer murder our victim?"

"I've no idea June, but ever since the good doctor said the murder weapon was probably round and struck with some force, I've been looking out for anything that would fit the bill, and that knobby-thingy would certainly fit."

June laughed, "It's called a knobkierie, Guv."

"Yeh, Whatever."

****

The day following the discovery of Thomas Carter's body the team were conducting their usual review of the case so far, with Paul perched on the corner of one of the spare desks, coffee in hand.

"Has anybody got anything new?" pleaded Paul, looking around the room hopefully.

"We've searched Carter's hotel room thoroughly now, but we haven't found anything of any further interest Guv," said Reg "and we've tracked down his ex-wife, Charlotte Carter, nee Clark. They married in 1988, but it only lasted three years. She says she hasn't seen or heard from him since he went to Australia in 2000."

"Did you believe her?"

"Yes, I did Guv. He was only twenty when they married and she was only seventeen, she said the marriage never stood a chance, it turned out that they both wanted different things from life, the usual story. She's moved on and re-married, got a couple of kids now, and she seemed genuinely surprised to learn that he hadn't re-married and started a family."

"Anyone else?"

"I've just put the pathologist's report on your desk Guv." volunteered Peter Cook, the youngest member of the team, "She's confirmed that the cause of death was a massive blow to the back of the victim's head from a round wooden object."

"Round and wooden," repeated Paul, looking over at June and smiling knowingly, "Ask her to look at the possibility that an African....." Paul turned to June again, who finished for him, "Knobkierie Guv", "thank you June, that an African....what she said, could have caused the damage, will you."

"Yes Guv." continued Peter, grinning, "She also said there is a mark on the victim's forehead caused by a straight wooden object with indentations. She speculated that the blow from behind caused our victim to fall forward and hit the front of his head on the edge of a piece of carved furniture."

"Something like a Chippendale desk perhaps," speculated Paul, again looking sideways at June.

"Could be Guv."

"OK Peter, let me know what she thinks about the knobby-thingy, as soon as, will you."

Peter looked sideways towards June, who mouthed back to him smiling, "Knobkierie."

John Campbell was the next to contribute to proceedings, "I've still not had any response to my calls to Peter Newbridge, whose name was in Carter's address book, so I googled him. Turns out he's a freelance investigative journalist. He's written a lot of stuff about corruption in the corporate world and has a good reputation in media land, but that's all I have at the moment, Guv."

"Well that's interesting, keep on to it John. Phillip, have you found out anything about our victim's movements since he's been here?"

"I've been in touch with the taxi firm, Guv. and interestingly, the only place he seems to have visited is Winchester's auction rooms, twice, once on the 12th June, that's the day after he arrived in this country and once again the following day."

"Now that's very interesting, our Mr Winchester has some explaining to do, he said he didn't recognise our victim.

"Just the fact that Carter visited the auction house doesn't mean he met Winchester Guv." pointed out June.

"That's true June, but I'd like to know the reason for his visit anyway, I'm more convinced than ever that the Wilberforce bronze is at the heart of the matter. Reg, get a court order to seize any paperwork pertaining to the auction the Wilberforce bronze was sold at, and I want our forensic team to look at that Knobby-thingy in Winchester's office, in fact, let's have a look at the whole office, especially that nice desk of Winchester's, I have half a feeling it could be our murder scene. The pathologist said our victim struck the front of his head, possibly on the edge of a piece of carved furniture, well our Mr Winchester's desk fits that description to a tee."

"You really fancy Winchester for the murder Guv?" asked John, there have to be lots of things that would fit the description of our murder weapon, and, as June said, we don't know that Winchester lied about seeing Carter."

"I know John....and we all have to keep an open mind and pursue enquiries as we normally would, it's just that something I can't put my finger on is telling me it's him. Now if I'm right and he did kill our victim in his office, he would have to have moved the body up to the Sea Walls in something, so let's have the forensic team go over his car as well, and any other vehicle he would have had access to."

"We'll have to start calling you, Columbo, if you turn out to be right Guv." joked June.

"Columbo?"

"Yeh, you must know Guv....the American detective off the tele....he always knows who the murderer is as soon as he meets them."

"I think we might all be better off if you stopped watching the tele, June. Now come on, let's visit my prime suspect again."

****

Paul and June entered Winchester's auction house for the second time, but this time with Reg and a forensic team in tow. After showing the receptionist a search warrant for Winchester's office and any auction vehicles, they ascended the stairs and entered his room. Winchester was just hanging up the phone, on which his receptionist had informed him of the police presence. Pauls face fell as soon as he entered and saw the room had changed.

The desk behind which Winchester was now sitting, was not the beautiful Chippendale one that had been there on their first visit, and Paul instantly turned to the display of African weapons on the wall opposite. All appeared unchanged, except that the knobkierie Paul suspected was the murder weapon had been replaced with another. The replacement was of a similar shape and size as the one he had seen, but this one was a slightly different colour.

"Changed your desk I see," said Paul, finding it difficult to stop his annoyance from showing, "and the

African club I admired as well, where's that gone?"

"Yes, as I think I said during your first visit Inspector, that desk was much too good for in here, but you're mistaken about the knobkierie, that's the same one you saw last time."

Paul saw no point in arguing about the club and simply enquired, "What have you done with your old desk, where is it now?"

"Oh, we had a German dealer in, just after you left actually, he gave me a very good price for it and I would think it's in the back of his van on its way to Germany by now, probably on a ferry, crossing the Channel as we speak Inspector, why? You seem disappointed, were you going to offer me a price for it?"

"Right, well we have a warrant to search this room, your car, and any vehicles belonging to the auction house, so I would like you to accompany us back to the station to answer some more questions, and I want all the paperwork you have pertaining to the auction the Wilberforce bronze was sold in."

"Well this is very inconvenient Inspector, I have a great deal of work to do, we have one of our general sales next week so it's a very busy time for us. But if you insist, I suppose I have no choice."

"I do insist. Where's the paperwork I asked for?"

"That will all be in the main office across the hall."

"Reg take Mr Winchester across to get all the paperwork will you, then bring him down to the car. June and I will have a word with the receptionist downstairs." Then turning to Steven Wyatt from the forensic team, "The two items I was most interested in are no longer here but I still want you to go over the room, I think it's possible someone was killed in here so there has to be some trace. I also want you to examine the vehicles, because it is possible one was used to transport the body."

"If there's anything here we'll find it Sir," said Steven.

The receptionist looked anxious as Paul and June approached her desk. "Do you keep records of client's visits?" asked Paul abruptly.

"If they've had a meeting with one of our valuers or of course, if they're a buyer or vendor, yes."

"We have evidence that a Mr Thomas Carter came here on the 12th June and again the following day, can you tell me what the nature of his visit was and who he spoke to?"

"Let we see," she replied nervously, tapping the keyboard and looking at the screen of the computer that adorned the reception desk. "Yes, here we are, Mr Carter brought in a couple of rings to be valued on the 12th and then he came back the next day for the results of the valuation."

"And where are the rings now?" asked Paul, sounding suspicious.

After consulting the computer for a second time she replied, "We have them here, Mr Peters, our jewellery expert, valued them at £100 to £150 each and Mr Carter left them to be sold in our specialist jewellery auction next month."

"Well, I have to ask you to withdraw them from the sale, they are now evidence in a murder enquiry. If you would like to let my constable here have them, she'll give you a receipt."

"I'll have to get a porter to fetch them for you, I have no idea where they are." she said, picking up the phone and asking for a porter.

"Tell me, I understand this place used to be Winchester Farm and a family home. I know Mr Winchester has a place in Leigh Woods now, but does your boss ever stay here overnight on the premises?"

"No....I don't think so, although he could if he had to for some reason, there is still a bedroom and bathroom upstairs."

"Let my constable have Mr Winchester's full address as well then please, together with the rings."

Paul was a little surprised when a porter appeared in the reception area carrying a small box and announcing, "Here are Mr Carters rings, what do you want me to do with them?"

"I'll take those," said June, just as Reg descended the stairs carrying several large folders and accompanied by John Winchester.

Back at the station, Paul asked Reg to conduct the initial interview with Winchester, while he himself collected his thoughts and considered their next move. He was angry that Winchester had managed to get rid of the desk and club, but still confident that forensics would find something in the office, or, if not, the vehicles.

Reg asked Derrick Price to conduct the interview with him, they had done several with each other over the years and had usually obtained good results. The two of them now sat in the interview room opposite John Winchester, who was
looking surprisingly calm for a man in his position.

"You understand why you're here, John, and you've been informed of your rights while being interviewed under caution?" asked Derrick.

"Yes, yes, I understand all that....what I don't understand is why I am here in the first place....am I being accused of something?"

"You're being questioned in connection with the murder of Thomas Carter."

"Murder!.....what, the man with the rings? That's got nothing to do with me, I never even met the man."

"You've never met him, but as soon as we mentioned his name you knew he brought rings in for sale, how is that?"

"I know the name, that's all, I couldn't put a face to it because I've never met him."

"It's odd, don't you think?"

"What's odd?"

"That a man who lives in Australia should come all the way to England to sell a couple of rings. I mean, the journey alone is going to cost more than the rings are worth, at least that's the case according to your valuer. Why do you think he would do that?"

"I have no idea why he would do that sergeant. Perhaps he intended staying on in England until after the sale, or even permanently...I really don't know...and I really don't care, like I say, I never met the man!"

"OK, let's move on."

"Oh! please, yes, let's move on by all means."

"Now, I have to say," stated Reg "that I'm very unimpressed with the state of your record keeping. We've been trying to find out who it was that put the Wilberforce bronze into your auction on 25th May, and there is nothing in any of the files you gave us. Can you explain that....can you now tell us who the bronze belonged to?"

"No, I can't, as I explained to your inspector, the vendor wants to remain anonymous."

"Yes, I understand that, but I'll bet that whoever he was, he wanted to be paid, and that doesn't appear to have happened. In fact, the money from the sale of the bronze is still in the auction's bank account. A cheque has been deposited from The Metropolitan Museum of Art, in New York who purchased the bronze, but no payment has gone out to a vendor, why is that?"

"It often takes several weeks between us being paid and cheques going out to vendors. Various charges and commissions have to be calculated first, and we have to make sure that cheques we receive clear the bank before we pay out. These things all take time."

"OK, but just for the sake of argument, let's say the time has come for you to pay out on the bronze, how are you going to do that, if you don't know who the vendor is?"

"In the case of the Wilberforce bronze, we will send a check to an intermediary agent."

"But presumably there has to be a name on the cheque, so what name will that be!"

"I'm not going to break a confidence and tell you that, and in any case the cheque will most probably be paid out initially to the intermediary. It will then be up to he or she to pay the vendor, minus their commission of course."

"Then tell us the name of the intermediary," urged Reg.

"I don't know off hand who that is, but it will be in the files there somewhere, you can look it up."

"Well, then there's the trouble with your record keeping again, we've been through the files and there's no mention of an intermediary, if fact, there's hardly any mention of anything to do with the bronze at all."

"Well I can't explain that, there must be some kind of a clerical error…. perhaps it's been mis-filed."

"You'll be charged with obstructing a murder enquiry and we will get a court order, requiring your bank to tell us who the payment is to be made to."

"Well there's your solution then sergeant....Oh! but wait a minute, if we haven't made the payment yet, the bank won't have a clue who we're going to make a cheque out to, will they? After all, they're not mind readers."

Changing tack, Reg continued, "Bit of a coincidence wasn't it, some German dealer making an offer for your desk just after our Guvnor had seen it?"

"Stranger things have happened, I'm sure."

"Your paperwork seems to have gone astray yet again. Can you tell me the name of this German dealer?"

"Sorry no...look to be honest, it was a cash deal, and I didn't bother putting it through the books, you can do me for tax avoidance if you like, but not for murder."

"You know that we're going to have a forensic team go all over your office and any vehicle you've access to."

"Help yourselves, perhaps you'd like to search my home as well, while you're at it? But I shall be suing for any damage you do, and I will expect any mess you make to be cleared up to my satisfaction, so knock yourselves out."

"Just to be clear for the tape Mr Winchester, you did just give us consent to search your house in Leigh Woods?"

"Well, I was being sarcastic actually....but yes, why not, let's get it all done in the one go shall we, and then you can all leave me alone. Yes....for the tape...I give you permission to search my house, OK. Can I go now?"

"Thank you for your cooperation, Mr Winchester, I'm sure our Guvnor will be pleased."

Chapter Three

Paul was wondering if his stomach could cope with another cup of the canteen's coffee when John Campbell stood in the open doorway of his office and tapped on the glass.

Paul looked up expectantly, "Have you got something for me John?"

"Call it a coincidence if you like Guv. but that reporter chap that I've been struggling to contact, you know, the one whose phone number was in Thomas Carter's address book. Well his wife has reported him as a missing person!"

"Has she indeed, do we know where she is?"

"Home at the moment Gov I've got her address, 36 Eastfield Road, Weston-Super-Mare."

"OK, let's go and see her, we'll see if she can shed any light on why our murder victim had her husband's number in his book. We'll take June with us, it might be good to have a female officer present if Mrs.......?"

"Newbridge Guv. the missing reporter's name is Peter Newbridge."

As Paul, June and John Campbell were walking down the main corridor on their way to interview Mrs Newbridge Reg and Derrick were returning from their interview with John Winchester.

"Reg. how did it go with Winchester?" asked Paul hopefully.

"About as well as I think you expected Guv, he's a slippery customer and no mistake. He's still refusing to say who put the bronze up for auction, and there's nothing in the files to give us a clue."

"OK Reg. June and I are off to see Mrs Newbridge, the wife of our investigative journalist who she's just reported as missing."

"Blimey! do you think he went to see Winchester when Carter's body turned up, because if he did we could have another body on our hands?"

"I don't know Reg but let's not bury him before we know he's dead, he could still just have gone off with some other woman. I'll leave it up to your discretion as to whether you have another go at Winchester or not"

"I really don't think we're going to get any more out of him Guv., not until we have something else to confront him with, anyway."

"OK, Reg. let him go for now then."

****

The Newbridge's house turned out to be a fairly ordinary Victorian terraced house. Because he'd understood that Newbridge was a well-known and successful journalist, Paul had visualised him living in something a little grander, but he speculated, perhaps home comforts weren't his priority, or perhaps he wasn't as successful as they'd been led to believe, but either way, it was a bit of a surprise.

June sat on the settee beside a somewhat distraught Mrs Newbridge, while Paul and John Campbell sat in separate chairs facing them.

"When did you last see your husband Mrs Newbridge?" asked Paul.

"My name's Mary Inspector. Peter left home about 9.30am on Monday, and that's the last time I saw him."

"That's the 18th June?"

"Yes, the 18th, that's right.

"Do you know where he was going or who he intended to see?"

"He left home about 9.30am....Oh I'm sorry, I already said that didn't I....well, he said he was going to interview somebody, I don't know who, I'm sorry."

"Do you know if he was working on anything in particular at the moment?"

"Well yes, no, well not exactly, what I mean is that it is a new investigation, I know that, and I think it had something to do with that bronze sculpture that fetched so much money the other week. He seemed quite excited about it."

Paul, June and John all exchanged glances, "Do you have any idea how the bronze featured in your husband's investigation, Mary?"

"No, just that it had something to do with it, oh... and Peter said something about a man being cheated by an auction house somehow. Peter often spoke to me about what he was working on, but this case was very new, so there hadn't been a lot of opportunity for us to talk about it."

"Where did your husband keep his files and notes, Mrs Newbridge, are they here or did he have an office somewhere?"

"They'll all be here Inspector, Peter always worked from home." said Mary Newbridge, beginning to cry, "His office is the little front bedroom upstairs if you want to look."

"That would be very helpful Mary, thank you. Constable Campbell and I will take a look now, if that's alright, did Peter have a laptop?"

"Yes, but I imagine he has that with him," she said bringing on a new bout of crying."

"I'll leave June here with you. June, perhaps Mary would like a cup of tea or something?

"Yes of course. Would you like a cup of tea Mary? I can make you one and you can tell me a little about Peter, what sort of man he is. Is it possible that he has got so involved in something that he has gone off somewhere and just not told you?"

"No! no he wouldn't do that, he always let me know where he was going to be, and what time to expect him back." She tried hard to stop sobbing, "if he was going to be late, he would always ring to let me know," she said reaching for a box of tissues.

June place a comforting hand on Mary's shoulder and said, "You take your time Mary, I'll go and put that kettle on."

Upstairs, Paul and John looked through Peter Newbridge's desk and filing cabinets. There were four, two of which were marked, ARCHIVES, the other two were marked respectively, RESOLVED CASES and PENDING. "He seems a very organised man, by the look of things." said Paul, admiring the general neatness of the room. "any sign of a laptop?

John looked up from the filing cabinet drawer he had been searching and claimed triumphantly, "Just the desktop computer that I can see in here Guv. but this is interesting."

"What's that?"

"There's a file here Guv. labelled "Thomas Carter."

"That's good, I've got his diary, but as there's no laptop, I say we get it back to the station and go through it, there's no need to put Mrs Newbridge through any more questioning at the moment. We can send someone down to pick up the desktop computer."

"I can get it down to the car now if you like Guv. save bothering Mary again."

"Yes OK, John, do that."

Back downstairs, Paul explained, "We'll be going now Mary, and we're going to take Peter's computer with us if that's alright, John's just bringing it down now, is there anyone you'd like us to contact for you, I don't like leaving you on your own when you're so upset?"

"That's alright Inspector, you go and find my Peter."

****

Back at the station Paul filled the rest of the team in with the contents of the file they had found at the Newbridge house. "It would seem that Thomas Carter was aware that Peter Newbridge was an investigative reporter," began Paul, "and would appear that he contacted him by phone from Australia, as soon as he saw the newspaper report covering the sale of the Wilberforce bronze. Now, Thomas Carter claimed, according to this file, that the bronze actually belonged to his late mother, Margaret Carter.

Now Margaret Carter died in April 2017 and Thomas came home then to sort out his mother's estate. The house was put in the hands of a local estate agent to be sold but the contents of the house were sold at auction, and I imagine you can all guess which auction house handled it."

"But if the bronze formed part of Margaret Carter's estate and was put in the hands of Winchester Auctions in April 2017, why did it only come up for auction in May this year?" asked June, posing the question that was on everyone's lips, "surely, when Thomas Carter received the statement from the auction, he would have noticed that the bronze hadn't been sold? They have to be two different bronzes, don't they, Guv?"

"Maybe Winchester lied to Carter and told him the bronze didn't sell," offered John Campbell, "after all, didn't Mrs Newbridge say that her husband told her a man had been cheated."

"Yes, but that's a hell of a risk to take, John, and if Carter thought his mum's bronze hadn't sold, he would have made other arrangements at the time, or simply requested that it be shipped out to himself in Australia."

"Maybe the bronze that Mrs Carter had was a cheap copy or reproduction of the Wilberforce bronze," offered Reg.

"That's a real possibility I suppose," replied Paul, "but if that was the case, surely Winchester could have just explained the situation to Carter? Why would it end up with Carter being killed?"

"Maybe our victim didn't believe Winchester's explanation, and maybe he was a violent man and things got out of hand," offered Peter Cook.

"If that was the case, it would have simply been a matter self-defence on the part of Winchester, and he could have just come to us, rather than trying to dispose of the body."

"Maybe he panicked Guv. people do strange things under stress," said June, "what about Newbridge's diary Guv. anything of interest in there?"

"Day to day entries stop on the 16[th.] and it looks as if his diary is clear of appointments until July 5th when he has a meeting in London with an editor. There are no entries indicating that he has had any meetings with either our victim Thomas Carter or our prime suspect John Winchester. It would be nice to locate his laptop."

"I think the fact that we haven't found his car yet, makes it less likely that he has just gone off with a girlfriend, Guv." said Derrick, "it seems to me the car has been hidden, and that spells something sinister to me."

Reg took it on himself to summarise what they had so far, "So at the moment," he began, "we have our victim arriving at The Clifton Gorge Hotel on the Monday 11th June and getting a taxi to Winchester's auction rooms on both the 12th and the 13th. The body is found on the 15th, so it must have been dumped Wednesday night because it would have been difficult to do it during daylight on the Thursday....that place is teeming with people during the day, especially this time of year."

Paul and Reg were interrupted when a figure who had just entered the main room, called out, "Inspector Paul Manley."

Everyone looked up to see a young man in shirt sleeves standing just inside the door, "I'm Inspector Manley," Paul replied, beckoning the new arrival over.

The new arrival introduced himself as, "David Phillips Sir, I'm part of the forensic team that checked out the office at Winchester Auctions, Steven Wyatt told me to come and update you."

Paul shook hands with the new arrival, "I hope your visit means you have turned something up?" queried Paul expectantly.

"A little, but I'm not sure how useful you'll think it is, Sir. There was a small trace of blood on the office carpet, but the carpet was still damp from having been thoroughly shampooed, so we don't think we will be able to match it to anyone, the DNA will be too degraded. However, we did find this just under the bottom edge of the filing cabinet," said David, "and it's odd for a couple of reasons," he continued, handing Paul a small evidence bag containing a spent cartridge case.

Paul shrugged his shoulders and looked even more expectant as he took the bag from David Phillips, "What reasons?"

"Well first I suppose, because we'd been briefed that the murder weapon was likely to be a heavy round wooden object of some sort, not a bullet."

"And second?"

"And second, because it's obsolete ammunition, an old rimfire cartridge probably dating from the 1860s."

Paul frowned, "You did say the 1860s and not the 1960s, David?"

"That's right, Sir.....it's the sort of thing Smith & Wesson produced in the 1860s, instead of the fulminate primer being located in the centre of the cartridge case base like later rounds, it was spread around the rim. It was made for one of the first, if not the first, of the successful breech loading revolvers."

"Well, I suppose the place where you found it is an auction house, and presumably they have sold their fair share of antique guns there....surely, it could just have belonged to one of those early revolvers that was sold at the auction sometime in the past?"

"Yes, that's right Sir, but although you do sometimes come across boxed guns with ammunition in the form of unfired rounds, you would normally only find spent cartridge cases where the gun was fired and reloaded.

"How do you mean?"

"Well Sir, a gun of that vintage, like most revolvers, would need to have the spent cartridge cases removed manually from the cylinder before it could be reloaded, it's not like a semi-automatic pistol, where the cartridge cases are ejected when the round is fired, with a revolver, they stay in the cylinder. You would expect the cases to be discarded or disposed of after removal, they wouldn't be kept with the gun.

"I see what you mean. You're saying that even if the gun was fired in that room, there would be no reason for the case to be lost there."

"That's right, like I say, it's not like a modern semi-automatic pistol that ejects the cartridge case as soon as it's fired, these cases stay in the cylinder after firing. Anyway, I'll leave that with you, shall I?" said David, turning to leave.

Everyone had been listening to the exchange between Paul and David from forensics with interest, but it was John Campbell that broke the silence, "So what do you make of it Guv? Do you think it has anything to do with our case? Our victim wasn't shot after all, he was bashed over the head."

"Walloped, I think you'll find is now the preferred term," said Paul.

"Maybe our missing reporter has been shot though Guv," volunteered Reg.

"Hold your horses Reg. We don't even know if our missing reporter has been murdered...he may just have decided his life wasn't what he wanted and walked out on his wife. We need to look into his life more closely, and Derrick, can you organise an appeal in the media for any information on his whereabouts or that of his car, and see what missing persons are doing to try and find him. Do we know what his car is by the way?" asked Paul, turning to John Campbell

"A Hyundai Tucson Guv, six months old, champion blue."

"We are working on the assumption that Winchester has murdered Carter and Newbridge though, Guv aren't we?" asked June.

"Certainly, if our reporter turns up dead, it would seem to be too big a coincidence to be otherwise, June, but let's not rule anything out at the moment. As I say, Newbridge could be shacked up with some girlfriend for all we know. OK, John, you concentrate on trying to locate Winchester's missing desk will you. I don't believe for one minute he sold it off to some German dealer that just happened to call in, it's too neat. It was a valuable desk, I wouldn't be surprised if he has shipped it off to some other auction house or maybe called in a local dealer.

Derrick, you concentrate on trying to find our missing reporter. Interview friends and neighbours, see if you can find out if his marriage is as good as we think. Has he ever gone missing before? You know the drill."

The phone on June's desk rang and she picked it up, after a moment she announced, "There's a girl just come into the station, Guv. she says that she and her boyfriend were walking up at the Sea Walls on the night of the 13th, she's in reception, shall I go and speak to her Guv?"

"Put her in an interview room June and I'll come and join you in a minute."

The interview rooms seemed to be a low priority with the station cleaners and it was beginning to smell more like a gymnasium and the young girl sitting opposite Paul and June looked uncomfortable.

"I'm sorry," began Paul, I know these aren't the most hospitable surroundings, and we'll get you on your way as soon as we can. Thank you for responding to our appeal by the way."

Paul looked sideway towards June, and she began, "Can I have your full name and address for our records?"

"Sylvia Davis, 18 Long Meadow Road, Horfield."

"Thank you, Sylvia, can you tell us exactly what you remember about that night."

"Well, I'm not sure exactly what time it was, but early morning, maybe two or so. Bob and I were just out walking after having a meal at a restaurant in Queens Road. He'd proposed to me in the restaurant and I suppose neither of us wanted to go home. Anyway, when we got to the Sea Walls, there was a man standing on the wall. I thought he was going to climb over, but he didn't...in fact, he must have read my mind because he actually told us that he wasn't going to jump, and that he was just getting some air."

"Did he have an accent of any kind?"

"No, he just sounded normal, well normal for around here I suppose I mean, I was born in the west country so I don't really notice west country accents, you know, they don't stand out for me like a London or north country accent would, so I'd say he was probably local."

Sylvia appeared to become upset, "Was he the one that jumped? Was it his body you found?"

"No Sylvia," Paul assured her, "the man we found had been killed before his body was put over the cliff, so it couldn't have been the man you saw, you have nothing to reproach yourself with, there was nothing you could have done, it wasn't the man you saw."

Sylvia looked as the weight of the world had just been lifted from her shoulders, "Thank you, it's been worrying me ever since I read about a man's body being found up there, thinking we may have been able to stop someone jumping but didn't do anything."

"Well you can put those thoughts from your mind. Could you describe the man you saw?"

"Not really, Bob and I talked about it last night. He was tallish we think, but then he was standing on a wall in the dark when we saw him. I do remember that he had a good head of hair, because I thought he had a woolly hat on at first....so he wasn't too old I don't think, middle aged maybe."

"Was there a car nearby?"

"Oh yes, a posh one, Bob joked that we would have a car like that one day....he's really into cars and all that."

"That's good, do you know what make it was?"

"Oh dear....what did Bob say it was now?.....A posh German car of some sort, he said."

"A BMW perhaps?"

"No."

"Audi maybe, or a Mercedes?"

"That's it!....that last one you said...That's what Bob said it was....a Mercedes."

"Can you remember the colour?"

"Oh, I don't know, it's difficult to tell, all those greys and silvers look the same in the dark don't they."

"So, it was grey or silver, you think?"

"Well I think so, yes, although it did look a little unusual, it may have had a funny tint to it, I sorry, I'm not being much help, am I?"

"Actually Sylvia, you've been an enormous help, thank you ever so much for coming forward, and if you remember anything else...anything at all, please give us a ring."

"I will, I promise."

As soon as they were back in the office Paul asked of everyone, "Does anyone know what sort of car Winchester drives?"

"Mercedes C class Saloon, Guv," answered Peter Cook, who had just joined them, "Brilliant Blue, I believe the colour is called."

"Is that a light or dark colour?"

"It's a light metallic blue, Guv, why?"

"Our witness at the scene says there was a silver or grey Mercedes parked there. Would light metallic blue look silver or grey at night, I wonder?"

"I think that's quite likely Guv. she didn't get a registration number I suppose?"

"She had other things on her mind, Peter, her boyfriend had just proposed to her."

"Oh! that's a shame."

"You never were the romantic sort were you Peter." said June, smiling.

Chapter Four

With the meal inside them, the women chatting between themselves about future holiday plans, and a glass of wine in hand, Paul and his good friend Richard Drake retired to Richards den, leaving Elizabeth Drake and Margaret Manley clearing the dining table.

His den was in fact a small office, full of reference books on everything antique and those odd things that Richard wanted to keep but Elizabeth disapproved of, two of which were, an 1860s Navy Colt revolver and an iconic Winchester rifle. Both of which were proudly displayed above his desk.

Paul stood looking at the weapons and said, "Do you know John Winchester, Richard, the auctioneer I mean, not the gunsmith?"

Richard smiled somewhat smugly, if he had one fault, it was that he loved showing off his knowledge, "Actually," he began, Oliver Winchester, the owner of The Winchester Repeating Arms Company was a shirt manufacturer and business man, not a gunsmith. But in answer to your question, I know all the local auctioneers Paul, why do you ask, is it to do with the Wilberforce bronze you asked me about the other day?"

"Yes, how well do know him?"

"I've spoken to the man on several occasions of course, but always about business, I have no idea what he is like as a man…..although having said that, I don't think he is a man I would trust particularly. But as I say, I don't really know him, so I could be doing the man a grave injustice. Are you going to tell me what this is all about? You've got me intrigued."

Paul stopped looking at the rifle and sat in a leather wing chair facing Richard, who had taken up residence in the only other chair in the room, a white leather swivel chair in front of his desk.

The two men each took a sip of wine before Paul began, "Our victim, a Mr Thomas Carter from Australia, claims that the Wilberforce bronze that was sold on 25th May, just gone, at Winchester Auction Rooms, was the same bronze that formed part of his mother's estate, and that he put into auction, along with the rest of her house contents, back in April 2017. My question is, could it possibly be the same bronze? and if it was, why did Winchester not sell it back in 2017? And if he didn't, why did Carter not question it at the time?"

Richard sat and pondered for a while before asking, "When did Carter say he put his mum's stuff up for auction?"

Paul took a small notebook from his pocket to ensure he had the exact date, "18th April 2017," he answered.

Richard rose from his chair and looked on the shelves that covered the entire far wall of his office. After a few moments of searching he announced, "Yes, here it is," he said, returning to his seat opposite Paul, "I keep the catalogues from all the big important sales stored in the attic, but for the first year or so after a sale, I keep all my catalogues in here for easy reference. This is the catalogue of the sale Carter's mum's stuff would have been in."

"You're an asset and no mistake Richard, does that mean you were at the auction?"

"Not necessarily Paul, as a frequent buyer I get sent catalogues from most local and London houses. As it was so local, I probably would have viewed it, but I don't remember actually going."

Richard had been going through the catalogue as he was talking and now said, "Here we are, this is interesting."

"What?......what have you found?"

"Lot 113.....is listed as, A figure of a slave girl in spelter."

"Do you think that's significant? I mean we're talking about a bronze figure here remember, not one in spelter."

"Yes, I know Paul, but just let me think a moment......What if Carter took his mum's possessions to Winchester, and that they did indeed include the lost Wilberforce bronze. Suppose then, that Winchester recognised it from descriptions he'd read, but instead of sharing the good news with Carter, told him it was just a spelter figure of no real value. Lot 113 listed here has a guide price of only one to two hundred pounds."

"Don't you think Carter would have smelled a rat? I mean, even I know spelter is a lot lighter in weight than bronze."

"Yes I know Paul, but just because you've picked up some knowledge from me over time, doesn't mean that Carter would know the difference, and in any case, a lot of spelter figures have lead incorporated in the base to give them weight and some stability."

"OK, but that doesn't explain it being in two different sales a year apart."

"Well perhaps it does. Let's assume for a moment that lot 113 is the Wilberforce bronze. Well Carter's not going to be much of a problem, because he's presumably going back to Australia before the auction, and will just expect a cheque to arrive after everything is sold. Winchester's problem is putting it in the sale without anyone else recognising what it actually is. But even then, all he has to do is catalogue it as a spelter figure and not have it on display on viewing days. It's easy enough to arrange for the internet to be down on the day of the actual auction, or simply to not include it in the online catalogue, he could even just withdraw it on the day of the sale. I think it's significant that there is no photograph of the figure in the catalogue, looking through, most decorative items with a guide price of over one hundred pounds have photographs included.

Now, when lot 113 comes up for sale, he can take a few bids off fictitious bidders and knock it down to a

Mr Smith or Jones or whoever, while actually purchasing it himself.

All he has to do then is send a cheque for a couple of hundred to Carter in Australia, after all, that's what he's expecting. Then Winchester can hang on to it for a year or so and then put it back up for auction, this time with a true description and publicise it on the net. That way he gets to pocket a sizeable sum of money when it fetches its true value."

"Well that's quite a scenario Richard, but Winchester must have known that anything fetching over three million pounds was going to be in the papers, and that there was a good chance Carter would get to see it, as of course he did, it was a big risk."

"Well let's see, the Wilberforce bronze is by John Edward Carew, an Irish sculptor working in England, he's quite well known and respected, in fact, I think he did one of the plates on Nelson's Column, but his work doesn't usually realise anything like the price this bronze sold for. Winchester probably didn't expect it to realise more than eighty to a hundred thousand or so, maybe not even that. In which case it would have made the trade papers for sure, but not the nationals necessarily, and even if it was reported in the nationals, it may not have warranted a picture. Winchester was lucky in one way, that it fetched such a huge sum of money, but unlucky in so far that it generated an enormous amount of publicity surrounding it."

"Stone the crows, Richard, you lot are worse than second hand car dealers!"

"Don't tar us all with the same brush Paul, and anyway, this is all speculation on my part and Winchester is probably as honest as the day is long."

"Yeh, maybe. What did you mean about, taking bids off fictitious customers, how does that work?"

"When an auctioneer takes a bid in the saleroom, it's usually quite difficult to see who is bidding. After their initial bid, most dealers will just nod their head slightly when the auctioneer looks at them. At big international art sales, it's not unusual for a potential buyer to have a pre-arranged signal to show he's bidding."

"What sort of pre-arranged signal, how do you mean?"

"Well, it could be anything, one chap I know has the agreement with Christies that he will tell them prior to the sale which items he's interested in, and the auctioneer knows when he's selling one of those items, that if the client is stood up, he's bidding, and when he sits down, he's stopped bidding, or you could arrange that if you have your hands in your pocket you're bidding, anything like that."

"That all seems a bit dramatic and cloak-and-dagger to me Richard, what's the point?"

"You have to remember Paul, that hundreds of thousands of pounds can be changing hands and it's all about knowledge. For instance, a couple of years ago one of my clients said he was interested in a piece of silver being auctioned at Sotheby's. He asked me to look at it and bid on it for him but he left me to decide how far to go. Now I would have dropped out at twelve thousand because I wasn't sure if it was worth more than that, but I'd noticed that one of the buyers from the Victoria and Albert Museum were bidding on it as well, so I was confident to go a bit further. Now I still didn't get it, the V and A did, but the point is that the V and A, would have got it for less money, if I hadn't known they were bidding and kept going. Anyway, does what I told you help with your case at all?"

"It certainly does, it answers an awful lot of questions, thank you Richard. Now I suppose we should join the ladies again."

"We're having coffee on the patio as it's such a lovely evening," said Elizabeth, as the four of them strolled into the large garden.

The Drakes house is one of a row of similar 1930s build detached houses, which have large front gardens set back from the main road and separated from it by a strip of grass some twelve feet in depth. The back garden, where the four of them now sat, is some twenty four feet wider than the house itself and surrounded on all sides by a three-foot-high fence.

Just as Elizabeth finished pouring out the coffees for everyone, all four became aware of the sounds of raised voices coming from next door. "Oh no! not again," sighed Elizabeth."

Richard apologised to his guests, "I'm sorry, you two, but we have new neighbours, Jack and Sandra Williams. They only moved in a couple of weeks ago and they seem to spend most of their time shouting at one another. I've had to call in to see them about it, it happens so often, but the husband, if that's what he is, is so aggressive I thought he was going to throw a punch at me. It's all very unpleasant."

"My friend Mary, who lives over the road, so quite a distance away, said that even she and John can hear them when they get going," put in Elizabeth.

"Wow, that's awful for you both," said Margaret, "how often do you have to put up with it?"

Elizabeth sighed, "Well it seems like every other day to some extent or another, sometimes it just lasts an hour and he storms off in the car, but sometimes, if he doesn't leave the house, it can go on for hours. The worst thing is that sometimes it finishes quite abruptly.....and I think that's because he's hit her."

"Is there nothing you can do Paul?" asked Margaret, "as Elizabeth says he hits her, surely that's a police matter?"

"Before you say anything Paul," cut in Richard, "some of our neighbours have called in the police...on two occasions now, so they are aware of the situation, but I don't think they can get the wife to make a formal complaint."

"What're their names Richard? I'll see if I can find out if anything is being done, you can't put up with that all the time, just how bad does it get?"

As if in answer to Paul's question the patio doors at the back of next door flew open and a woman in her early thirties ran into the garden shouting, "Don't you come near me with that thing again."

The four friends stood up and looked over the fence into next door. The woman was now backing away from the doors and they could see that she was holding a large kitchen knife out in front of her in a posture of defence.

A man, who looked somewhat older, had followed her out of the house and was approaching her in a threatening manner holding a stick or cane of some sort. It seemed obvious that the man had intended hitting his wife with the cane, and that she had picked up a knife to defend herself.

Paul and Richard approached the fence as Elizabeth and Margaret looked on in distress.

"All right you two....just calm down and take a deep breath....this is getting out of hand and somebody is going to be injured," shouted Paul.

"The man stopped his advance and looked across, and seeing the two men, answered in an aggressive voice, "Well well, if it isn't our favourite meddling antique dealer again....you just keep out of this.....it's got nothing to do with you, so mind your own business....both of you."

81

"Of course, it's to do with me," said Richard, "your involving the whole neighbourhood in your rows, they're so loud."

Without turning around, Paul called to his wife, "Margaret, go to the car and get my brief-case would you....I may need it....my handcuffs are in there, and call the police, tell them what's happening and that I need backup, tell them there's a knife involved."

"Get inside and put that knife back before I give you what-for," Jack shouted at his obviously terrified wife.

"Come near me with that again and I'll stick you with it....I swear I will," sobbed Sandra.

"Just take a deep breath and calm down the two of you," repeated Paul, "I'm a police officer and I'll arrest the pair of you if I have to," he continued, preparing to climb over the fence.

"I'll show you, you stupid bitch," roared Jack, as he made to lash out with the cane he had now lifted over his head, he lunged forward with it towards his wife. She turned away putting her hands up to shield her face, and he took the opportunity to grasp the hand that was holding the knife and wrench it from her. She cried out in pain as he twisted her wrist.

As Paul practically leap over the fence, Sandra broke free of her husband's grasp and ran back into the house, closing and locking the patio doors behind her.

Seeing that Sandra was now, at least temporarily out of danger, Paul stopped his advance and stood still

the fence to fill them in with the facts of what had been happening, as Jack just sat and watched, knife in hand.

Constables Colin Jones and Jean Hargreaves introduced themselves.

"Where is Sandra now? constable Hargreaves enquired.

"She's seems to have locked herself in the house at the moment," replied Paul.

"OK, I'll call at the front door and see if she'll open it for me, are there any children on the premises?"

"No, they don't have children," answered Elizabeth, "it's just the two of them."

"At least that's a blessing," she offered, "if Sandra lets me in, I'll come to the patio doors so you can see me and know I'm in." she said as she set off.

"I think I'll just wait to see if the woman lets Hargreaves in before I approach her husband," mused Constable Jones, "as he seems quiet at the moment, what do you think Sir?" he asked Paul.

"You do what you think best Constable, but as the man is armed, you might consider calling for more backup."

After a brief period of inactivity and uncertainty, the male officer took a call on his radio and then looked over at the patio doors to see his partner standing just inside.

Turning to Paul, he said, "Hargreaves is with Sandra now Sir, she's very frightened, afraid that her husband will hurt her if we leave, so I intend arresting him. We can keep him at the station for twenty-four hours and get Sandra to a place of safety. Hargreaves has alerted our domestic abuse officer and she's on her way now."

"He's armed Constable," said Paul, "and I don't intend getting involved any more than I already am, I'm with my wife and friends and I don't have a stab-vest, but I'm cautioning you not to tackle him without backup."

"Understood Sir, my colleague will assist in the arrest if required, I can see her at the patio doors now, I think we can handle it, I've got my baton, and Hargreaves is deadly with a pepper spray, it won't be the first time we've arrested a suspect with a knife, Sir."

Constable Jones climbed over the fence as his partner unlocked and opened the doors to the garden with her pepper spray at the ready. Jack stood up as constable Jones took out his baton and approached him, and despite his assertion that he wouldn't get involved, Paul went with him, much to Margaret's dismay, but Paul was concerned that constable Jones, who looked as if he should still be in school, had exaggerated his experience to impress a superior officer.

"Mr Williams, I want you to put down the knife and come with us to the police station, do you understand, I'm arresting you on suspicion of assault. You do not have to say anything, but it may harm your defence if you do not mention when questioned something which you later rely on in court. Anything you do say may be given in evidence."

Jack looked at the young officer and at the baton he was holding, he was also aware of the fact that the female officer behind him was holding what he assumed was a pepper spray. Realising that resistance would probably only result in a badly bruised arm and possibly sore eyes, he placed the kitchen knife he had been holding on the garden table and stepped away from it. The spectators all breathed a sigh of relief.

"Turn around and place your hands behind you," said Jones as he deftly placed handcuffs on Jack Williams. In order to avoid Jack and Sandra coming into contact with each other, constable Jones and Paul assisted Jack in climbing over the fence and the officer led him out to the car through the Drake's residence.

During this time another female plain clothed officer appeared at the door and after a brief chat with her colleagues strolled over to Paul, who had now re-joined his wife and friends in their garden.

"Inspector Manley is it?" she asked.

"Thant's right.

"My name's Jillian Simmons, Sir, I specialise in domestic abuse cases and as this is now the third time police have been called to this address, I shall be getting involved. I should like you to provide me with a statement of exactly what you witnessed, tomorrow if that's possible. I will stay with Sandra until I can get a relative or friend to stay with her tonight, and I'll find her a place of safety before her husband is released."

"That poor woman," said Elizabeth, "There have been rows and shouting almost every night."

"Do you know if he has ever physically assaulted her in the past?" asked Jillian.

"Well we can't be absolutely sure," said Elizabeth, "but sometimes the shouting stops very abruptly,"

"OK, you can leave it with me now."

The four friends sat down to finish their drinks after Jillian Simmons had left, but the joy had gone out of the evening and Paul and Margaret headed home before ten.

Chapter Five

Paul had just finished bringing the team up to date with Richard's speculations from the previous evening."

"Is there any way we can prove that the spelter figure sold in 2017 was in fact the Wilberforce bronze?" asked June.

"Not unless we can find someone who was at the auction and happened to photograph it June."

The team were just about to resume their various tasks when John Campbell entered the room with a somewhat smug look on his face, and strolled across to his desk, "Mirror mirror on the wall, who's the cleverest of them all." he chortled as he sat at his desk.

"This had better be good," said Reg "you've been gone for hours, we were just about to report you as missing."

"Well at least that means you've all missed me," he said taking his jacket off and hanging it on the back of his chair, "anyway, I've just arranged for them to be brought down to our forensics department."

"Arranged for what to be brought down?" asked Reg irritably.

"Winchester's desk of course.......and wait for it."

John was determined to prolong his moment of triumph as long as he could, but at least three rolled up scraps of paper hit him before he'd finished, "Winchesters desk, and a certain African knobkierie that was put in the auction by the same lady."

"You're kidding…. Are you telling me he didn't destroy the club!" exclaimed Reg "what an idiot!"

"Well only if he did it and it is the murder weapon," cautioned Derrick.

"That's right," countered John, "but both items were put into the auction by a Miss Louise Brown, and Louise Brown just happens to work as a secretary at Winchester Auctions."

"Our Mr Winchester doesn't appear to be the cleverest of murderers, does he Guv? said June.

"Well only if he is……" started Derrick again, before being interrupted by Paul.

"No, he certainly doesn't appear to be June……Well done John, where did you find it?"

"It was easy in the end Guv, bearing in mind what you said, I rang all the auction rooms within a hundred miles radius, asking if they had a Chippendale style desk coming up for sale, and if they did, where had it come from. Wotton Auctions in Wotton-under-edge had a desk matching my description and I went to see it. As soon as I saw it, I knew it was the one you had described Guv. and when I asked if anything else had been entered by the same person, they showed me the knobkierie. I couldn't believe it."

"When is it arriving," asked Paul.

"The desk will be with forensics in the morning, but I brought the knobkierie back with me in the car and they're working on it now Guv."

"Well done John, if you were better looking, I'd kiss you."

"Yeh, but as you're an ugly old sod, so you're out of luck," said Reg. to everyone's amusement.

****

Constables Derrick Price and John Campbell had been knocking on doors in Eastfield Road, Weston-Super-Mare, for nearly an hour and interviewing neighbours of Mr and Mrs Newbridge. There had initially been no reply from the house directly opposite the Newbridge's, but as the two men returned from opposite ends of the road, a woman in her sixties was letting herself in while struggling with two heavy looking bags of shopping.

The woman looked worried as the two men approached her, but John flashed his warrant card to reassure her, "Here, let us give you a hand with that," he said, as he and Derrick each relieved her of a bag. "Is all this shopping just for you or do you have a large family?"

"Thank you, those are heavy," she replied, "normally it's just me, but my son and daughter-in-law are visiting for the weekend so I've had to get more in. Did you want me for some reason? I haven't forgotten to pay for anything have I?"

"Oh, it's a little more serious than that I'm afraid," joked John, with a big grin on his face, "We've had a tip-off that you're the mastermind behind a big jewel robbery."

The woman, who turned out to be Gladys Simmons, smiled back, "Oh damn!....You've got me, and that was going to be my pension as well, how many years do you think I'll get....would you boys like a cup of tea?"

"Well now that depends."

"On what?"

"On whether or not you can tell us anything about the couple opposite, Mr and Mrs Newbridge?"

"Mr and Mrs Newbridge......oh well, I'll put the kettle on then, shall I?"

Derrick and John looked at each other and grinned as they followed Gladys into her little kitchen.

"One of you boys put the kettle on while I put away my frozen bits," said Gladys, as she started putting contents from one of her bags into the small undercounter freezer. "What is it you want to know about Mary and Peter Newbridge? they used to be such a devoted couple."

"Used to be," repeated John.

"Yes, used to be. Now you boys have to understand, I'm not an old busy-body snooping on all my neighbours, or anything like that, it's just that I'm an old lady living on my own and I take an interest in what's going on around me, a bit like Miss Marple...you know…Agatha Christie's sleuth.   I'm not as good as her….."

"What can you tell us Gladys," interrupted Derrick, keen to avoid hearing Gladys's life story.

"Oh yes, I'm sorry, I was about to start rambling, wasn't I?" Gladys had finished putting away her frozen shopping and John had put three cups of tea on the large kitchen table as she sat down, "Well, what is it you want to know about them?"

"Anything you can tell us would be helpful Gladys, how long have they lived here?"

"Oh, let me think, it must be nearly fifteen years now, just before their little boy Jason was born. They were a really lovely couple and I liked them very much. I used to look after Jason quite often for Mary. Well, Peter was out working all the time you see, he's a journalist you know, quite well known in those circles I believe, I think he's even been on the television, so if Mary wanted to go shopping without the hazzle of taking a young child with her, I would look after him. They were very happy times."

"You say they were happy times, Gladys…..what happened….when did things change?"

"Oh," Gladys took a tissue from the box on the table to wipe a tear from her eye, "Well that was about three years after they moved in, Jason died you see….it was so sad, some sort of infection I think, Mary never really spoke of it, not in any detail anyway. Everything was different after that and they never got over it. Well you wouldn't would you, not the death of a young child."

"But they're still together, aren't they?"

"Yes, and I have to say that, although it took some years, Peter seems to have moved on....he had his work I suppose, but Mary has never come to terms with losing Jason. She's not the same person that she was before, I'm sorry to say it, but I don't like her very much now, and although, as you say, they are still together, they live very separate lives. Why are you so interested in them, has one of them done something wrong?"

"No, not as far as we know, it's nothing like that Gladys, but Mrs Newbridge has reported her husband missing, she hasn't seen him since Monday 18th June."

"Oh, Monday, I think that's the day I saw them leave together...quite early."

"Are you sure Gladys? Mrs Newbridge said her husband left for work at 9.30am and that she's not seen him since."

"Well I thought it was Monday....now let me think....now I did get up early on Sunday as well.....so I suppose I could have my days mixed up. One day is very much the same as another now I don't work anymore, even the weekends. So there we are, I thought it was Monday I saw them together, but if Mary says Peter left for work on his own that day, then I must be mistaken, mustn't I? Yes, now I remember, it was the Sunday they left together, that's right, I remember the church bells were ringing."

"Don't worry Gladys, we all get days mixed up sometimes, especially looking back in time, is there anything else you can tell us?"

"Peter's gone missing you say…..well I wouldn't have mentioned it normally, as I say, I not one for idle gossip…."

"Go on Gladys, tell us what you're thinking."

"Well now, you have to understand that everything I've told you so far is correct, there is now doubt. But what I'm going to say now is speculation on my part, I don't want you to get the impression that I know what I'm telling you is true, because it may not be."

"It's all right Gladys, we understand, what is it?"

"It's just a feeling you understand."

"Go on Gladys, get it off your chest, what is it you want to say?"

"Well, over the last few months, Mary has started going out after Peter has gone to work. Now I know she has always gone out during the day, she has shopping and things to do the same as anyone else, but the pattern has changed. Twice a week now, on different days depending on what time Peter goes out, Mary leaves the house within half an hour of Peter and is picked up by a man in a car just around the corner."

"Is it a taxi, do you think?"

"No, it's a Ford C-Max, Dark grey and it's driven by a man of about Mary's age.

"If this happens just around the corner Gladys, how do you know so much about the car and driver?"

observing Jack, who was now in possession of the knife. Jack turned and walked slowly back to the doors and tried them, smashing the side of his fist against them in anger on discovering that he was now locked out of his own house. After a while, he tired of ineffectually pounding on the doors, and walked over to the garden furniture that was located on the sunnier side of the patio, where he took up residence in one of the chairs, still holding the knife that he had taken from his wife, and seething with anger.

Looking over towards Paul, who had narrowed the distance between them while Jack had been pounding on the doors, he said calmly, "Time for you to get off my property now, or when the real police arrive, I'll have you arrested for trespass."

"I am the real police, Jack, now put down the knife."

"That still doesn't give you the right to invade my property…..what goes on between a man and his wife is none of your damn business."

"If you physically assault your wife then I'm afraid it's very much my business, and….."

Paul was interrupted by the arrival of two uniformed officers that Elizabeth had let through, one male and one female, who now stood with Richard, Elizabeth and Margaret in the Drake's garden. Elizabeth had been standing out at the front of the house waiting for the arrival of the police, so she could show them through to the back garden. Paul walked back over to

83

"Oh dear....now I really am going to sound like an interfering old busy-body." Gladys looked embarrassed as she continued, "Once I realised what was happening, I'm ashamed to say I left my house just after Mary one morning, and I saw the car and driver up close. Before that, I had only noticed that the same car was pulling in as it passed the end of our road you see, only a few seconds after Mary had turned the corner. I thought it must be picking her up, but I had to walk to the end of the road myself to confirm it. I feel so ashamed of spying on Mary like that, but I had to know for sure, because we used to be so close, I suppose."

"Did you get the number of the car Gladys?"

"No, I'm sorry, I didn't think there was any point."

"Never mind.....what do you make of it, Gladys? What do you think is going on?"

"Well the only reason I can think of for the secrecy is that Mary is seeing this man behind Peter's back, otherwise, why doesn't he pick her up outside the house?"

"When was the last time you saw Mary picked up by this man, Gladys?"

"Not for a few days now, unless I've missed it of course, I'm not looking out for it."

The two detectives finished their tea and stood to leave, "Well thank you Gladys, that has all been very helpful," said John, "now if you remember anything else that might help us, or if you see this man again, give me a ring," he said, passing Gladys his card.

"Do you think Peter found out about the affair and has walked out on her, is that why he's missing?"

"We don't know Gladys, but we are going to keep looking for him, even if he doesn't want to be found."

"Well what do you make of all that John?" asked Derrick as they drove back to report what they had discovered.

"Personally.... I still think our Mr Winchester has bumped him off....but you seemed like you had a few doubts, back at the station I mean."

"No not really, John, I was just playing Devil's Advocate.....Gladys is great isn't she?"

Chapter Six

Paul was updating his DCI, William Blake, or Blakey as he was affectionately referred to around the station.

"You're convinced this auctioneer is your man, are you Paul?" asked DCI Blake.

"I am Sir, yes, I'm convinced he cheated our victim over the bronze, and that when Carter returned to confront him, they got into some kind of a fight and Winchester used the African club to kill him."

"OK, what about this journalist chap that's gone missing, how is he involved?"

"Well we know that Carter contacted him even before he returned to Britain, there was a file on Carter in Newbridge's office, so it's possible that Newbridge confronted Winchester after Carter's body was found. At the moment we can't locate Newbridge or his car so it seems plausible that Winchester has killed him as well and hidden the body."

"Well you seem to have everything in hand Paul, just keep me updated as usual."

"Will do Sir."

On his return to his office Paul was greeted by June, who looked as if she had bad news.

"You look as if you've just found a fiver and lost a tenner June, what's up?"

She passed Paul the file that she had been holding, "It's the forensic report on Winchester's desk and the knobkierie Guv."

Paul beckoned her to follow him into his office, "From the look on your face June, I think I'd better sit down before you tell me what it says."

June waited for Paul to get comfortable behind his desk before she began, "The knobkierie has been scrubbed clean with household bleach as well as the desk, it's taken the polish off both. The knobkierie is exactly the right size to be the murder weapon but it can't be proved that it is, and carved moulding on the edge of the desk is a match for the marks on our victim's forehead but no more than a lot of other carved mouldings they tried. So, in short, it could have made the marks but there is no proof of that either."

"Marvellous!"

"Sorry Guv."

Just as June was leaving Paul's office, Clive Pascoe stuck his head around the door, "We've had quite a few responses to our appeal for information on the whereabouts of Peter Newbridge Guv."

"Tell me there's something promising, Clive," said Paul hopefully.

"Lots of sightings, both of him and his car, but one does stand out from the rest."

"Go on."

"Unfortunately, it's from an anonymous caller, but one woman who rang, says that she saw him getting out of his car in the carpark of......guess where."

"You're kidding me!.....Winchester auction rooms!"

"Got it in one, Guv."

"What time of day was that?"

"Around 11am apparently, Guv."

"Get back there Clive, show that receptionist a photograph of Newbridge, see if she recognises him. Check to see if they have CCTV in the carpark or reception area, and while you're there, bring in a Miss Louise Brown, she's one of the secretaries there and the woman who put Winchester's desk in Wotton auctions. Take John and a WPC with you."

"My pleasure Guv."

****

Miss Louise Brown had been waiting in the interview room for almost quarter of an hour and was very agitated when Paul and June entered the room and sat opposite her.

She looked anxiously from one to the other and asked, "Should I have a lawyer with me?"

"Why?" asked Paul, "have you done something wrong?"

"No....so why am I here?...shouldn't I have a lawyer if I'm being interviewed?"

"You're not under arrest and you're not under caution, you can call a lawyer if you like, but we've just asked you in for a little informal chat, that's all."

"Oh… so I can just leave if I want?"

"Yes of course you can, but then we would have to bring you back in for questioning under caution. So, it's up to you Louise, you can have a chat with us now or be questioned under caution later, what do you want to do?"

"Well OK, I'll answer your questions, I've not done anything…..what's this all about?"

"Well Louise, can you think of anything that it might be about?"

"I only know what I've heard through office gossip."

"And what have you heard?"

"I know that you have questioned Mr Winchester about a man who visited the auction rooms and that the man is dead, that's all."

"Has Mr Winchester asked you to do anything out of the ordinary lately, anything that wouldn't normally be part of your duties as a secretary?"

"No…..oh well, unless you mean the business with his desk, that was all a bit strange."

"Well tell me about that, all of it from the beginning."

"Well, Mr Winchester arranged for two of our porters, Alan and David, to take the desk from his office, to Wotton auction rooms, in Wotton-under-Edge, and he asked me to go with them and put the desk and an African club into the auction under my name, with my address and contact details."

"Why did he ask you to do that, do you think?"

"I don't know. When I asked him, he just said he didn't want anyone to know it was his desk."

"What did the porters make of it, did you ask them?"

"Yes.....they thought it was strange as well, especially as they had been told to use the van with no markings and not to mention what they'd done to anyone."

"What do you mean....the van with no markings?"

"We have three vans, one very big one that we use if we're picking up the whole contents of a house, like with a deceased estate or something, and there are two transit sized vans, one with, Winchester Auctions, sign-written on the side, like the big van, and one that has no markings at all. He also told the porters not to wear their work overalls, because they have Winchester Auctions, written on the back."

"If this was all to be such a big secret, how come we found out from Wotton Auctions that you worked for Winchester?"

"Well, it was all a bit awkward really, what with Mr Winchester wanting it kept a big secret and all. But the girl who booked the desk and club in for me knows me. We used to work together before I joined Winchester's.

She knew where I worked now but she had changed her job since I saw here last and I had now idea she was working at Wotton.   You don't have to tell Mr Winchester, do you?"

"Probably not."

"Thank you, can I go now?"

"In a minute Louise, why do you think he decided to change his desk so suddenly?"

"I don't know, no one does, he was always very protective of it, I know he spent a lot of money having it restored a few years ago.   It's a mystery."

"How long have you worked at Winchester's?"

"Nearly three years now."

"So you were working there in April of last year."

"Yes...why?"

Paul placed the 2017 April antique auction catalogue on the table in front of Louise, "Do you remember this auction, Louise?"

"Well not particularly, I work in the office, so I don't have much to do with the auction room itself."

"But I expect you all have a look around don't you, just to see if there is anything you'd like to buy?"

"Yes, sometimes."

"Well do you remember seeing lot 113, catalogued here?" asked Paul, pointing to the entry, "a spelter figure of a slave girl."

Louise shifted nervously in her chair, "I don't remember it, no."

"Are you sure you don't remember it Louise, I believe it would have born a striking resemblance to the Wilberforce Bronze that was sold recently."

"I've told you...I don't remember it...I'd like to go now please, I've answered all your questions."

"OK, Louise, you can go. But remember we are investigating a murder here, so it would be very unwise to lie to us."

After Louise had left June turned to Paul, "There's not much doubt that Winchester killed Carter in that office is there Guv?"

"No doubt at all in my mind June...I just wish we could prove it."

On their return to the main office, Phillip informed Paul, "There's a Jillian Simmons waiting to see you Guv. something to do with an incident at Richard Drake's house."

"Yes, thank you Phillip."

Jillian stood up as she saw Paul enter the room and greeted him, "I thought you would like to be kept up to date on developments concerning Mr and Mrs Williams Sir."

"Thank you, Jillian, as a matter of fact if you hadn't called in I was intending to contact you. Come into my office, can I get you a coffee or anything?"

"No thank you Paul I've drunk coffee here before." Paul smiled.

"I just wanted to let you know that Jack Williams has been released without charge and will be returning home."

"What about Mrs Williams?"

"At the moment she is in a refuge until we can find her somewhere."

"Can she manage financially?"

"I think so, she has a job doing the books for a small firm and her husband pays money every week into her personal account, that payment may stop of course if he decides to cancel the standing order, but even then she should be able to manage on her own....if that's what she decides to do."

"You don't think she will go back to him surely."

"I really don't know, but it's a possibility, she didn't want to bring charges against him."

"What about the police, are we pressing charges?"

"The problem is, he is saying that it was her that was the aggressor. He says that she threatened him with the knife and that he was forced to take it off her, and actually, that sort of fits in with your statement. You didn't see him with the knife until he took it off her did you."

"That's true, but she was telling him not to come near her with the cane again. It was obvious that she had picked up the knife to defend herself and it was him that chased her into the garden."

"Well, that's the situation at the moment, I just think.....no look I'll keep you updated if you'd like."

"Please...but what were you about to say?"

"Strictly between you and I....I have looked into Jack Williams past, he's not unknown to the police, he has a conviction for actual bodily harm. I don't think your friends next door should get involved with him at all. He's a man with a short fuse and a nasty temper, and my advice would be to stay well away from him."

"Thank you, Jillian, I'll certainly pass on that advice."

****

Constable Christopher Foulkes had been nearing the end of his shift when he received the call to investigate an abandoned car in Leigh Woods. The caller had said the car was a blue Hyundai Tucson and not very old so it had probably been taken for a joyride by youths and left in the woods. He was, however, surprised that the vehicle hadn't been burnt out, that was how most of them ended up.

It had taken him the best part of an hour to locate the car because the directions had passed on to him through a third party, and been like a game of Chinese Whispers. If only he'd been told that it was at the end of an old track it would have made his life a lot easier. When he did finally locate it, he looked at his watch, and was dismayed to see that his shift had finished five minutes earlier.

When he eventually got to the car, he found the driver's door was wide open, as if whoever had been driving it had got out in a hurry. He peered in. The keys were in the central well between the seats and nothing appeared to be damaged. It was seeming odder by the minute, joyriders don't usually have the keys, and why did whoever took the keys out of the ignition then leave them in the car? If they weren't going to take the keys with them why take them out of the ignition in the first place? Something was wrong with the whole scenario he could feel it.

Standing up straight once more he walked around the car checking for damage to the bodywork but there didn't appear to be any. This didn't feel at all like joy-riders, perhaps the car hadn't been stolen at all, and the owner was out exploring the woods somewhere. The only thing wrong with that idea was the fact that the call about the car had come in nearly four hours ago now, and that was a long time to be exploring, unless of course they'd had an accident and were lying injured somewhere, but then surely the rightful owner would have locked his car and not left the keys in it?.....no, something was badly wrong.

He walked to the back of the car and opened the tailgate. There was something bulky in the back covered by a large blanket, and there was something about the shape of whatever was underneath the blanket that unnerved him. He pulled the blanket away, and even though he'd been half suspected what he was going to find, he still let out a gasp of surprise. The body was lying on its side with its knees drawn up to the chest and there was a lot of dried blood on the side of the head. He leaned in and felt for a pulse mostly out of habit as the man had clearly been dead for several hours, if not longer.

As he took out his radio to call in his discovery, he cursed, realising that his shift was going to be extended even longer now. This wasn't the first body he had discovered in his six years on the force, but the others had all died from natural causes. It was true that one had been dead for some weeks and had been an experience he didn't want to repeat, but this was different again, this looked like anything but natural, and there was a tremble in his voice as he reported his find.

After calling in his discovery, Chris leaned into the boot once again and felt for the man's wallet. After finding one in the man's back trouser pocket, he took it out and went through its contents until he found a driving licence in the name of Peter Newbridge. Bloody-hell! he thought, that's the chap they've all been looking for.

****

After Paul had finished talking with Jillian Simmons, he walked her to the door of the main office and as he did so he bumped into Inspector Roy Darnley who was just entering. "Afternoon Paul, can I have a word with you?" Roy asked.

"Yes of course, Roy..." and then shaking hands with Jillian, "goodbye Jillian, I appreciate the update."

After Jillian was out of earshot Roy said, "What's this Paul, are you getting involved in domestic abuse cases now?"

"No, Jillian was just keeping me up to date on an incident I witnessed the other night, it's not a case of mine."

Inspector Roy Darnley followed Paul into his inner office and took a seat as Paul assumed his place behind his desk, "What can I do for you Roy?"

"Well the boot's rather on the other foot actually Paul, it's more what I can do for you. We were called out this morning to Leigh Woods. There's a spot there that was once a clearing used by charcoal burners back in the eighteen hundreds, it's still just about reachable from the main road via an old cart track. Well a couple of locals out walking their dogs came across an abandoned car and called us in. When a local uniformed officer arrived he discovered a body in the back covered by a blanket."

"So, it sounds as if you've got a murder on your hands as well, Roy, how is this of help to me?.....Unless of course, you're going to tell me it's Peter Newbridge you've found," said Paul jokingly.

Roy said nothing, he just allowed the significance of Paul's statement to sink in, "My god!.......that is what you're telling me isn't it...you've found our missing reporter."

"Yep...no charge this time Paul, you can just buy me a drink when we're next at the pub together." said Roy, enjoying the moment. "Do you want me to stay with it as a separate case or do you think the fact that he seems to have been murdered connect it to yours? Why were you looking for him in the first place, anyway? Surely it was just a missing person case?"

"We had no idea whether his being reported missing was connected to our case or not, Roy, but there was a connection between him and our murder victim. And as it now looks as if he has been murdered as well, I think there is a good chance he was killed by our prime suspect, so I'll gladly take it off your hands. How was he killed, do you know yet?"

"We've not had the official pathology report back yet, but my money is on it being something to do with the bullet hole in his head."

"He was shot!"

"Yeah, you seemed shocked, is the fact that he's been shot significant?"

"Well, it's just that our original victim was struck, or rather walloped over the head and most multiple murderers tend to stick to the same method of dispatch for all their victims....but we do have a stray cartridge case to account for, although it may be a red herring and nothing to do with the murder at all."

"Your case sounds more complicated than an Agatha Christie novel, it also sounds as you've been talking with our new pathologist, Dorothy Lansbury."

"Yes, the one that works on a ranch, she actually seems OK, I think she could be a real asset."

"I agree, and the good news, as far as you're concerned is that our body....or rather your body now....still has the bullet in it, so once our new rancher gets that out, at least you'll be able to compare it to your shell case."

"That's right, thank you Roy, I was beginning to think we'd never get a break in the case and you're right, although the whole case looks simple on the surface, I have a feeling it's going to get very involved and complicated."

"Well you know me Paul," said Roy with a grin, "always willing to help out a fellow officer if he's struggling. Anyway...this is everything we have so far," Roy continued depositing a brown folder on Paul's desk, "not much in there at the moment I afraid, and you've probably already got most of it anyway. Just give me a ring if you need any other cases solved for you."

"You've hardly solved it for us Roy....you've just made it more complicated, and we're perfectly capable of doing that ourselves, thank you very much."

Paul smiled at his friend and colleague as he thanked him, but also made a rude gesture as Roy left his office smiling.

After Roy had gone Paul addressed the team, "OK girls and boys, listen up," roared Paul, anxious to get everyone's attention so he could share the news with them, "We now definitely have a second murder on our hands. Peter Newbridge's body has been found in the back of his car in Leigh Woods, and he's been shot in the head."

"Shot, Guv." queried Reg, "not bashed....or, I'm sorry walloped, over the head?"

"No Reg...shot....Derrick, get down to the morgue as soon as Dr. Lansbury has the bullet, and get forensics to see if they can match it to the cartridge case found in Winchester's office. John, his car should be in soon so keep on top of that for me would you, if he wasn't actually shot in the car then I want anything forensics can give us that can place him in Winchester's office or auction rooms or his house. June, I'm going to have a look though the file Roy just gave me, but then I want you to drive me to Weston-Super-Mare. I would like your assessment of Mary Winchester's reaction when we break the bad news to her about her husband."

"Guv? You don't think she has anything to do with his death, do you?"

"No, I just want your assessment of her reaction that's all."

An hour later, Mary Newbridge opened the door to Paul and June, and stared at them with a blank expression on her face.

"Mary Newbridge? Inspector Paul Manley and Constable June Kelly again, we spoke to you about your husband's disappearance the other day, do you remember?"

"Yes, of course I remember, have you found Peter?....is he all right!"

"If we could just come in and talk Mrs Newbridge, I'll explain everything."

Mary turned away from the door and led them into the same small lounge they'd sat in before. It was furnished with a small two-seater settee, two arm chairs, a television and a coffee table. June thought the room was very spartan and gave the impression of being unloved, she looked around for family photographs but could see none.

Mary sat on one of the arm chairs with her hands clasped in her lap. She was the picture of a woman expecting bad news and looked on the verge of tears.

"I'm sorry to have to have to inform you," began Paul, but the obviously distraught woman opposite him burst into tears and sobbed uncontrollably before he could finish. June stood beside her chair and put a hand on her shoulder in a gesture of comfort.

"Where did you find him? How....how did he die? He didn't suffer did he...please tell me he didn't suffer."

"He was found in his car in Leigh Woods, Mary, and he didn't suffer....I can assure you of that."

"How did he die?"

"I'm sorry Mrs Newbridge, but it seems that your husband was shot."

"Shot!....how could he be shot....he didn't own a gun...who shot him?"

"We haven't got all the answers yet I'm afraid, but believe me, we will. Can you think of anyone who would want to harm Peter?....did anyone have a grudge against him? maybe somebody he investigated."

"No...well no one I know of, he did sometimes expose people who had done wrong or broken the law, but not for a while actually...unless it has something to do with what he was working on at the moment.....this thing with the auction.

"Well, we'll be looking in to that along with other things. At the moment though.....is there anyone you would like us to call for you? a friend or family member than can come and be with you."

"No, I shall be alright Inspector...you just concentrate on finding whoever did this to Peter, don't worry about me."

"We will get to the bottom of it, Mary, I can assure you of that. Are you sure there is no one you'd like us to call?"

"No, no one."

As Paul and June said goodbye to Mary Newbridge and left the house Paul said, "It doesn't feel right, leaving her alone like that."

"I know Guv, I'll put in a call to victim support as soon as we get back," said June, as they got into the car to return to the station."

"Yes June, do that. How did you judge her reaction? She seemed genuinely upset to me."

And to me, Guv, were you expecting her not to be?"

"No, I suppose not...she did seem natural, I mean it didn't look like an act or put on at all, I suppose I was just thinking about what Gladys said the other day, to Derrick and John, that she thought Mary was seeing someone behind her husband's back."

"I know Guv, but even if she is having an affair, that doesn't necessarily mean she didn't love her husband. It's possible for their marriage to be still in emotional turmoil because of the tragedy of losing their son, and them still to have feelings for each other. Lots of women have affairs for all sorts of reasons and still love their husbands."

"Your right, of course June, as you so often are."

"Thank you, Guv." said June smiling.

"Don't let it go to your head...just drive."

Chapter Seven

Paul had been optimistic that forensics would find Thomas Carter's DNA on either Winchester's desk or the knobkierie from his office and had been bitterly disappointed that they were unable to do either. He was now hoping that at the very least they'd been able to match the bullet taken from Peter Newbridge's body to the cartridge case found in Winchester's office but the expression on the face of Steven Wyatt, the forensics officer did not bode well.

"What have you got for me," asked Paul, hoping that the look on the young man's face was down to him just having stubbed his toe.

"Not exactly what you were hoping for I suspect, Sir. The bullet taken from your victim is certainly consistent with one that would have been fired from a cartridge case like the one found at the auction house, they are both from an early Smith & Wesson rim fire revolver, but I can't state for certain that that particular bullet came from that particular case, or even that they were fired from the same gun.

"Damn it!...why not? surly there are markings that correspond?"

"I'm sorry Sir, if you could give me the gun that fired them, I would certainly be able to match them to it, both the bullet from the gun's rifling and the case from marks it would have received in the chamber, but even then I couldn't connect that particular bullet with that particular case...all I could do is say they were both fired by the same gun...but not necessarily at the same time."

"Any chance you could look at the desk and the club again?" asked Paul, realising that he was beginning to sound desperate

"I could do of course, but believe me Sir, if there was anything to be found, we would have found it already."

"OK, Steven, I know you've all done your best, I wasn't trying to imply otherwise, I'm just clutching at straws. I'll just have to find the gun for you, I guess."

The bad news from forensics went down as well with the rest of the team as it had with Paul.

"Do you want us to pull Winchester in again and have another go at him Guv?" asked Reg.

"No, I don't want him to think we're desperate, but you could take a team back and interview all the staff again, keep on at them. If Newbridge was there someone would have seen him. John, do a bit more digging with the rings Carter is supposed to have taken in for valuation, we know the receptionist lied about the reason for Carter's visits, put some pressure on her, if she thinks she's in trouble she may change her story. Why is she so willing to lie for her employer? Is he threatening her or paying her, or is there something going on between them?"

"Ok Guv."

"Phillip Strange was another constable on the team and had been away on holiday for the start of the case. He had spent his first morning back going through all the files in order to bring himself up to date.

"I've been going through all the paperwork relating to the sale of the Wilberforce bronze, Guv. but none of the names relating to its ownership are traceable, they all appear to be fictitious, but I don't see any way we can prove Winchester owned the bronze. However, if we obtained the paperwork for the sale Carter put his mum's belonging in, we may be able to show that Winchester bought it."

"Good Phillip, I don't know why we haven't done that. Good to have you back by the way...how was Scotland?"

"Wet."

"Well come on, let's get busy, I don't intend letting our cheating auctioneer get away with two murders."

After Paul had returned to his office a uniformed officer knocked on the door and looked in, "Inspector Manley?"

"That's me constable, what can I do for you?"

"Well there seems to have been an incident involving your car Sir."

"An incident, what sort of incident?"

"One of our officers going off duty, saw a man in the carpark, Sir, and when he asked him what he was doing, he said he thought there was a shortcut through the carpark to the road behind the station. The officer saw him out of the park, but then walked back to where he had seen him coming from and discovered that your car had been vandalised Sir."

Paul stood up, "Vandalised how?"

"Well it looks as if someone has poured something corrosive on it, Sir."

"Have any other cars been damaged, or is it just mine?"

"It seems to be just yours Sir."

"OK, log the incident in the book and I'll come down and have a look," said Paul, wondering if the day could get any worse.

"Yes Sir, do you want me to come with you Sir?"

"No, that's alright Constable, I think I can find my own car.....you go back to work. Did anyone think to go after the man that was seen?"

"After the officer saw your car, he went after him Sir...but he was long gone."

"Any description?"

"Not really Sir.......medium height wearing a hooded top...but not a youth, a man in his thirties probably."

Paul walked to the carpark to take a look at his car and despaired when he saw it. Both nearside doors were affected and would need a re-spray but at least that seemed to be the extent of the damage. The thing that concerned him was the fact that no other cars had been damaged. If whoever had caused the damage had a grudge against the police why had he only targeted one car? It seemed to Paul the he was the only victim, and he wondered who could be targeting him.

****

Susan Whitehouse, John Winchester's receptionist, stared back at Paul and Reg over the interview room table, fidgeting with the eternity ring on her left third finger.

"You seem nervous Susan, can we get you a cup of tea or coffee?" asked Reg.

"No thank you, I've just never been interviewed by the police before that's all."

"There you are Reg" said Paul, "Susan's just never been interviewed by the police before, she's no reason to be nervous." then, leaning forward towards her over the table he confirmed, "you haven't done anything to be nervous about, have you Susan? You haven't lied to us about anything have you?"

"No...no, of course I haven't. Why would I lie....about what?"

"Well, you see, my sergeant here, well he has a very suspicious nature, he doesn't trust anyone, there are times when I don't even think he trusts me, isn't that right Reg?"

"Oh no...I always trust you Guv. it's other people I don't trust."

"Well that aside, the thing is Susan, Reg here doesn't believe that Mr Carter…that's the chap that you told us came in to have some rings valued and then came back the next day for the estimate, and left them to be sold, do you remember?"

"Yes…."

"Well Reg doesn't believe that was the real reason he came in."

"But I gave you the rings."

"Yes, I know. But the thing is…." Paul turned to Reg, who handed him a sale catalogue, "I have a friend who goes to lots of auctions and is sent catalogues of upcoming sales. Now it just so happens that he has a copy of the catalogue for your specialist jewellery auction next month and the rings are catalogued in there."

"Susan seemed a little relieved by the question, "Well yes that's right, they would be, wouldn't they, that's what I told you at the time, Mr Carter left them to be put into that auction."

"The confusing thing is though Susan, that we have been going through a lot of paperwork from the auction house and we've found out that the photographs of those rings, that were taken for that catalogue, were taken on the 9th June, now that's three days before Mr Carter's first visit to the auction house. How do you explain that?"

"Well….no that can't be right, they can't have been photographed before they came in, can they!"

"Well, that's what we thought, Susan, thank you for confirming that....so why did you lie to us?"

"Me!....Oh! well look, it's nothing to do with me, I just gave you the information that is on the system."

"We've also spoken to Mr Peters, your jewellery expert, about the rings, and he is somewhat confused as well, he seemed to think that the rings were part of an unsold lot from a previous auction that are due to be re-offered. Does Mr Peters often get confused like that?"

"I don't know, I told you, I only know what's on the system."

"Who is normally responsible for updating the system and putting this sort of information on there?"

"Well, pretty much any of the office staff have access to it, as well as Mr Winchester of course."

"Yes, but Reg here thinks that you knew the rings didn't belong to Mr Carter, so why did you lie Susan? lying to the police in the course of a murder inquiry is a serious offence."

"Oh, look, I only do what I'm told, I'm not in any trouble really....am I?"

"Not if you tell us the truth now. Who told you to lie to us about the rings?"

"Mr Winchester, you're not going to tell him I told you...are you, I could lose my job."

Paul and Reg stood up, "OK Susan, you are free to go," said Paul, as they left the room, and then to Reg. "Well I think we should pay our Mr Winchester another call Reg, take John and go and get him will you."

"It'll be my pleasure Guv.

****

Elizabeth Drake was pouring out the tea when Richard entered the kitchen, "Is Margaret opening up the shop for you this morning Richard?"

"Yes, why, is there something you want me to do before I leave?"

"Well you did say you were going to get rid of all that old decorating rubbish from the shed, the black wheelie bin is only half full this week and it's being collected this morning, I thought it would save you a trip to the tip."

"Yes OK, I'll do it before I leave, it will save me a trip."

After two cups of strong tea and his usual round of toast, Richard loaded a black bin liner with bits and pieces of old decorating rubbish from the garden shed and carried it around the side of the house to where Elizabeth had put the waste bin, near the front gate, ready to be put out for collection.

Richard and Elizabeth's house is a large detached property with a single iron gate on the right hand side that has a path leading to the front door. Over on the left of the house are double iron gates giving access to the driveway which leads up to a double garage that is set back from the front line of the house. The driveway also sweeps around in front of the house so that there is room for four cars at a push.   Because they live on a busy main road, Elizabeth drives her small car in and to the right, parking in front of the left side of the house. Richard always reverses his estate car in and parks in front of the garage. This arrangement means that neither of them has to reverse onto the main road, as, once Richard's car is gone, Elizabeth can reverse her car around and up to the garage and drive out forwards onto the main road.

Richard now carried his bag of rubbish past his garage and then down past the near side of his car to the rubbish bin. After depositing the rubbish and wheeling the bin out onto the strip of grass outside the gate where it would be collected, he retraced his steps, however on the return journey he walked up the off-side of his car between the driver's side and his neighbour's fence.

He stopped in his tracks and stared in disbelief at the side of his car. The paintwork along the whole side of the car was bubbled and flaking. Instinctively he looked to his left over the small front fence into his neighbour's garden. Jack Williams, whom Paul had warned him would be returning to the house, had also put his black bin near the front gates ready to put out for collection.

Richard's eye was drawn to the five-litre yellow tin that was stood beside his neighbour's bin, "Nitromores Paint and Varnish Remover" was printed on the side.

"The bastard!" cried Richard out loud.

It seemed that not only had Jack vandalised Richard's car, but he thought it funny to leave the incriminating evidence in plain sight so that there could be no doubt about the perpetrator.

Having heard Richard's cry of anguish, Elizabeth emerged from the house, "What is it Richard, are you all right?" she asked, concerned, and half expecting to see her husband had fallen over or cut his hand on some rubbish.

"Look at the car." instructed Richard, regretting having such a harsh tone in his voice.

Elizabeth did as she was bid and stared in horror at the damage, "What's happened to it, Richard. why is the paint like that?"

Richard looked again at the yellow tin of paint remover in their neighbour's garden and Elizabeth's eyes followed his gaze. She was just about to say something when Jack Williams came out of his front door.

"Good morning Richard...Elizabeth," he cried cheerfully, "I thought I heard someone cry out. Are you putting your bins out as well," then appearing to notice Richard's car for the first time he continued, "good lord Richard!...what on earth has happened to your car?"

"Well I don't know Jack," said Richard sarcastically, it looks as if some pathetic moron has poured paint remover over it.....what do you think?"

"Wow...yes....I think you could be right, that is just what it looks like, who do you think would do an awful thing like that, have you upset one of your customers do you think. Wow…that's going to cost a pretty penny to put right as well I expect, if you claim on your insurance you'll lose your no-claims bonus won't you….unless you've got protected no-claims of course, I always think it's worth paying the extra for that….have you got protected no-claims Richard?"

As if catching the direction of Richards gaze for the first time, Jack now also turned to look at the yellow tin in his garden. "Oh! Richard, I can see what you must be thinking, but I can assure you I had absolutely nothing to do with it. That empty tin was left in our garden shed by the people we bought the house from, and I'm only just now getting around to clearing it all out."

All the time Jack had been speaking there had been a grin on his face and his tone of voice had been overly apologetic.

"Well, no Jack, I know you wouldn't do anything as stupid and childish as to vandalise a neighbour's car, I don't think even you could be that pathetic. I'll get it sorted anyway, and I expect whoever was responsible will get what's coming to them in the end, they usually do I find."

Elizabeth, who had been holding Richard's arm throughout the exchange now pulled him towards the house, "Come inside Richard, you need to ring the police….and the insurance."

"Bye Richard, Elizabeth, hope you can get it sorted soon." said Jack, who now proceeded to put his bin out for collection.

"Was it him Richard, did Jack do that to your car?"

"Yes, I think so, but I have no proof, so I don't think there is any point in ringing the police."

"Yes, you have to ring them, don't you.....to get a crime number or something for the insurance company. I think you should ring Paul and let him know what has happened as well."

"Paul won't be able to do anything, I don't think we should involve him, he's got enough on his plate at the moment."

"I still think we should let him know."

"OK, I'll ring him later today, I promise, and I'll ring the insurance company from the shop. The car is still drivable and Margaret is there on her own at the moment."

As Richard drove to his shop he wondered if he and Elizabeth were going to have any more trouble from their new and unwanted neighbours.

Chapter Eight

Sergeant Reg Evans and Constable John Campbell walked up to the reception desk at Winchester Auctions, to see a man standing behind the desk.

Reg realised that the receptionist that he and Paul had just interviewed was probably not yet back at work, so he asked the man, "Is Mr Winchester in his office? we'd like to see him."

"Are you the police?" the man asked, causing Reg and John to look at each other and wonder just what it was about their appearance that gave them away.

"That's right.," replied Reg, "and you are?"

"David Adams, chief valuer, and no Sir, Mr Winchester's not in his office, he hasn't turned up for work today, in fact I've been trying to contact him all morning, but he's not answering his home phone or his mobile, It's not like him at all. In fact, I was just thinking of calling the police to see if he's been in an accident or something."

"John, pop up to his office will you, see if there is anything in his diary for today, I'll ring the Guvnor and let him know."

As John made his way up the stairs to Winchester's office, the man looked on, troubled, "Oh...I'm not sure I should let you..."

"It's alright," said Reg reassuring him, we just need to know if he has an appointment that he's not told anyone about. You won't get into any trouble."

Paul picked up his mobile from the desk and saw that the call was from Reg. "Reg, what's up, I thought you and John were bringing Winchester in?"

Afraid not Guv, he hasn't turned up for work today and his chief valuer is worried something may have happened to him, he's not answering his mobile or land line. What do you want us to do Guv?"

"Have you got his home address with you, if not, get it from his staff, get to his house and June and I will meet you there."

"OK Guv, we're on our way now.

"Twenty minutes after putting down the phone, Paul and June pulled up outside the large and impressive front gates of, "The Oaks" the home of John Winchester.

"Wow! That's an impressive entrance Guv," commented June, looking at the six foot high oak gates, on either side of which were stone walls of similar height. The gates were very modern in appearance and the walls looked to have been recently repointed.

"Somebody's been spending money," said Paul as he and June exited the car and approached the gates together, looking for a way in. There was no obvious handle or keyhole of any kind on the gates themselves, but on the right-hand side, mounted in the stone wall was an electronic entry system and intercom.

Paul pressed the button and waited for a response that never came. Standing back, he looked for a way to climb over but there were no suitable hand or foot holds to be seen.

"The man lives in bloody fortress,"

Making a decision that he hoped he wouldn't regret, he turned to June and said, "Bring the car over and park it across the front of the gates will you June, I'll see if I can get over by standing on the roof."

"Oh, your poor car, Guv, it doesn't look like you've been looking after it very well,"

After doing as she'd been bid, June got out of the car and stood watching as Paul climbed onto first the bonnet and then the roof of his car and peered over the top of the gates.

"I think I can clamber over and drop down onto the drive, what shoes have you got on?"

"They're rubber soled Guv but they do have a small heel, why Guv? Do you want me to follow you over?"

"That's the idea June, just be careful with the paintwork on the roof and bonnet, I don't want to have to get them resprayed as well as the doors."

"I was going to ask you about the car Guv, what happened?"

"It's a long story June, and one for another time."

"Fair enough."

Paul proceeded to climb over the oak gates and hang from the top on the far side before letting go and dropping onto the gravel drive. He had only just straightened himself when he looked up to see June completing the same manoeuvre.

"It's a good job I'm wearing trousers today Guv. or we might have had to get married," laughed June as she too dropped to the ground.

Both smiling and a little red in the face from their exertions the pair began walking up the long driveway to the house.

"You never mentioned your car being vandalised Guv what happened?" June persisted.

Somebody threw paint remover over it, I'll tell you about it another time, June, let's concentrate on finding Winchester for now."

Realising Paul wasn't in the mood to talk about his car, she continued, "Someday, I intend to marry a man who owns a house with a driveway I can get into fourth gear on."

Paul shook his head, "Most women say they want to get married for love, June, but you just have to be different, don't you."

"I could learn to love a man with a long driveway, and well, you know what they say Guv....Big driveway.... Big...."

"Big what?" asked Paul, not sure if he really wanted to hear the answer.

"Big driveway.....big bank balance, Guv."

The gravel drive took them up a slope through part of the woods and when they reached the top of the slope the house appeared before them. It was not what either of them had expected. The house was in fact, a large 1960s chalet-bungalow, double fronted with a large porch in the middle and a double detached garage to the right.

"Do you think all the houses along here are like this," asked Paul.

"Is that not what you expected to see Guv?"

"No, I was expecting a conventional Georgian or Victorian manor house, not this."

"Me neither Guv. it's nice though, I could see myself living somewhere like that."

"Well it has got the right length drive for you."

Paul rang the front door bell, but as with the entry system at the gates, there was no reply. The gardens, which again seemed to consist mainly of woodland that wrapped around both sides of the house, with only a small lawn and flower-beds to the front. After peering through the front windows to no avail, Paul walked around to the left of the house as June circled to the right, trying doors and peering through more windows.

"Did you see anything," asked Paul as they met up at the back of the house.

"No Guv, do you think we should break in?"

"Well, he does appear to be missing and his employees are worried about him, so...yes, I think we should, I'd like to have a little look around anyway and this gives me an excuse, and he did give us permission to search." Casting an eye over the back of the house Paul continued, "The front door looked pretty solid, as does this back one, is there a suitable size window around your side?"

"There's a fairly large frosted one Guv. I think it's probably a downstairs cloakroom, we could try that."

June led Paul to the side window she had mentioned, "It still looks pretty secure Guv. how will you get in?"

"I think we'll have to smash it with something, can you see anything suitable lying around? A large stone might do it."

June and Paul both looked about for a large stone or anything heavy with which to smash the window "How about the garage June, did you try the doors?"

"No Guv."

"Well let's give them a try, if we can access the garage there should be some tools we could use in there."

The double garage was fitted with an up-and-over door that surprisingly, proved to be unlocked. As Paul lifted the door, they both became aware of the unmistakable smell of carbon monoxide fumes. They looked anxiously at one another as Paul lifted the large double width door. The only car inside the garage was Winchester's Brilliant Blue C-class Mercedes, and after the noise of the garage door being opened had stopped, it was replaced by an eerie silence as they peered inside.

As they walked into the garage, they both put their hands over their mouth and nose, but most of the carbon monoxide had already dissipated. They both spotted the hosepipe running from the car's exhaust, in through the rear window of the car at the same time, as well as the body slumped in the driver's seat.

"The engine's not running Guv." shouted June, somehow hoping that the fact meant they were in time to save the occupant of the car.

"The car has run out of petrol June, maybe hours ago now.

"Yes of course, Guv, sorry….Is it Winchester?"

"Yes, it's him." said Paul, even before he had opened the driver's door and instinctively felt for a pulse, despite the fact that it was obvious the man was dead.

Just as Paul had confirmed to June that John Winchester was in deed dead, his mobile rang.

Seeing that the call was from Reg he answered it, "hi Reg, where are you?"

"We're at the gates now Guv," said Reg. "why is your car blocking them?"

"We used the car to climb over the gates, I'll send June down to let you in, but it's quite a long drive, you'd better bring both cars on up to the house once you're in." Then turning to June he said, "Reg and John are at the gates, there must be some method of opening them from the inside, go down and have a look for it, I'd prefer it if the whole station doesn't take a turn at climbing over my car. Throw the keys over to Reg and get him to move my car away before you open the gates…it would be just my luck if they opened out. Once the gates are open you can drive both cars up here."

"On my way Guv." said June as she set off back down the driveway.

After June started back down the drive, Paul turned his attention back to the interior of Winchester's car. Perched on the passenger seat as if intended to be found was a brass bound wooden box, and on top of the box a folded sheet of A4 paper. Paul put on a pair of latex gloves as he walked around the car and opened the passenger door.

He picked up the folded note and read it to himself with a feeling of anger rising within. The short note read.

"To whom it may concern.

"I can no longer live with the guilt of having murdered two men, Thomas Carter and Peter Newbridge. Tell Mary I'm sorry

John Winchester"

Paul was disappointed, he hated the thought that the case was over, and yet he and the team had no one that they could arrest and take to trial, it felt unfinished. Having read the note, he returned it to the passenger seat, but placed it beside the wooden box, so that he could lift it out and examine it.

Even before he lifted the lid of the box, he knew what it would contain, and sure enough, there it was, an early Smith & Wesson revolver, and almost certainly their sought for murder weapon.

He looked out of the garage as two cars now pulled up outside. "What have we got Guv?" asked Reg. as he exited the first car and approached the garage.

"It would seem as if our auctioneer friend decided to end it all today instead of turning up for work." answered Paul.

"Damn! Did he leave a note?" asked Reg who was every bit as disappointed about the turn of events as Paul.

"A very brief one Reg, just saying he couldn't live with the guilt of killing two men, and he even named them for us, Thomas Carter and Peter Newbridge. And he was kind enough to supply us with the murder weapon that he used on Newbridge as well."

"Well I guess that wraps it all up then Guv. we knew it was him all along." said John.

June grinned, "Yeh, just like Columbo."

John and Reg turned to look at June enquiringly, "You know, Columbo, off the television....I told you before but you couldn't have been listening, he always knows who the murderer is right from the start, and it's just a matter of finding the proof. Well the Guv. knew that Winchester had done it right from the start, and we just had to find the proof."

"The trouble is June," said Paul, "we didn't find the proof, did we? It has only just now been provided for us by Winchester himself, and I'll bet this Columbo of yours gets to arrest his culprits."

"It's still a result Guv even if we have no one to prosecute. It's still two murders solved."

"OK......But I want forensics to go over this with a fine-tooth comb. I want it established beyond any shadow of a doubt that Winchester killed himself and I want to know for sure that the gun that killed Newbridge is the one in there," said Paul, pointing towards the open garage door.

"You sound as if you have doubts Guv?" queried Reg.

"I don't know Reg perhaps I'm just disappointed with the outcome, it just seems so neat and tidy."

Paul walked back to the car in the garage and felt through Winchester's pockets until he found his keys, "Come on June, let's have a look around the house."

****

Paul pulled onto the driveway of Richard and Elizabeth's house after finishing his shift. Elizabeth had rung him and asked him to call in on his way home and she now opened the front door, obviously having seen him pull onto the drive.

She appeared distraught when she saw the state of his car and Paul thought it strange that she didn't enquire as to what had happened.

"I'm really glad you could come Paul, Richard is in the lounge.

Richard stood up when his wife and Paul entered the room, "Hi Paul, can I get you drink?"

"Just a coffee for me Richard, but don't let me stop you and Liz having one."

"I'll make a coffee for you Paul," said Elizabeth, turning to leave the room, "Richard and I have already started on the wine."

Paul sat himself down on the settee beside his friend, "Why did Liz want me to call in Richard, is there something I can do for you both?"

"I don't think there is anything you can do Paul, but Elizabeth thought we should let you know that our esteemed next door neighbour has vandalised my car."

"Vandalised how?" asked Paul, concerned that he may already know the answer.

"The same way as yours, by the look of it," said Elizabeth, returning with Paul's coffee.

"Has yours been done as well?" asked Richard, genuinely surprised.

"Yes....where is your car Richard? when I didn't see it on the drive, I assumed you were still at the shop."

"I put it in the garage earlier, why, do you want to see it?"

"No, that's all right, I assume it's had something corrosive poured on it, is that right?"

"Nitromores paint and varnish remover, to be precise, the cocky little swine next door left the bloody tin out so I could see it."

"Jesus.....he's got some nerve, he did mine in the police carpark, can you believe that!"

"You believe he's responsible for both cars as well then Paul, yours and Richard's?"

"It has to be him Liz, it would be one hell of a coincidence otherwise, both our cars vandalised in the same way on the same day."

"What should we do about it?" asked Elizabeth.

Paul thought for a moment, "It's difficult Liz, we can't prove it was Williams that did it, and if we kick up a fuss about it, he'll just laugh at us."

"So, are you saying we should just ignore it!"

"Outwardly I think that's the best policy at the moment yes, we don't want to give him the satisfaction of thinking he's angered us or put us out at all. But if I were living next door to him, I would get some security cameras installed, try and catch him in the act if he tries anything else."

"Do you think he will.....try anything else, I mean? Why don't we call the police and tell them that we know it was him....tell them about the paint-remover tin, and your car, and why we think he did it? If they question him, it might put him off from doing anything else."

"It might Liz, and I'm not going to tell you not to do that, it's your decision, but all they would be able to do without proof, is just give him a warning. The trouble is that it might have the opposite effect, it might make him angry enough to do something worse. It could trigger a vendetta. I don't know the man, so I can't predict how he will behave."

Richard had remained quiet throughout the exchange between his wife and Paul, but he now said, "I think I feel the same way as Paul, Elizabeth. I think we just go on as if nothing has happened, but take some precautions, like have some cameras installed as Paul suggested, and just staying vigilant. Let's hope that damaging the cars has got the revenge out of his system and he'll let things rest now."

Elizabeth took hold of her husband's hand and squeezed it, "It goes against the grain to think of him getting away with it, but if you think that's best Richard, then OK, but I want those cameras fitted yesterday."

Paul finished his coffee then shook hands with Richard and gave Elizabeth a hug before leaving, "Call me if he causes any more trouble but let's hope that's an end to it." And with that he left his friends and drove his own sad looking car home, wondering if he had heard the last of Jack Williams.

****

The body of John Winchester was laying on the mortuary table covered by a white sheet and Paul was

139

talking to Doctor Dorothy Lansbury, "How did he die Doctor?" asked Paul.

"Well I understand you were the one that found him Paul, but if that's not enough for you I can confirm that the cause of death was carbon monoxide poisoning. Did you have any doubts?"

"I suppose not, but is there any chance he could have been murdered?"

"Well there are no signs of him being involved in a struggle of any kind, and there are no ligature marks to indicate that he was restrained, but I suppose it's possible he was given a sedative of some sort before being placed in the car, I'll have another look at his bloods if you think it's worth it, I didn't look for a sedative, and to be honest even if I find one it could easily have be self-administered. Some suicides do take things to calm their nerves before doing the business."

"Would you mind though," answered Paul, "I know all the signs point to suicide, he just didn't strike me as a man with that much of a conscience for it to prey on."

"OK Paul, I'll have another look."

"Thank you, Dorothy, I'll owe you one," said Paul as he left the mortuary and made his way to the forensic laboratory.

The head of the forensic department, Steven Wyatt was holding the Smith & Wesson revolver in his hands as he spoke to Paul, "You'll be pleased to hear that this is definitely the gun that fired both the bullet we retrieved from Peter Newbridge's body, and the one belonging to the cartridge case we found in Winchester's office."

"But you can't say the bullet and the cartridge case belong together?"

"No, only that they were fired by the same gun...but it could have been on separate occasions."

"What about the suicide note?"

"That's not completely conclusive either, I'm afraid. There was a Hewlett Packard ENVY 4524 printer in the house and that is the type of printer the note was printed by, but I can't say for certain it was that particular one. We also took samples of the ink and they are a match as well. But all I can say is that, the note could have been printed on that machine."

"What sort of odds?"

"I'd say there was a sixty-five percent probability that was the printer, no more than that. What I'm confused about is why you would doubt it in the first place? after all, it's Winchester's suicide note and Winchester's printer."

"I know, everyone feels the same Steven, but the note doesn't ring true for me."

"Why on earth not?"

"Well there are several things that worry me. Firstly, why would he commit suicide? He didn't strike me as the sort of man that would let guilt bother him, and he knew we had nothing on him.

Secondly, why name the two victims in the note? He could have just left it that he had killed two people, we would have known who he was talking about, and why go to the trouble of providing us with the gun as proof? Did he think we would doubt his word, or not find the gun in the house? Most people who confess to a crime simply say, I did it, they don't say, I did it and here's the proof.

Third, why go to all the trouble of trying to dispose of the body of your first victim well away from everything, and then dump the second within walking distance of where you live!

Fourth, most murderers stick to one method of killing, after you've been successful with it once, why risk using a different method…why whack one over the head and shoot the next."

"Well, the guilt thing could have just built up over time, or perhaps you just misread him…no offence."

"None taken."

"As for the note and providing proof, perhaps he was just being tidy. I know that most multiple murderers tend to stick to one method, but the first one here was spur of the moment thing, and he probably didn't have the gun with him. I'm sorry Inspector, but I think you are reading more into these things than are there."

"Yeh, you're probably right."

Chapter Nine

Paul sat facing DCI. William Blake, or Blakey, as he was affectionately known throughout the station, who now said, "Well done Paul, that's another murder case under your belt, well, another two in fact. You've had three previous to this since you've been an Inspector, so with four cases now, and a hundred percent clear up rate, you must be as happy with your performance as I know the top brass are....aren't you?"

"Yes, I guess so Sir, I just don't like loose ends."

"What loose ends? The man left a suicide note confessing to the two murders and left you the evidence to prove it...what loose ends are you talking about?"

"I know Sir, but it worries me that he disposed of Newbridge's body so close to his home, and if he had a gun, well in fact the search of the house shows that he had several guns, why didn't he shoot both his victims?"

"Take your team out to the pub tonight Paul, and I'll join you all there after a bit and get some rounds in. I know you would have liked to have been able to take the man to trial. But at least you know he didn't get away with it. Now off you go, I've got tons of paperwork to do and I'd be surprised if you haven't.

Paul left his DCI's office with his mind in turmoil, everything did seem to fit, he just wished he could shrug off his nagging doubts.

****

The celebrations after the closing of a high-profile case always involved far more drinking than was sensible and Paul was anxious to get home, and when he eventually did, it was already approaching midnight. When he entered the house, he found that his wife Margaret was already in bed and asleep so he went into the kitchen and made himself a very large mug of strong coffee.

Paul knew he would be unable to sleep, despite the fact that he had broken his own rules and consumed two pints of beer before driving home. The coffee would keep him awake, as well as his mind being torn between worrying about his friends and their nasty neighbour, and the fact that deep down he had serious doubts as to whether Winchester had been responsible for the deaths of both Carter and Newbridge. Sleep was going to be a stranger tonight.

Having finished the mug of coffee he made himself a second and just sat at the kitchen table going over the facts of the case again and again in his head.

During the time Paul was drowning in coffee and reviewing the case Richard and Elizabeth Drake were fast asleep in bed.

All was quiet except for the gentle ticking of the Georgian bracket clock in the lounge until some unusual noises from the back garden caused Elizabeth to stir. A light sleeper, she was used to waking in the night if some nocturnal creature decided to visit the garden. Recently she had become aware of the fact that a hedgehog was in the habit of calling, and she had decided to encourage it by putting out food on the decking outside the back door.

The mistake she had made was in choosing to put the food into a shallow metal bowl. Sultanas, small pieces of fruit, cooked potato, fruitcake, plain biscuits, cooked chicken and even raw mince were all on Elizabeth's hedgehog menu.

The metal bowl however, tended to make a noise and wake her whenever the visitor came to dine. She had been meaning to change the bowl for a wooden one that she hoped would solve the problem, and now regretted that she hadn't already done it.

She looked at the digital alarm clock beside the bed, it was three in the morning. There was something different about the clock this morning, or not so much the clock, as the light falling on the clock....it was flickering.

It took Elizabeth a moment or two to realise that that the flickering light was coming in through the window and that the sound that had woken her was not the sound of the metal feeding bowl, but a different sound entirely, it was more of a crackling noise.

She shook Richard's shoulder to wake him up, "Richard wake up, I think someone has lit a bonfire in the garden."

Richard took a moment to fully wake up, but as soon as he saw the flickering light coming through the window he jumped out of bed and crossed quickly to the window, pulling back the curtains.

"Oh my God! It's the decking….it's on fire…..ring the brigade quick, I'll see what I can do with the extinguisher."

"Be careful Richard! don't take any risks, let the fire-brigade take care of it," cried Elizabeth, anxiously reaching for the phone beside the bed.

"Put something on quickly and ring from downstairs," called Richard from the landing cupboard where they kept their CO_2 fire-extinguisher, "I don't want you upstairs in case it takes hold of the house," he shouted, entirely forgetting that the phone Elizabeth was using was cordless.

Extinguisher in hand, and closely followed by Elizabeth, phone in hand, and now in her dressing gown, Richard descended the stairs. The fire was directly outside the back door and Richard quickly decided it would be better not to open it, so he headed into the television lounge at the back of the house, where there are patio doors opening on to the other end of the decking, which runs the full width of the back of the house.

Once outside, dressed only in pyjama bottoms and vest he quickly assessed the situation. The decking outside the kitchen and utility room was well ablaze, and the back door and water downpipe had also caught.

146

Richard pulled the pin from the extinguisher and cautiously approached the fire. He could feel the heat, not just on his upper body directly from the fire, but also under his feet. Realising suddenly that the fire could well be spreading along beneath the decking, he stepped off it and onto the lawn.

Once close enough he pulled the trigger and fired a jet of CO_2 towards the fire. From where he was on the lawn, he could reach only about half way back towards the house but he had no intention of venturing back onto the decking, especially not that end.

Running back towards the patio doors he was grateful to see that Elizabeth had not put away the garden hosepipe after she had been watering earlier in the day. The hose was on a plastic reel and the end was still attached to the outside tap. Turning on the tap, Richard played out the hose and directed a jet of water over the fire, successfully extinguishing it in a matter of minutes. He continued to dampen down the whole area until a very relieved Elizabeth followed two firefighters out of the house.

Richard put an arm around his wife's shoulders and led her back into the house, "I think I could do with a cup of tea now Elizabeth, and I'll bet these chaps wouldn't say no either," said Richard, indicating the firefighters.

Elizabeth put the kettle on while Richard took orders for teas and coffees from the assembled firefighters, one of whom was a young lady no older than his daughter Rebecca.

"What do you think could have started it," Richard asked one of the men.

"Maybe a discarded cigarette under the decking," one of them speculated, "do either of you smoke?"

Richard shook his head.

"Difficult to say then, unless it was started deliberately, would you like our investigator to take look, it could have been a much more serious incident if your wife hadn't woken up when she did."

"Yes, I think I would like someone to look into it, we've had a couple of things happen lately."

"I'll give him a call for you, he'll most likely be in touch in the morning."

"Thank you."

After the brigade had left, Richard and Elizabeth stood outside the patio doors and surveyed the damage. Over two thirds of the decking, much of which had been unaffected by the fire, had been taken up so that the firefighters could ensure nothing was left smouldering and likely to re-ignite underneath. The downpipe from the roof had melted to a height of six feet and the back door and kitchen window were so badly damaged that they would need to be replaced.

The Drake's neighbours to the right, Mr and Mrs Robins, had come out into their garden and Elizabeth was explaining to them what had happened and reassuring them that everything was under control and that they could return to bed.

Richard strolled onto the lawn and looked back at the house next door. There were no lights on at all, but the curtains to both back bedrooms were open and Richard was sure he could just make out the figure of a man, standing back a little from the window out of the moonlight, and watching proceedings with interest.

"It's him again isn't Richard? that bloody man, he could have killed us."

Richard put an arm around his wife and led her back indoors, "I arranged for a fire investigator to call to find out how the fire started, and if it was deliberate, I shall call the police and tell them of our suspicions."

"But they're more than just suspicions, aren't they? We know it was him."

"One thing at a time Elizabeth, let's get the proof that it was started deliberately first and I'll ring Paul in a while and let him know if he's continuing to target us, he may be planning something else against Paul as well, so I have to warn him. Now try not to worry, the contractors are coming to fit the security cameras tomorrow as well remember."

The day following the fire, Richard, Elizabeth and Paul sat around the kitchen table as they filled Paul in with the details of exactly what had happened.

"What did the brigade investigator say," asked Richard.

"We won't get his actual report for a day or two, but he said there was definitely signs that an accelerant had been employed and he's reporting his findings to the police,"

"He's not going to let it go Paul," said Elizabeth, "we have to go to the police and report him now."

"Yes, I agree, I was hoping he would think he had done enough, but clearly he is a much bigger threat than I thought. Call the police, but don't mention that you've spoken to me. Leave me out of it as much as you can."

Elizabeth looked at Paul with a slightly hurt expression on her face but said nothing.

Seeing her expression Paul said, "It's not that I'm opting out Liz, believe me, I shall do everything I can to rid you both of this odious man. It's just that to do so, I may have to bend a few rules a bit, so the less people who know about my involvement the better. So, no mention of me, agreed."

Elizabeth gave Paul a hug and said, "I knew you wouldn't let us down Paul."

****

Jack Williams stood six foot tall with a mass of brown wavy hair. He regarded himself as an entrepreneur. He owned a car dealership with three outlets in Bristol, Bath and Swindon, he also had investments in several other companies.

He looked at his Rolex watch and decided that he had time to visit all three of his dealerships today, before getting home ready for his wife to turn up at 4pm. He had rung her several times on her mobile and had eventually persuaded her to return home, as he'd known she would, he was fed up with the house being so dirty and untidy and fed up with takeaway meals.

He was in fact in quite a good mood, he'd trashed the cars of his interfering neighbour and the meddling copper and last night had been a hoot. The sight of that antique dealer, desperately trying to stop his house from burning down had been priceless, he wished he'd thought of taking some pictures.

The knock at the front door caught him totally by surprise, he wasn't used to visitors, he thought for a moment that perhaps his wife had decided to come home earlier than they had arranged, well that was alright, she could get the place cleaned up while he was doing his rounds.

When he opened the door, the two men standing outside flashed warrant cards, but so quickly he was unable to see any names, and they failed to introduced themselves "Mr. Jack Williams, we have a warrant to search these premises," declared the first man as they both pushed past him into the hall.

"What the hell's this all about....a warrant to search for what?" Jack demanded.

The first officer to enter the house now took hold of Jack's arm and led him towards the front room, "Why don't we go in here and I can explain everything, Mr Williams."

Jack wrenched his arm away from the officer but did as was suggested and followed him into the front room.

"I'll make a start upstairs," called the second man as he ascended to the stairs.

Jack sat facing the officer as he explained, "Your neighbour, Mr. Drake, has made a very serious complaint against you. He says that as revenge for him having called the police the other day to an incident of domestic violence you have carried out two acts of vandalism against his property. Firstly, he says that you vandalised his car with paint remover, and then more seriously, he claims that it was you that set fire to the decking at the back of his house, thus endangering life and property."

"That's rubbish, for a start, he and that copper he's friendly with got the whole thing the wrong way around, it was my wife that threatened me, and now all is forgiven and she's returning this evening so I've no reason to carry out any acts of revenge, and just what are you expecting to find searching the house....firelighters?"

"The fire-brigade said they believe an accelerant was used to start the fire, do you keep any petrol on the premises, Mr Williams?"

"I'm a car dealer, so yes, I keep a couple of gallons of petrol in the shed, but that doesn't prove anything."

"Well you don't mind my colleague having a little look round upstairs do you, we've also had a tip-off that drugs are being sold from this property."

"Well you're not going......."

The door opened and the second officer entered clutching a bag of white powder and declaring, "Look what I've just found upstairs."

"What the hell's that?" asked Jack, gazing in disbelief at the bag....you didn't find that here...Christ! are you fitting me up....is that it?"

"Calm down Mr Williams," advised the first officer, then turning to his colleague, "is that what it looks like?"

The second man dipped his finger into the white powder, and put a small amount on the end of his tongue, "Yep," he replied, "I'm pretty sure it's cocaine, quite a bit too."

"That's not mine...I don't do drugs, it's a mug's game...I've never seen that before in my life and you know it, you bastards are fitting me up!"

"So, you're saying that you don't use drugs, is that right, Mr Williams?"

"Yeh.....that's damn right!"

"Well in that case Mr Williams, as it's not for your own use, I'm arresting you on suspicion of drug dealing, will you come with us please."

"This is that bastard police friend of next door's doing, isn't it? Well he won't get away with it, I'll create such a stink, he won't know what hit him." Williams

153

continued to protest as the two officers handcuffed him and led him out to their car.

Elizabeth was just in the act of calling the men fitting cameras to the house, in for tea and cake, when she saw Jack being led away in handcuffs. "Looks as if the police are arresting your next door neighbour, Mrs Drake, what do you suppose he's been up too?"

"He's actually the reason you're here," said Elizabeth, leading the men into the house and preparing to relay the events of the past few days.

Back at the station Jack Williams paced up and down inside a detention cell, cursing Richard Drake, Inspector Manley, his wife and anyone else who had ever crossed his path. The cell smelt of something Jack couldn't quite make out, but knew he didn't want to ever smell again, and the bench, which was the only place to sit except for the toilet, was the most uncomfortable he had ever come across.

Eventually the cell door was opened and Paul Manley entered. Paul just stood and stared at Williams as the door was close and locked behind him.

"What the hell do you want?....oh wait a minute, I get it, you can't prove that I had anything to do with the cars or the fire, so you decide to fit me up on a drugs charge, is that it? Well bad luck Manley, or whatever your bloody name is....I've never used drugs in my life and you'll never get it to stick in court."

"I've been looking in to your background Jack," said Paul, calmly, "you've got quite a reputation for violence haven't you."

"I stick up for myself if that's what you mean."

"Stick up for yourself, is that how you describe it. You put a chap who worked for you in hospital a few years back, what was that all about?"

"Oh what, you talking about Jimmy, he worked for me, not on the books you understand, he was self-employed. I used to pay him to keep the cars on my forecourts clean, he'd do them twice a week on a regular basis, and we'd call him in if they got dirty in between. Well, we went through a stage when we seemed to be in need of his services an awful lot, and it was costing me money. One of my managers filmed him one day, and saw that after he had cleaned the cars, he spread breadcrumbs around the forecourt to encourage the birds down. Well of course they crapped all over the cars and we had to call him back and pay him again, crafty little beggar. Well I couldn't let that continue could I, I had to persuade him to stop doing it, didn't I?"

"You put him in hospital."

"He deserved it, he was costing me money and having a laugh at my expense, so he had to be shown the error of his ways. Now do you think that what you've done is entirely sensible? I mean, being in possession of some drugs isn't the end of the world is it, I'll pay my fine like a good little boy and be back home in no time. If you and your antique dealer friend really believe I'm

155

capable of the things you say, don't you think this will just egg me on to do even more horrible things? I'd be worried if I were you, I'm not a man to be messed with."

Paul closed his eye for a moment as if considering what Williams had just said, "Well I also have a couple of observations to make about the situation we find ourselves in Jack. Firstly, we're not talking about just possession of drugs here, it was quite a large amount they found in your house, and you admit that you don't use it yourself, so it must have been your intention to sell it on, and that's a charge of drug dealing....that's much more serious than just possession, and I think it would involve some time inside. Maybe not a terribly long sentence for a first offence, but it could seem a long one to you if rumours of wife beating get bandied around, wife beaters tend not to have a very good time inside.....but then on the other hand.....this whole thing could all just go away."

"Ah! Now the truth is out, you're looking for a deal, I see. Well go on, what would I have to do to make this all go away."

"Move house Jack, you can afford it, and I reckon you could have the place sold in, what? six weeks, if you're not too greedy with the price. But you have to move out straight away, I know you have places you could go."

"Move house! You have to be joking, it sounds to me like you're the one taking substances, there's no way I'm moving....I'll tell you what, I've got an alternative

156

scenario, suppose I just tell everyone the truth, that I was angry and damaged the cars and set the fire....and that you then got your mates to fit me up on a trumped-up drugs charge. I may not be able to prove it but mud sticks inspector and I'll bet it wouldn't do your promotion prospects any good.....be a blot on the old copy-book I should think....so pick the bones out of that and see what it gets you. Move house, why don't you get your pet Lovejoy to move house."

Again, Paul close his eyes as if weighing up the options, "Well, I can see that's an option for you Jack, and yes, it would possibly hold my career back a bit, although I have to tell you that I have a pretty good reputation at the moment and a lot of friends in the job with influence so I think I could ride the storm as it were, after all, who are they going to believe, a police officer with an impeccable record, or a scumbag with a record for violence and wife beating?   But, you could do that if you wanted, it's certainly an option for you.....oh!.... but then.....what if they were to discover all that child pornography on your computer....oh, now that would be very bad! Time inside as a wife beater wouldn't be good....but time inside as a child abuser, well, I hear they can come up with some pretty nasty ideas about what to do with them."

Jack just stared at Paul for a moment, taking in the significance and the enormity of what he had just said, "You'd really do that wouldn't you, Christ! You're even more of a bastard than I thought."

"Do we have a deal or not Jack? House sold in six weeks and you move out straight away." Paul held out his hand to shake on the deal.

Jack declined the offer of a handshake but said, "OK, it seems I have no option, but my wife is due back tonight, you have to give us a couple of days to move out."

"Be gone by the weekend then, agreed?"

"Agreed," responded Jack reluctantly, realising, possibly for the first time in his life that he'd met his match. The thought of being in prison as a paedophile filled him with horror.

Paul knocked on the cell door and the custody sergeant opened it, "All done Inspector?" he asked.

"All done sergeant, I'll be leaving now, and I believe Mr Williams here is free to go as well."

"Right you are Sir."

Paul exited the cell and Williams followed close behind with the custody sergeant. At the desk, the custody sergeant returned Jack's belonging to him and Jack asked, "Do I have to sign anything, or what?"

The sergeant looked on the desk in front of him, and shuffled some papers as if looking for something, "Well that's strange...there doesn't appear to be any paperwork here at all...oh well, never mind, I should just go if I were you Sir."

The two men watched as Jack left the station.

"Everything right as rain, is it Paul," asked the duty sergeant.

"Everything's right as rain, Ernest," answered Paul, who smiled and returned to his office.

Chapter Ten

When Paul returned to his office after his visit to Jack Williams in the cells Constable Phillip Strange was waiting to see him and he didn't look happy.

"What can I do for you Phillip, is everything alright?"

"I'm sorry Guv but I have a massive apology to make….I've messed up big time."

"Go on."

"Well, we had a huge number of calls and sightings of Peter Newbridge when we put out the appeal, if you remember."

"Yes, I remember, you were more than a bit bogged down and I was going to get you some help."

"That's right Guv so, I had everything stacked in my in-tray so I could take them in order but when that anonymous call came in putting Peter Newbridge at Winchester's Auctions on the day he disappeared, well that seemed to be what we were hoping for and I stopped following up on the ones left in my tray. I'm sorry Guv, that was lax of me, I should have checked the rest but I forgot all about them."

"Well OK, so we had what we were hoping for, I take it you've chased up the rest of them now, is there a problem?"

"That's right Guv and the problem is that amongst them was a report I received from Somerset Traffic Division. Apparently, Peter Newbridge's car was caught on a speed camera leaving Minehead on the 18th June at 11.04 in the morning."

"I see, that's the same day as the anonymous call puts him in Winchester's car park, at what time?"

"At around 10am, Guv, so there's no way he could be in Winchester's car park at 10am and driving out of Minehead at 11.04. So, either the anonymous caller got the time very wrong or it was a bogus sighting."

"What car is on the camera, is it his Hyundai?"

"That's right Guv."

"Did the anonymous caller mention the type of car he was in?"

"No Guv."

"Right, well we need to check that it was indeed Newbridge driving his car out of Minehead because if it was his wife or a friend, it could still have been him at the auction car park, just in a different car."

"That's true."

"So, get a look at the speed camera picture, I doubt it will be any use, but get it anyway. See on a map exactly where the speed camera was located and follow the natural route in and out of Minehead from Weston-super-Mare. Find every filling station on the route and hope that they have CCTV of the car being filled with petrol, going in or out of Minehead. Let's hope that whoever was driving didn't start out with a full tank."

"I'll get on to it right away Guv. I'm really sorry I missed it."

"Don't dwell on it Phillip, at least you followed it up in the end."

Early the following day, Phillip Strange once again entered Paul's office, "I've got some updates for you Guv."

"OK, let's keep the rest of the team up to date as well shall we," said Paul, leaving his office and calling for everyone's attention, "Phillip, do want to bring us all up to date with what you have."

"Yes, thank you Guv. I now have a copy of a speed camera photograph showing Peter Newbridge's car leaving Minehead on the A39 at 11.04am on the 18th June. Now obviously that means that he, or at least his car, could not have been in the carpark of Winchester Auctions at 10am. After discovering the report yesterday, I drove the most direct route from Newbridge's house in Weston-super-Mare to Minehead, although I have no idea of his final destination there."

Reg interrupted Phillip's flow, "Hang on a minute Phillip," he said rummaging through some paperwork on his desk," "Yes here it is......I knew Minehead rang a bell for some reason, Mr and Mrs Newbridge have a caravan in Minehead, so that would probably be where he was coming from."

"Do we know what sort of caravan Reg?" asked Paul, "is it a touring one?"

162

Reg checked his notes again, "No Guv. it's more of a mobile home, you know the sort of thing, I think they refer to them as static caravans."

"Thank you, Reg," continued Phillip, "Well I called into all the filling stations along the route and acquired all the CCTV footage I could get hold of. Now it makes for very interesting viewing."

"Yeh, I can imagine," said June, yawning, and eliciting a round of muffled laughter from the assembled team.

"Because," said Phillip, ignoring the laughter, "I have footage of the same car being filled with fuel at a station on the A370 going south the day before, that's the Sunday at 10.30 am, and there are quite clearly two people with the car, a man and a woman. The man who gets out to fill the tank is quite clearly Newbridge but it's difficult to positively identify the woman who remains in the car. However, the photo taken by the speed camera leaving Minehead shows only one driver in the car...no passenger."

"A man or a woman driving?" asked Paul.

"It's not clear enough to be absolutely sure Guv but it looks like a woman to me."

"What made you think to check footage from the Sunday, Phillip," asked Paul.

"I don't know Guv, just a feeling I suppose, and the fact that Gladys was confused as to whether it was Sunday or Monday she saw Mary and Peter leave together."

"That was good thinking Phillip."

"Wait a minute," cautioned Reg, "are we now saying that Mr and Mrs Newbridge drove to their static caravan on the 17th and that Mrs Newbridge then killed her husband and drove home with him in the boot on the 18th and then abandoned the car in Leigh Woods! Is that what we're saying?"

"Well yes, I think we are," replied Phillip.

"Well that would mean not just that it wasn't Winchester who killed Newbridge.....that would also mean that Winchester didn't commit suicide.....that his death was murder as well! Guv, are you on board with this?"

"Yes, I think I am Reg, most of you know that I've had my reservations all along about Winchester killing Newbridge, ever since we discovered his body."

It was June who spoke up next, "Do you really think that Mary Newbridge is capable of killing two men and staging a suicide...and where would she have got hold of an antique gun, Guv? We know Winchester was interested in antique weapons so I can see him owning one, but Mary Newbridge?"

"Well here's the thing about the gun," said Paul, "it's true that Winchester had a modest collection of antique weapons including one or two guns, but I've gone through the files on his computer and every single item in his collection is catalogued and photographed but there is no mention of a Smith & Wesson revolver. I just don't think the gun was his."

"His fingerprints were all over it, Guv."

"Oh! come on June, I sympathise with your point of view about Mary Newbridge, but don't forget that we have a mysterious boyfriend on the scene now...do we know anything about him?"

"Nothing at all Guv."

"OK, John, give Gladys Simmons a call will you, you seem to get on well with her."

"He certainly does, Guv" said Phillip, "I wouldn't be surprised if he was chatting her up, they got on so well."

"Yeh, he's desperate enough," said Reg.

"That's a little harsh," said June laughing.

"Getting back to the case, boys and girls...See if the boyfriend is still on the scene continued Paul, "Phillip, follow up on that speed camera photo, see if you can get it enhanced so we can say for sure whether it's a man or a woman driving back. Derrick, get down to the caravan park where the Newbridge's have their van. See if they have CCTV there. Find out what the procedure is when people turn up, do they have to book in, or can then just go straight to their van? Ask around the other residents and see if any of them remember the Newbridge's turning up on the Sunday or the Monday."

John Campbell put down the phone on his desk and announced to the room, "I've just spoken to Gladys Guv and not only is Mary's boyfriend still on the scene....he's moved in.....and the house is up for sale."

"OK, well we need to find out who this boyfriend is."

"Well you all laughed," said John, "but I knew Gladys would make a decent source, she's a regular little Miss Marple. Boyfriend parks his car outside the house now and Gladys has given me the number. I'll get on to the DVLA and find out the owner's name."

Paul slid off the end of the desk he'd been sitting on, "Right, let's see if we can finally tie this all together, shall we?"

Chapter Eleven

Detective Constable Derrick Price pulled his car in outside the reception cabin at Seaview Caravan Park and looked about for any signs of CCTV. There appeared to be just the one camera, positioned on the facia board just below the flat roof at the far end of the cabin facing the entrance, it would film those entering or exiting the reception building, but he didn't think it would record any vehicles accessing the park direct.

Inside he showed his warrant card to the receptionist and asked, "Do people have to come to reception when they turn up to stay in their vans or can they just go straight to their vans and let themselves in?"

The receptionist, a young woman in her twenties, put down her phone on which Derrick noticed she'd been playing poker, and replied, "We like and encourage everyone to book in and let us know they are here in case of emergency but not everyone complies," she said, and picked up her phone again.

"I see, well can you tell me if Mr and Mrs Newbridge booked in on the 17th or 18th of June."

The receptionist sighed and put her phone down again to check her computer screen, "No, they didn't book in, but their van was cleaned on the Tuesday, that's the 19th and the maid said it looked as if someone had been in there, even though the beds hadn't been slept in."

"If they had come here and not booked in, is there any way they or their car could have been picked up on any cameras?"

The receptionist thought for a moment before replying, "Not really, the camera here only picks up the fronts of cars that park directly outside, it's really trained on the doorway, and the only other place there are cameras is at the onsite club and restaurant, oh! and the outdoor swimming pool of course. So if they only visited their van we would have no way of knowing if they were here or not."

"Thank you, can you show me on the site map exactly which van is theirs and is there any way I could get a look inside?"

She passed Derrick a site map and pointed out the Newbridge's van, "I can't really let you in to anyone's van without their permission," she said, anxious to return to her game.

Derrick decided not to pursue the point until he'd had a look at the outside of the van, "Well thank you anyway, I'll just pop down and have a look at the outside if that's alright."

"Yes of course," she said, and then realising that her boss might want to know what was going on, "is there a problem of some sort."

"No, no problem, it's just in the course of an enquiry that's all, you get back to you game."

Derrick easily located the Newbridge's static van that was located on the outskirts of the park with a view overlooking the coast. Nice spot he thought as he parked in one of the parking bays on the opposite side of the tarmacked track. He walked up to the side of the van and peered in through the window, delighted to see that the interior was once again being cleaned. Walking back down the other side of the van, he opened the door and walked in, causing the maid to scream out in surprise.

Taking out his warrant card to show her he said, "I'm sorry I didn't mean to scare you, I'm Constable Derrick Price and I'm making enquiries about the owners of this van. Was it you that cleaned it on Tuesday the 19th?"

The maid thought for a moment, "Yeh, that would have been me...why?"

"It's just that the owners didn't log in at reception and they didn't let anyone know they were coming down. But you said you thought they had been here, is that right?"

"Well I didn't see them, but somebody had been in the van for sure...it was a mess."

"In what way, a mess?"

"You know, a mess....Well there were feathers on the floor for a start, it looked as if someone had taken the stuffing out of a feather cushion and spread it round the floor and there were two cushions missing as well as a couple of blankets off the foot of the bed. Oh yes! and a vase had been smashed and put in the waste bin, and they'd cut their themselves on it as well"

"How do you know that?"

"Well the broken vase is normally on that cabinet in the corner over there," said the maid, pointing, "and there was blood on the carpet in front of it, and some on the little mirror, it must have been a bad cut."

"Where is the vase now?"

I emptied the waste bin into the big container behind the main building but that would have been emptied yesterday for sure."

"Show me exactly were the blood was, would you?"

The maid pointed to a spot on the carpet and said, "I cleaned it all off the mirror but you can still see it on the carpet a bit, I'll have another go at it before I leave."

"Actually," said Derrick, "I'd like you to stop cleaning now, and I don't want anyone back in here until we say, so would you mind leaving now."

"I'm not finished cleaning yet."

"I know, but I don't want any more cleaning done this could be a crime scene."

"Can I just finish dusting?"

"No, I want you to stop what you're doing now and leave please, and tell them at reception that no one is to be allowed in here until further notice."

"What is wrong?....nothing is missing in here except the cushions and blankets I didn't take anything and I didn't break the vase, it was broken when I came in to clean."

"I know, you're not in any trouble, nobody has accused you of anything....really, there's nothing for you to worry about."

"You sure? Because I've been falsely accused before, I need this job."

It took some more assurances on Derricks part before the maid reluctantly picked up her box of cleaning materials and left the van, looking back over her shoulder questioningly.

Derrick rang Paul, "I think it's possible Newbridge was killed in his caravan Guv, there's a blood stain on the floor, that unfortunately the maid has tried to clean up, and there are cushions and blankets missing and apparently, when the maid cleaned on the 19th there were feather on the floor that may have come from one of the missing cushions."

"Good work Derrick, any evidence to show that the Newbridge's were there?"

"Nothing other than the mess in the caravan at the moment, Guv."

"OK, you hang on there until backup and SOCO arrive, don't let anyone near it, I'll pay another visit to Mrs Newbridge and see why she lied to us about the last time she saw her husband."

"Ok, Guv. I hope SOCO won't be too long though, I skipped breakfast this morning and I'm starving."

"That'll teach you to skip the most important meal of the day, but don't you leave my crime-scene."

"I won't, even though SOCO may find me starved to death on the steps of the van."

"Oh! come on Derrick, I must have told you a million times, not to exaggerate."

"Very funny Guv." said Derrick as he sat on the steps of the van, wondering how long he would have to wait.

Back at the station Paul asked, "What do we have on Mary Newbridge's boyfriend now Reg?"

"He's a chap by the name of Raymond Travis, Guv. aged forty-two, he runs a small building firm, employs six men full time and they have a good reputation by all accounts. He owns a small lorry, a transit van and he drives a Ford C-Max, dark grey. He has a son and a daughter from a previous relationship but they never married, she and the children now live in Scotland but he has no contact with them.

"OK, June and I are just off to see Mary Newbridge again, can you keep up to date with what's happening at the caravan park and let me know if anything of significance turns up? and ring Derrick and keep him up to date, I don't want him getting bored, hanging about down there all on his own, and you might suggest that he orders himself a pizza and gets it delivered if he's still hungry."

"Will do Guv."

When Paul and June parked in Eastfield Road, they both noted that a dark grey Ford C-Max was parked outside Mary Newbridge's house.

"Boyfriend's here as well Guv, said June.

"Yes, I shall look forward to meeting him, Raymond Travis, wasn't it?"

After they'd rung the bell, the front door was opened by a tall balding man in his forties, "Hello, what can I do for you?" he asked in a not too friendly tone.

Paul took out his warrant card and showed the man, who barely gave it a glance, "We were hoping to have a word with Mrs Newbridge, can we come in."

"Wait there, I'll see." he said, pushing the door back until it was almost closed and wandering off.

"He seems pleasant enough Guv." said June sarcastically.

After a few minutes in which time Paul and June could hear a conversation in somewhat whispered tones the man returned, "Come in, Mary will see you, but you must understand that she is very emotional at the moment, so don't stress her out."

"Of course," said Paul as he and June followed the man into the room they'd been in before and the four of them sat down, Mary and her companion sharing the settee.

"What news have you got for me Inspector?" asked Mary anxiously

"I'm sorry Mary, not very much I'm afraid, but before I start, could I enquire who you are?" Paul asked of Mary's male companion.

"Yes, of course, I should have introduced myself right away, I'm sorry," he replied trying to sound a little friendly, "my name is Raymond Travis, I'm an old friend of Mary's, and as she is understandably upset and not coping very well at the moment, I said I'd stay for a while and help out."

"I see, well that's very good of you Mr Travis, did anyone from Victim Support turn up? we did request that they call in."

"Yes, they did Inspector," said Mary, "thank you for that, but now that Ray is here, he's giving me all the support I need, but thank you anyway."

"I see you've put the house up for sale Mary, have you somewhere in mind to go?"

"Ray is helping me look for somewhere Inspector, I don't want to live here anymore, there are too many memories."

"Well I can understand that. The reason we've come to see you, is just to check a couple of details really. Firstly, in your statement to us before, you said that the last time you saw Peter was when he left for work about nine-thirty on the Monday, is that right? That's the 18th June."

"Yes, around nine-thirty, it could have been a few minutes either way."

"But definitely the Monday?"

"Yes Inspector, why?" asked Mary as she and Raymond exchanged glances.

"Well it's just that a neighbour of yours, said she saw you and Peter going out together that day, although to be fair, she was a little uncertain as to whether it was the Monday or the Sunday."

"Oh, well yes that's right, we did go out in the car together on the Sunday, we drove out to the Mall in Bristol, to do some shopping."

"Well that explains it, your neighbour obviously got the wrong day, she did say it could have been the Sunday. What were you looking for, was it something specific?"

"What?"

"Were you shopping for something specific?"

"Look....I don't see how knowing what Mary was shopping for the day before her husband went missing is going to help you, Inspector." said Travis, angrily, "shouldn't you be out there looking for whoever killed Peter, rather than here asking pointless questions?"

"Yes, I'm sorry," responded Paul, "but I'm a police man and I just ask questions, it gets to be a habit I'm afraid. But there is another anomaly here, and please believe, it's not pointless."

"And what's that Inspector," asked Raymond.

"Well, we have an anonymous report that Mr Newbridge was seen at around 10am in a car park in Chipping Sodbury."

Both Raymond and Mary appeared a little relieved, "Well I don't see how that is an anomaly inspector," said Raymond, "a half an hour is plenty of time to get from here to Chipping Sodbury, what's the problem? Whoever he was due to meet must live in Chipping Sodbury."

"Actually, I think you'll find that half an hour from here to Chipping Sodbury is almost impossible even if there was no traffic."

"Well perhaps Peter left a little before 9.30 Inspector," said Travis, "Mary didn't exactly check the clock, and perhaps your anonymous caller got the time wrong as well, where are you going with this, your just stressing Mary out."

"The problem is that Peter received a speeding fine coming out of Minehead on Monday 18th, at 11.04 am. And I just don't see how that is possible…..do you?"

"Well no," said Mary, "there must be some kind of a mistake."

"I agree, there must be a mistake somewhere, either he was at Chipping Sodbury or he was coming out of Minehead, he certainly wasn't in both places at the same time."

"OK, so the anonymous caller was wrong and Peter went to Minehead on the Monday that's possible, we've driven from here to Minehead in that sort of time, Inspector," argued Mary, now sounding somewhat flustered.

"Look Inspector, whether Peter was in Chipping Sodbury or Minehead that morning....what has this got to do with Mary, why are you badgering her like this? Wherever he went that morning he left here at around 9.30 or perhaps a little earlier like Mary said. Now I don't think she is up to answering any more questions at the moment, so I think you should leave."

"We'll go in a moment, Mr Travis, but I just want to confirm where you and Peter went on the Sunday, Mary, when you went out shopping to The Mall, together."

"Yes, I've told you Inspector, we went shopping at the Mall, that's Cribbs Causeway, just north of Bristol."

"Well that's what I thought you said, but there's another one of those anomalies."

"What is it this time Inspector, are you going to tell us that the Mall doesn't open on Sundays?" asked Raymond.

"No, not at all....I'm going to tell you that we have CCTV footage of Peter's car at a filling station on the A370 heading south, on that day, and some forty miles south of Bristol. Can you explain that, Mary?"

Mary looked at Raymond pleadingly, "Well perhaps it was another day we went to the Mall....That's right, I think it might have been the Saturday."

"So where were you going on the Sunday?"

"I don't know Inspector.....you're getting me all confused, Peter must have been on his own that day, I don't know where he was going."

"No...you see there we are again; the footage clearly shows two people in the car."

"I think Mary has answered all the questions she's going to today, Inspector, I think you should go now, you shouldn't be badgering a grieving woman like this."

"OK, we can leave it there for now, but these questions aren't going to go away they need to be answered. Now if you would be kind enough to give us your full address, Mr Travis and the address of your former partner, Miss Christine Parks, I believe, is that right? We'll leave you to think about things and we'll be in touch again shortly. In the meantime, I'm telling you both not go anywhere, if you have any holidays planned I'd like you to cancel them, even if it's just down to the caravan in Minehead that you forgot to mention, I'm afraid that's off limits until our forensic boys have finished with it."

Mary Newbridge and Raymond Travis just sat staring at Paul and both now looked worried and angry, "I don't see what any of this has to do with me Inspector, I'm just here to comfort Mary over the death of her husband, which I can tell you has hit her very hard. Wherever Peter's car was seen on the 18th Mary was home here, I know because I was with her. If you've been speaking to the neighbours, as you obviously have, then you will probably already be aware that Mary and I are seeing each other. Now I know that you are thinking that that gives us a motive to kill Peter but nothing could be further from the truth. The truth is that Mary and

Peter haven't been close since their son died, and Peter was well aware of our relationship and we have no doubt he was seeing someone, that would explain two people in the car on the Sunday, wouldn't it. Now I think we would like you to leave."

"We'll go for now Mr Travis, but not before you have furnished me with your full address and that of your previous partner."

"What the hell do you want with Christine's address, we haven't been in touch for years…do you think she might have been jealous of my seeing Mary? if so, surely she would have killed one of us not Peter!"

"I don't think for one minute your previous partner is involved, as well you know, but we shall be speaking to her about her relationship with you."

"Well you're welcome to my address, it's 162 Henleaze Walk, but I have no idea where Christine is living, other than the last I knew it was in Scotland somewhere, but you're the police, I expect you can find her if you put your minds to it, her name's Christine Parks like you said."

"Are you telling me you don't even send your children Christmas or Birthday cards?"

"That's right inspector, I would do of course, and get them presents, but like I say, I have no idea where they are."

"OK, we're going now, but we will be back.

****

"I've got an address for Christine Parks, Guv," said June," she's living with an Alan Thatcher, in Edinburgh."

"Good work June, get us booked on an early flight up and back tomorrow, we'll see what Christine Parks can tell us about her old partner and why she doesn't seem to want him to know where she's living."

It was a hot sunny day when Paul and June touched down at Edinburgh airport and they were grateful that the taxi they took had air-conditioning. It turned out that Christine Parks lived with the head teacher of a large comprehensive school on the outskirts of Edinburgh in a large detached stone-built house.

"Fallen on her feet by the look of it Guv."

"Well if her partner is head of a large school, he'll be alright for a bob or two June, and don't forget property can be a lot cheaper up here."

Having rung the bell, they only had seconds to wait before the door was opened by a smartly dressed woman who greeted them with a smile.

"Inspector Manley, is it," she enquired of the pair.

"That's right, and this is Detective Constable Kelly, thank you for agreeing to see us, Miss Parks."

"No problem Inspector, and it's Christine please," she said as she led them into a spacious front room furnished with a white leather three-piece suite and expensive looking oak furniture. "I'm curious as to why you want to know about Ray? Has he been up to no good?"

As they all sat down Paul asked, "Why do ask that, did he used to get up to no good, as you put it, when the two of you were together?"

"Ray is one of those men that never really grow up, Inspector, he thought I was happy holding down a job, cooking his meals, washing his clothes and doing the housework, while he went off playing with his mates. When the twins arrived, everything just got too much for me and I left. The mistake I made was letting him know where I'd gone, he came around and got quite nasty. It was a side of him that I hadn't seen before. Well I realised then and there that I had to get far away, so I moved up here and when the twins started school, I got friendly with a couple of the teachers, one of them introduced we to Alan and lifes been pretty good ever since. You won't tell Ray where I am, will you?"

"No, we just need some background on him, we need to know what sort of a man he is, and whether you think he might be capable of killing someone."

"Wow!....killing someone, my God!....I didn't realise it was going to be about anything that serious. Do you really think he's killed someone?"

"We don't know, that's the reason we're talking to you, do you think he's capable of it?"

"If it hadn't been for that time he came to see me after I'd taken the twins away, I would have said no, capable of hurting someone, yes maybe, but not killing them. After that visit, I'm not so sure, maybe, given the right motivation, I'd have to say yes, and he did have all those guns of course."

Paul and June exchanged glances, "What guns would that be Christine?"

"Oh, all sorts, back in the early days, before they changed all the laws about gun ownership, he used to belong to a couple of gun clubs, he used to go shooting most weekends."

"What did he shoot?"

"It was mostly target shooting I think, although he did sometimes bring back a pheasant or two. He also had some handguns, and he belonged to a black-powder club, where they would shoot antique muskets and the like."

"What guns did he own, do you know, and where did he normally keep them?"

"The rifles and handguns he would keep at the club, although he did bring them home on occasion, the antique muskets and pistols he kept at home. He had the small bedroom looking like an arsenal."

"Do you know what antique handguns he had?"

"No, only that they were old, and some of them had their own boxes, he owned a pair of duelling pistols, I think. I'm sorry, but I never really took any interest, I hated the things."

"Do you know where the clubs were located."

"No, and they will all be gone now, I remember Ray being angry when they changed the law on gun ownership and the clubs had to close."

"Did Ray get rid of his guns when that happened?"

"The more modern ones he did, he had to, but he kept the antique ones, I suppose he may even have kept some he shouldn't have, knowing him."

"Did he still keep shooting then, after the clubs closed?"

"Yes, I think he did now you come to mention it, but I don't know where he would have shot them, in a field somewhere I suppose."

"Did he keep any sort of a list or record of the guns he owned?"

"No, I don't......, oh wait a minute, yes he must have done, because I know they were all insured, they were worth quite a bit of money I think, so the insurance company would have wanted a list, wouldn't they?"

"I suppose it is too much to ask for that you have any of his insurance documents from back then?"

"No, but I can tell you that we did all our insurance though a broker, Carl Williams Brokers, they had a place on Fishponds Road back then, I don't know if they're still there."

"Well thank you again for seeing us Christine, you've been extremely helpful."

"That's alright Inspector, and you promise me Ray won't find out where I'm living."

183

"Not from us Christine, and thank you again for your help."

On the way back to the airport Paul asked June to ring Reg before boarding the plane, "Get him to apply for search warrants for Raymond Travis's house and builder's yard, and Mary Newbridge's house and any vehicles either of them have access to" said Paul, "I'd like to find out what guns he has now, if any."

"You're obviously thinking that the gun used to kill Newbridge actually belonged to Raymond Travis, Guv."

"It seems the most likely scenario to me June, especially given what we've just heard from Christine Parks."

"What is it that you hope to find at his house and yard apart from any guns he still has of course?"

"Well it would be nice to find a list of insured guns that include an early Smith & Wesson revolver."

"Do you know what my dad would say to that Guv? He'd say, "You want jam on it, you do.""

"Well, I think we deserve a little bit of jam at the moment, June, it's been mostly dry bread up to now. When we get back I want you to find out what gun clubs there were in the area back then, see if you can find out which one Raymond Travis belonged to. If we can get hold of a membership list we should be able to track down some of his old shooting buddies and maybe one of them could tell us where he did his shooting after the club closed."

Chapter Twelve

During the search of his home it turned out that Raymond Travis owned quite a lot of guns, and a not insubstantial collection of reference books on them. As Paul surveyed the collection that was laid out around the small third bedroom, he though his friend Richard would probably be quite envious. There were several flintlock and percussion muskets mounted on the walls, together with an array of handguns in display cabinets, some in boxes and some on purpose made stands. Paul surmised that the whole collection must be worth a considerable sum of money, and was surprised by the apparent lack of any extra security.

He put down the little double barrelled Remington derringer he'd been admiring when Reg entered the room, "I've got some recent insurance documents here Guv that include cover for the gun collection. But unfortunately, there's no list of individual items included."

"Never mind, get on to the insurance company, they must have a list of what's covered, is there an insured figure on there?"

"It just says, collection of muskets, rifles and handguns, twenty-six items in total, valued at £88,000."

"£88,000, I know the place is alarmed, Reg but have you seen any additional security measures? I'm surprised the insurance company didn't insist on something."

"The place is actually pretty secure Guv. I did notice that all the window and door locks have been upgraded from the norm and the alarm is quite an upmarket one as well. It's more than enough to put off your opportunist burglar, so as long as nobody is aware of what's here and targets it specifically, I think it's safe enough."

"Yeh I suppose you could be right, Reg. Well as I say, the insurance company are bound to have a list of individual items, so get on to them would you."

I'll do that now Guv?" said Reg, looking a little aghast, as Paul took aim at him with a seventeenth century flintlock musket.

"You are sure that things not loaded, are you Guv?"

Paul grinned at his sergeant, "Your knowledge of flintlocks is somewhat limited I see Reg."

"How so, Guv?"

"Because otherwise you would know that the weapon has to be cocked and there has to be powder in the pan for it to fire, even if it is loaded."

"OK, Guv we can't all be experts, I thought you just had to pull the trigger…..but to be honest, if anyone points a gun at me, checking to see if there's powder in the pan, is not the first thing on my mind….Guv….it's fear!"

"Point taken Reg, I promise not to take aim at you with a musket again," said Paul, marvelling at how simply holding an antique musket in his hands had made him feel like a little boy with a new toy.

After Reg had left, he took aim out of the window at a passing car and June entered the room, "Nothing of any interest in the lounge or kitchen I can see, Guv." and then noticing her surroundings, "Woah!....you seem to have hit the jackpot in here though....how many guns has he got?"

"Twenty-six, according to the insurance, I'm just about to count them, because I'm hoping there are only going to be twenty-five here."

"I just don't understand why anyone would want to collect anything like this," said June, "they're guns for goodness sake, they're designed to kill people," then spotting the musket that Paul still held in his hands, "what where you doing with that one Guv. when I came in?"

Paul, now feeling a little sheepish, replied, "Oh what this one...oh...I was just checking it wasn't loaded before counting them, I wouldn't want you or Reg to shoot yourself accidentally in the foot with a smoothbore."

"Well that's very thoughtful of you of course Guv. although we'd have to prime and cock it first, wouldn't we, before shooting ourselves in the foot I mean, and in point of fact, the long-arm you're holding is a rifle and not a musket." said June, as she took the weapon from him and held it resting on the ground with the barrel pointing to the ceiling, "it's probably a fouling piece for shooting game birds, if you see here Guv." she continued, pointing "you can see the grooves of the rifling if you look at the muzzle."

"Yes, very good June," said Paul, somewhat impressed by her obvious knowledge and a little embarrassed by his lack of the same. "well seeing as how you are so versed in the ways of muskets and rifles, perhaps you'd like to count them for me."

After a quick count, June said, "You were right Guv. there are twenty-five pieces, sixteen muskets and rifles and nine hand guns, well ten hand-guns actually, but I'm assuming the insurance company would class the pair of duelling pistols as one item, seeing as how they share a box."

After Paul and June had finished searching the house, they returned to the station to find that Reg had just received an e-mail from the insurance company, listing the twenty-six items that constituted Travis's collection.

"Tell me there's a Smith & Wesson revolver among the items listed," pleaded Paul.

"One boxed rim-fire revolver c1860, Guv, but it doesn't attribute it to Smith & Wesson or any other maker specifically. And actually Guv I've just had another look at the murder weapon, and there's no makers name or mark on the gun itself, other than proof marks. The only reason for us thinking it's a Smith &

Wesson is because of the manufacturers label on the inside of the box lid."

"Yes, I know, but I've been speaking to my friend Richard about it, and apparently Smith & Wesson had a virtual monopoly on cartridge firing revolvers between 1856 until 1869 and they used rim-fire cartridges like the ones we've retrieved from Newbridge's body and Winchester's office. Now if the insurance company say that the gun insured by Raymond Travis is a rim-fire revolver of 1860, then it has to be a Smith and Wesson."

"Do you think your argument will stand up in court Guv?"

"No, I don't."

"Well then we're no further forward," said Reg.

"OK everyone, let's call it a day, if we sleep on it, perhaps one of us will come up with a way to prove that the gun we have, is the same one that was owned and insured by Raymond Travis."

"There's one other thing that bothers me about all this Guv." said Reg.

"What's that?"

"Motive....I mean, if Mary Newbridge was so unhappy with her lot, why didn't she just up-stakes and go off with Raymond Travis...why did they have to kill her husband? And it all seems very convenient them having Winchester to pin it on."

"I know Reg, it bothers me as well, but when we get to prove they did it perhaps we'll have a better idea of why."

Paul called in to see Elizabeth and Richard Drake on his way home and was happy to see a For-Sale sign up at the property of Jack and Sandra Williams.

Once he was inside Elizabeth gave him a friendly hug and a kiss on the cheek, "Thanks Paul, I knew you would be able to do something."

"What are you talking about Elizabeth, what am I supposed to have done?"

"Elizabeth thinks you're responsible for getting Mr and Mrs Williams to put their house on the market, didn't you see the sign as you pulled in?" said Richard.

"Yes, I saw the sign alright and was delighted, they must have been making your lives hell, but I can assure you I had nothing to do with their decision to move out, whatever made you think that?"

"Well I'm pleased they're going anyway," said Elizabeth, "although I am very concerned that Sandra has returned to him, she turned up late this afternoon. I'm convinced that it's not going to end well for her. I thought that Jillian Simmons had found her somewhere to stay."

"She had," said Paul, "but Sandra decided to return, it's her choice Liz, at least there are no kids to worry about."

"Yes, there is that, I suppose, I wonder where they'll go? You are staying for a coffee aren't you Paul?"

"Just a quick one then," said Paul following his friends into their spacious kitchen, Margaret's going out with some old school friends tonight, so I thought I might pop to the Chinese for a takeaway."

"Nonsense, why don't you stay and eat with us if Margaret's not cooking, I've got a lasagne in the oven and there's plenty to go around," invited Elizabeth.

"Well I don't want....."

"That's a marvellous idea," interrupted Richard, "give Margaret a call and tell her, so she doesn't panic when you're late, and you can fill me in with all that's been happening with our auctioneer friend."

"Oh, of course, you won't have heard yet," said Paul, as he took a seat at the kitchen table and Elizabeth placed a coffee in front of him, "We found our Mr Winchester sitting in the front seat of his car in his garage with a hose leading from the exhaust pipe."

"Oh, my word!" exclaimed Elizabeth, "how awful, is he dead?"

"Yes Liz, he is."

"So, it looks as if he did kill that chap from Australia then, the one you thought he had cheated out of the Wilberforce bronze?" deduced Richard.

Richard was the one-person Paul felt comfortable discussing cases with outside of colleagues, he often found it helpful to have the opinion of someone who was not involved in policework, so over a glass of wine and Elizabeth's lasagne, Paul filled Richard in with developments."

"So, you don't think you've got enough on this Raymond Travis for killing either Newbridge or Winchester?"

"That's about the size of it, Richard. I need to prove that the gun we retrieved from Winchester's car, and that we can prove is the gun that killed Newbridge, is the same gun that was insured by Travis and is now missing from his collection."

"I don't know how you can do that Paul; the only way would be if you had photographs of Travis's gun and there were some sort of distinguishing marks to identify it. Without that, all those guns look pretty much the same. There would have been presentation guns made of course with engraving or carved handles and the like, but you say the gun you've got is plain."

"That's right, Richard, well look, I'd better be heading off now, thanks for a lovely meal Liz, and you'll keep me updated on any movement from next door yeh?"

"Of course,"

Richard and Elizabeth saw their friend to the front door and seeing Paul's car, Elizabeth commented, "Richard's car is in for a respray at the moment, Paul, when are you going to get yours done?"

"As soon as I put Raymond Travis behind bars, Liz," and with that Paul made his way home.

****

Sandra Williams pulled her Ford Fiesta onto the drive of the house, and Jack Williams opened the front door to greet her. She knew that he would be kind and attentive, he always was for a while after she returned. As she exited the car, she wondered why she allowed herself to be sucked back into the same old cycle of overbearing love one minute and violent anger the next. It was like living with a paranoid dog and not knowing when you approached him whether he was going to lick your hand or bite it.

She calculated that this was the sixth time she had left him and returned and each time she had told herself that it would be the last, that if he hit her again she would leave and never return. Sometimes she thought there must be something mentally wrong with her, like a defective gene or something, or that maybe she had somehow become the unwitting host of a previously unknown parasite that depended on her being regularly abused to survive.

On the other hand, having spent time in refuges on several occasions, she knew she wasn't alone in her predicament, she actually had friends now who shared her experiences.

"Come on, let's get you inside and I'll put the kettle on," said Jack, "it's so good to have you back."

Sandra smiled, why was it good to have her back she wondered, did the toilets need cleaning?

The first few hours of her return went well, Jack was on his best behaviour, and for a while, she was reminded of those things that first drew her to him. He was capable of such warmth and affection.

Things went sour when it was time for bed however. She told him she wanted to take things slow and was going to sleep in the spare room that night but he had been angered by the suggestion.

"Oh for goodness sake, I've been leaning over backwards to be nice and now you throw that at me....Have you come back or haven't you?" he demanded, "because if you have come back then we live as a proper married couple, you made some promises when we got married, or have you forgotten?"

"No, I haven't forgotten Jack, I remember very well, and you made some to me and I don't recall any of them saying you would take a cane to me if I didn't measure up to your expectations or do exactly what you want. You're not going to start bullying me again as soon as I move back....oh, I've been so stupid, this is a mistake.....I should have known it, I'm going back to the refuge."

Jack caught hold of Sandra's wrist, "You're not going anywhere now or any other time, how dare you think you can walk in and out of my life just when you feel like it."

Sandra pulled away from Jack's hold and retrieved her car keys from the hall table, "Don't try to stop me," she shouted as she made for the front door.

Jack grabbed hold of her arm and pulled her back violently causing her to stumble and fall to the ground,

"That's it!" she exclaimed, "you've attacked me for the last time....this time I'm going to the police to make a complaint, I'll see you locked up for it this time, you bastard!"

As Sandra pulled herself up from the floor Jack shouted, "I don't think so," and struck her hard across the side of her head with the back of his hand. The blow caught her off balance and caused her to fall sideways and strike the other side of her head hard against the front room doorframe and pass out.

"Jesus!" exclaimed Jack as he stepped back, "now look what you've made me do."

He stared down at his wife, expecting her to start getting up again and having another rant at him, but she didn't move. He waited, still no sign of movement at all. He realised that he had struck her even harder than he'd intended, as hard as he could in fact. He shoved her leg gently with the side of his foot, thinking that she might be pretending to be unconscious, but still nothing. It was only then that he noticed the blood on the doorframe, she must have hit her head very hard.

He turned and walked away towards the front door wringing his hands and cursing his luck, wondering what he should do. He knew of course that what he should do was ring for an ambulance, but what would happen then? The ambulance crew would have to ring the police because they would assume it was a case of assault and he could do without that at the moment, they were already breathing down his neck thanks to the interfering couple next door. And then there was that bloody police inspector, he'd probably frame him for the Kennedy assassination if he got wind of it, certainly his threat about them finding child pornography on his computer has given him cause for concern.

He bent down beside his prostrate wife and felt for a pulse. He'd never been very good at finding people's pulses and he couldn't feel one now. He looked at his watch, it was almost eleven there was nothing he could do to turn back the clock if she was dead, and in some ways, he thought ironically, it would probably be better for him if she was dead. At least if she was dead, she wouldn't be able to make a complaint against him and he could always make her body disappear, it wouldn't be the first time he'd disposed of a corpse.

No doubt that nosey bitch next door would have seen Sandra turn up or at least have noticed her car on the drive. There was nothing he could do about that but she wouldn't be watching all night so if Sandra's car was gone by the morning she wouldn't be able to say what time she'd left. So that was that. If Sandra came round then he would have to cross that bridge but if she didn't, well....then he would just have to get rid of her body and brazen it out. He squeezed past his wife's body and entered the kitchen, walking over to one of the wall cabinets he took out a bottle of whiskey, what he needed most at the moment was stiff drink.

It was some hours later when Jack decided it would be safe to move his wife's body. She hadn't so much as twitched in all that time and she felt cold now. He opened the front door and went outside. It was two-thirty in the morning and all the houses he could see were in complete darkness. He opened the boot of his wife's Fiesta to assess the boot size. It looked small, too small, but he couldn't think of any other way, so leaving the boot open, he returned to the house and lifted his wife's motionless body.

He struggled picking her up but once she was in his arms she felt as light as a feather, and he was reminded of other, happier times, that he had carried her and he was overcome with remorse and with the enormity of what he had done, he actually began to cry for the first time since he was a child.

When he got her to the car he discovered that she fitted relatively well in boot although there was no space left over. He briefly wondered about rigor-mortis, it had been over three and a half hours since he'd hit his wife and he thought that was about the time it was supposed to set in. He had no idea how long it lasted for though, so perhaps it had come and gone. Closing the boot, he locked the house and drove off as quietly as he could, not wishing to wake the neighbours.

Late the next morning Jillian Simmons turned up to see Paul with a worried look on her face, "Paul," she said, "I know you're busy, but can I have a word? It's important."

"Of course, Jillian, what can I do for you, has there been a development? I know from speaking to Richard and Liz last night that Sandra has gone back to Jack and there's a For-Sale sign in the garden, it looks like they're planing to move."

"Your friend Elizabeth Drake rang me this morning, Paul. Sandra arrived back yesterday afternoon in her Ford Fiesta and parked it on the drive but Elizabeth was up at six-thirty this morning and noticed that the car was gone. She rang me because she was concerned that they'd had another fight and that Sandra had fled in the night. She asked if I would check up on Sandra to make sure she's alright.

The thing is Paul I can't locate her. She didn't go back to the refuge, she's not answering her phone and she hasn't been seen by anyone since she returned home last night. Knowing what he situation is I'm very worried about her. When I spoke to her husband he at first denied that she had returned home at all, it was only when I told him that her car had been seen on the drive that he admitted she had been back, but he says she just came back briefly to collect some things and left almost straight away. Now that doesn't tally with what your friend said. Mrs Drake says that her car was there when she drew her bedroom curtains at eleven thirty."

"Have you reported this to missing persons?"

"Yes, I have, but they won't treat it as a priority, because of the circumstances and the short time she's been gone. I know this is an imposition Paul, and I know

199

you have a lot on your plate, but do you think you could find some time to look for her? Something tells me she's come to harm."

Paul leaned back in his chair to consider Jillian's request. He wouldn't normally get involved in something that wasn't strictly his case, but as he had been sort of involved already, and in view of the conversation he had had with Jack Williams in the cells, he reluctantly agreed, feeling that he was being sucked into something that could possibly backfire on him.

"If I can clear it with my DCI, I'll do what I can, but I warn you Jillian, it may not be a lot."

"Anything you can do is better than nothing, thank you Paul, if I can ever return the favour, don't hesitate to ask."

Paul said farewell to Jillian, and made his way to his DCIs office. After knocking on the door, he waited only a second before the familiar voice of DCI Blake said, "Come in Paul."

"That was impressive Sir, you said my name before I came in, how did you know it was me?"

"I guess I must have recognised your knock Paul, take a seat, and tell me how I can help you."

"Well sir, I've just had a visit from Jillian Simmons, concerning a married couple who currently live next door to my friends Richard and Elizabeth Drake. To cut a long story short Sir, she wants me to try and help find Sandra Williams because she's gone missing and Jillian thinks she may have come to harm."

DCI Blake leaned back in his chair and studded Paul's face, "What are your feelings about it, Paul, do you want to get involved? You've still got two unresolved murders on your hands and it's not strictly our problem, not yet anyway."

"No, I appreciate that Sir, but I would like to give it a little time, if that's alright with you? I won't let it interfere with our murder enquiry."

"That's fine then, Paul, I'll see if I can rustle up a little extra help for you, shall I?"

Paul was a little taken aback, "Well that would be great if you could Sir, I have to say I'm a little surprised, I was thinking you'd tell me not to waste any time on it."

"Well, I'll let you into a little secret Paul, I know Jillian Simmons quite well, I've worked with her in the past, before she specialised in domestic abuse cases, and I have to tell you that she has the most uncanny instincts, if Jillian thinks there's cause to worry about this Sandra's wellbeing, then we should all be worried. And just to keep the record straight, Jillian called in to see me, before she saw you."

"Can I ask why, Sir?"

"Because she's a stickler for doing things right, and she didn't want you to be tempted into going behind my back. She said she wanted your help, and asked if I had a problem with you providing a little. I told her you had a lot on your plate, but that I would leave the final decision up to you."

"Thank you, Sir."

Paul stood to leave and just as he was exiting the door, Detective Chief Inspector Blake said, "And thank you for being up-front with me, Paul, I was hoping you'd came to me if you decided to help out."

"Wouldn't have been able to keep it from you anyway Sir, everyone knows that nothing happens in this station without you knowing about it."

"And that's one urban myth I would like to perpetuate," said DCI Blake, as Paul left his office.

The following morning was a bright sunny day and Paul was feeling up-beat, a feeling that was justified when a man who looked to be in his late fifties entered the main office and asked for Paul.

"I'm Inspector Paul Manley, what can I do for you?"

"Detective sergeant Christopher Foulkes, Sir, DCI Blake said you needed an extra pair of hands, so here I am, ready to undertake whatever task you have for me Sir."

Paul shook the new arrival by the hand, "Nice to have a new face about the place, Chris, I hope you've got a sunny disposition," said Paul, looking around the room and indicating the rest of the team, "these are a surly lot. I have to say that when the DCI said he'd get me some help I didn't expect a detective sergeant to turn up."

"No, well the truth is Sir, I'm retiring in a few weeks, so I think they've sort of put me out to pasture as it were."

"OK, Chris, well you introduce yourself to the crew and then I'd like you and Reg in my inner office in ten minutes, yes."

"Yes Sir."

"Oh, and one other thing, while you're here, everyone calls me Guv, not Sir, I didn't much like it at first, but now it would feel strange if they called me anything else."

"Understood Guv."

Paul studied the faces of the two men opposite him and after a moment said, "Reg, I'd like you, John and Phillip to take on the task of looking for Sandra Williams, you've shown a talent for tracking people down in the past. Work with Jillian Simmons, she feels that Sandra has already come to harm, so it may quickly escalate into another murder enquiry."

"What about Raymond Travis Guv?"

"I know Reg but I feel like we've come up against a brick wall at the moment, and I'm wondering if we've all just gone a little stale on it. I'm hoping a fresh pair of eyes and ears will come at it from a new angle. And if not, then maybe you having a break from it and coming back fresh will lead us somewhere. I don't want you thinking I'm doing this because I'm dissatisfied with your work in any way Reg, quite the contrary, I need an experienced man looking for Sandra."

"How about letting me have June Guv? It might be good to have a female officer on a domestic abuse case."

"I thought about it, Reg but I have a feeling it's going to be a murder case rather domestic assault, although of course I hope I'm wrong. You can have June if you need her for anything specific, but to be honest, she's the only one of you lot I trust to drive my car."

"What, even in the sate it is at the moment Guv?"

"Yes, thanks for reminding me Reg."

"Sorry…..is there something I should know," asked Chris.

"Somebody saw fit to pour paint remover over my car the other day, Chris. I'm quite upset about it, and that lot out there think it's funny to mention it at every opportunity. Now go on you two, hop to it."

Reg and Chris stood to leave the room and on the way out Chris asked Reg, "Do you know what make it was Reg?"

"What make what was?"

"The paint remover."

Paul picked up the empty plastic coffee cup that was on his desk and threw it at them as they exited his office, laughing, and instantly regretting doing so as the small residue of coffee splashed on the window and began to drip on the carpet.

"You're fired…both of you," he called after them.

Chapter Thirteen

Paul filled Sergeant Chris Foulkes in with the details of the case they were building against Mary Newbridge and her lover Raymond Travis and gave him the files to review on their way to Raymond's builders yard.

The yard turned out to be one of a number of medium sized industrial units alongside a disused railway embankment just south of the city of Bristol.

"It's a bit isolated out here for a builders yard Guv." commented Chris, "It's a bit of a journey for him too, if he lives in Henleaze."

"Yes, but it's not as if he and his men work here is it? It's just a depot where they keep all the materials and things, and park the vehicles overnight."

"I suppose so, I wonder where the railway line went when it was open?" asked Chris, pointing up to the top of the earth embankment.

"I've no idea," said Paul as he pushed open the large wooden gates at the front of the yard.

Inside the gates, a long drive stretched from the front of the yard all the way down the righthand side where it ended against the railway embankment at the far end. To the left there were several structures, ranging from no more than a covered barn type building to a modern porta-cabin that was obviously used as an office. Most of the structures had been erected simply to keep whatever was under them protected from the elements. One edifice housed an assortment of timber, while others contained tiles, sand, bricks and other building materials.

There was a flat-bed lorry and a transit van parked in the yard one behind the other and the two men gave them a quick inspection before opening the porta-cabin door and entering the office.

"So, did Travis give up his interest in shooting when the gun clubs closed Guv?" asked Chris, as he looked through one of the two filing cabinets in the room.

"Christine Parks didn't seem to think so, she reckoned he still used to go off shooting somewhere."

"There must be membership records of the clubs he belonged to somewhere, I'll see if I can locate where they are now. If we can speak to some of the other members they might know where he went to shoot, may even have gone with him."

"That's a good shout, Chris, but June is already looking into it, I'll check with her when we get back and see if she's had any success. Anything in the filing cabinet?"

"Not of interest Guv, just bills for materials and invoices for work done, that sort of thing....you?"

"Not much, although I have got a list of the men he employs, along with addresses and contact numbers, otherwise I think this is a damn waste of time...come on,

206

we'll have a quick scoot round the yard, then get back to the station and you can chase up those membership records with June. I can't believe we'll find anything of interest in the yard, but it's best to be thorough, we'll circle the yard in opposite directions and meet up back here," said Paul.

After the two men had looked about the yard and met up again, they both shrugged their shoulders, "I've got nothing" said Paul, "You?"

"No, but I am curious about the two posts down by the embankment."

"What posts? Show me."

Paul accompanied Chris to the end of the yard where it finished up against the earth embankment of the disused railway line. Just in front of the earth wall two six-by-six inch wooden posts had been cemented into the ground, standing some seven feet tall and set about eight foot apart.

"What do you suppose these are for Guv?"

Paul studied the posts for a minute, "Well I don't know, maybe they are to stop the lorry being reversed into the earth embankment."

"They're a bit too far apart for that Guv. unless they had some kind of cross-member at one time and in any case you'd do more damage reversing into those than you would the earth wall."

"That's true, but look here," said Paul, "there was something screwed to the face of them at one time, you can still see the screw holes, there must have been a notice board of some sort mounted on there. Maybe an advertising board, or perhaps a health and safety notice for the yard, you know the sort of thing, "Hard Hats must be Worn at All Times" that sort of thing."

"Yeh that's probably it, Guv. or maybe a dartboard for when the men have their break….."

Both men just stood in silence staring at one another for a moment, and then Paul gave voice to the thought that had crossed both their minds, "Or a target, for target shooting, you mean!"

They both turned and looked back towards the front gates, "If you take the van and the lorry out of the yard, you've got quite a nice little shooting range from here to the doors, plenty long enough to fire a flintlock musket I should think, and maybe even a small handgun." Paul speculated.

"But what about the noise Guv, I've never heard of a flintlock being fitted with a silencer. There would surely have been complaints?"

"Maybe not, you said yourself when we arrived about how isolated it is out here. There are no residential properties around that I can see, and after the other units have closed for the day, who is there to complain?"

"You could be right Guv or maybe the noise would be less intrusive during the working day, let's face it, the engineering units on either side are going to generate quite a bit of noise themselves."

"You're right, let's have a word with the neighbours, you take the one on the left, I'll talk to the ones on the right."

As Paul entered the small engineering works next door to Raymond's builder's yard, he realised that Chris had been right the noise level was very high. He stood inside the door looking around. Several men all dressed in overalls were working at benches or machines and all were wearing ear-defenders. After a few minutes the noise level dropped significantly as two of the men finished what they were doing at the machines they'd been operating and carried whatever it was they were working on, back to their bench. The only man Paul could see that was not wearing overalls spotted him standing by the door and approached him.

As the man got close, he indicated that Paul should step back outside the workshop, where he joined him, "Sorry to usher you out like that," the man said, "but it can get very noisy in there at times. How can I help you?"

Paul showed the man his warrant card and introduced himself, "I'm Inspector Paul Manley, and we're making some enquiries about Raymond Travis, the man who owns the builder's yard next door, do you know him?"

"Ray, yes, I've known him for years, what's the old chap been up to?"

"Well at the moment we don't know that he's been up to anything, it's just that his name has come up in the course of our enquiries, what can you tell me about him?"

"Well not a lot really, he had the yard next door before I had this unit, that's about twelve years now, how long he was there before that I don't know. He's got about half-a-dozen men working for him and seems to do OK, but I don't know anything about his home life or anything, although he did build an extension on the back of my house for me a few years back, did a good job too, I'd recommend him to anyone wanting work done."

"Have you ever had cause to complain about anything next door, loud noises or anything like that?"

The man laughed, "Like from the occasional gunshot you mean."

"Gunshot?"

"Yeh, is that what this is about? the guy's a, what do you call it, a black-powder enthusiast, really into his flintlock muskets and all that stuff, not content with just owning them, he likes to fire them as well, that's not against the law is it?"

"The law on antique firearms is quite vague and complicated and it's not my area of expertise, but if you intend to fire an antique weapon, rather than just keep it as curio, you need a licence to hold the powder or obsolete ammunition, no matter how old the weapon is."

"Oh, I see, so that is what this is all about, Ray firing the guns down here?"

"How often did it happen?"

"Every week for a while and then I think he found somewhere more suitable."

"But you don't know where that was, I suppose?"

"Sorry no."

"Did he shoot the guns on his own down here, or did he have people with him?"

"Again, I don't know, I only ever saw him or his workers down here, although he did let me have a go once."

"What did you shoot at?"

"He had a target set up on a board in front of the embankment."

"Thank you, you've been very helpful."

Chris joined Paul outside Raymond's yard after speaking to the manager of the unit the other side of Raymond's.

"Anything from your side?" asked Paul.

"Nothing at all Guv. They've only been there three years and it was an empty unit when they took over, how about your side Guv?"

"Yeh, they definitely remember Travis bringing his muskets down here to fire, but only for a brief period of time, and then he found somewhere else, presumably more convenient."

"Does it help us at all, Guv. knowing that he fired his guns down here?"

"Well.....if he was shooting at a target mounted between those two posts at the end of the yard...." started Paul.

"Then there just might be some bullets embedded in the earth behind them," finished Chris.

"Right," said Paul with renewed enthusiasm, "I want a forensics team down here as soon as possible, tell them to sift through the earth from behind that target area with metal detectors, I want every musket ball and bullet there is retrieved from there. If we can find, even one bullet from there that was fired from our murder weapon, then we've got the bastard!"

****

Back at the station Paul caught up with June, "Any luck finding Travis's old gun club, June?"

"Yes Guv, he belonged to The Long Ashston Rifle and Black Powder Club. I've spoken to the then Chairman, a Mr Andrew Mitchell. He told me that when the club closed, a few of the members, including Travis, applied for black-powder licences and got them. Mr Mitchell is a banker and owns a large property in Cleeve on the way to Weston-super-Mare. His place has over six acres of land, and he set some of it aside to set up his own firing range. It took a few months to get up and working apparently, but that's where they shoot now."

"Including Raymond Travis?"

"Yes Guv."

"That's great work June, Chris and I have also found out that he did some shooting at his yard. Chris is organising a forensics team to go down and examine the area behind where we believe he had a target erected. There's an earth embankment behind it and if we can find a bullet in there that was fired from our gun, then I think that should wrap it up."

"What about where they shoot now Guv? do you still want to follow up with that."

"Absolutely, ring this Andrew Mitchell, tell him we want to speak to him at the property."

June walked off to make the phone call, and for the first time in days, Paul was in a good mood, one that was made even better when Steven Wyatt rang to say that they had found blood spatter inside Newbridge's static caravan that was a definite match for Peter Newbridge.

****

June turned onto the driveway of, Five Acres the home of Andrew Michell and his family, and drove up to the impressive six-bedroom house. Andrew Mitchell himself opened the door and greeted them.

"Welcome, Inspector Manley is it? And you must be Constable Kelly, whom I spoke to on the phone, please do come in, can I get you anything to drink, tea or coffee perhaps?"

"No, thank you, Mr Michell, I don't want to take up too much of your time, we just have a few questions about Raymond Travis, and while we're here, I wonder if it would be possible to see your firing range?"

"Yes of course, I'm always happy to show off the range, I designed it myself, and the man you're enquiring about, Raymond Travis, his firm built it. If you'd like, we can talk on the way there, it's a bit a walk, do follow me, and please call me Andrew."

June and Paul followed Andrew out of the back of the house and walked along a neat paved path, past an assortment of flowerbeds, spacious lawns, greenhouses and vegetable patches, "We like to put the grounds to good use, as you can see Inspector."

"It's very impressive," said June, "how does the firing range fit in?"

"Do I detect a slight hint of disapproval Constable."

"You weren't meant to Andrew, but it's true, I'm not in favour of people shooting guns, not for any reason."

"Some people like collecting china, or old cars, constable, some of us like, not just collecting antique firearms, but shooting them as well, it's all strictly regulated, and I don't think anyone has held up a bank with a flintlock or a percussion pistol for donkey's years."

Paul was a little surprised to find that the range was enclosed inside a long narrow brick building and Andrew could see the surprise on his face.

"You thought the firing range would be out in the fresh air, Inspector?"

"Yes, I suppose I did?"

Well there are four reasons why the range is totally enclosed. Firstly, my children were living here when it was built and it was a sensible precaution that my wife insisted upon, secondly, I keep a quantity of black-powder on the premises and that needs to be kept both secure and dry, thirdly I needed a workshop for repair and restoration, and last, but by no means least, flintlocks aren't at the best in the rain, it makes it very difficult to keep the powder dry."

Andrew unlocked the oak door and led them inside. Once inside, Paul and June found themselves in a fully equipped gunsmith's workshop. There were two different sized metal working lathes, and various other machines that Paul had no idea of their purpose, and a large central bench.

"So, you do your own repairs in here," asked Paul.

By way of an answer, Andrew unlocked a metal cabinet that stood against the wall to their left and took out, what looked like, an antique musket and handed it to Paul.

"What do you make of that Inspector?"

Paul examined the weapon closely, "Well I can see that it is in remarkable condition for its age, in fact, it looks to be in mint condition, is this one you've restored?"

"You've got a good eye Inspector. Well I can tell you that it's a Baker Rifle, that would normally date to around 1800, but that particular one is only two years old, and I'm very proud of it."

Paul looked at it with fresh eyes, "You made this?"

"I did indeed, in this very room, with my own two hands." announced Andrew proudly.

Even June was a little impressed,

"Well you're to be congratulated," said Paul," I'm no expert, but the workmanship looks top quality to me. Have you fired it?"

"Oh yes, last month for the first time."

"Why did it take you so long to fire it," asked June, puzzled, "you said you made it two years ago?"

Andrew loved nothing, more than showing people his workshop, "Let me show you something else," he said, leading them to the far end of the room and pointing to another bench, in the centre of which was mounted a musket on a wooden frame, "this is our proofing bench. None of us would be stupid enough to fire an antique weapon without being sure it wasn't going to blow up in our face, so we proof fire them first."

"What does that entail?" asked Paul, who was truly interested.

"Well if you want to, you can of course send your gun to the London or Birmingham proof house and get it officially proofed and proof marked, a legal requirement for shotguns or any gun that is to be sold in the UK, other than antique weapons. Or we can do it here on an unofficial bases, you don't get an official proof mark of course, but you do know the gun is safe to fire.

"How do you go about proofing a gun?"

"We take the bench out to the range, that I'll show you in a moment, clamp the gun to be proofed to the frame you see there and load it with five time the normal charge, like a superimposed load if you will, five times the powder and five balls or bullets. Then we attach a cord to the trigger and pass it through this small hole in the wall here, he continued, pointing. Then we retire back inside here and pull the cord. If, when we examine the gun afterwards, it is undamaged, then we feel confident enough to fire it with a conventional load."

"That's why you didn't fire the Baker Rifle you made for two years."

"That's right Inspector, I'd invested hundreds of hours of work into making it, and I was immensely pleased with the result, so the thought of potentially destroying it, if it failed the proofing test, was hard to come to terms with, but I bit the bullet, so to speak, the other week and as you can see, it passed with flying colours. Now I know my Baker is OK, I will sometime send it to be proofed officially and get it stamped. Now, I've bored you for long enough, come through here and I'll show you the range."

Once through the end door and into the shooting range proper, Paul asked, pointing to the target at the far end "What's directly behind the target?"

"It's rather like a large wooden trough on legs and it's filled with sand. The front of the trough slots into a groove and is easily removeable, and every now and

217

again we have to replace it, when it becomes too damaged."

"Do you ever collect the spent bullets from the sand?"

"Of course, when we change the front board, most of the sand falls out so we sieve it before returning it to the trough."

"What do you do with the bullets you recover."

"We melt them down and mould new ones, Inspector."

"Have you sieved the sand recently?"

"Just two days ago actually, why?"

"Please tell me you haven't melted the bullets yet!"

"No, they're all in that big box over there, waiting to be melted," said Andrew, pointing.

Paul walked over to the box Andrew had indicated and started to look through the contents. Pulling out a handful of assorted projectiles, he asked, "Some of these are bullets, rather than balls, what were they fired from?"

"Some will be from rifles, like my Baker, others will be from percussion rifles and maybe the odd percussion pistol, one of our group has an early Adams revolver."

"I'm wondering if any could have come from an early Smith & Wesson revolver? I understand that Raymond Travis owned such a gun, is it possible he ever fired it here?"

"No, I know the model of gun you're talking about, Inspector, but it's not a muzzle loading weapon, it takes a fully contained rim-fire cartridge, and although the law recognises that anyone who owns an antique weapon of that sort as a curio, may want to also own some authentic ammunition, it is strictly controlled and it would be illegal to fire such a gun."

"So, Travis never fired his gun here, you're sure?"

"Absolutely not, I wouldn't even allow such a gun on the premises, it wouldn't be worth risking my licence."

"OK, thank you for your help, Andrew, I can truly say this has been an extremely interesting visit."

"Would you like to fire one, Inspector?"

Paul and June both turned back, "No, that's OK," said June, but Paul replied, "Well...yes, I think I would actually, thank you."

June looked at him with her hands on her hips, "Guv. really?"

"Yes June, really, don't they say that all experience is good experience."

"Having your leg chopped off would be an experience Guv."

"OK, so there may be one or two exceptions, but this is one I'd like to have."

Well in that case you can have the privilege of shooting my Baker, Inspector. Wait there and I'll fetch it for you."

After a brief wait in silence for Andrew to return, Paul was taken over to a metal cabinet to the side of the range. Andrew took some keys from his pocket and opened the cabinet. Inside, Paul and June could see an assortment of powder horns and flasks. Andrew selected two, which he placed on top of the cabinet and then took out a wooden box and placed that beside them.

"Now Inspector, place the butt of the rifle on the ground between your feet and grasp it between your knees, so you have both hands free."

Paul did as he was instructed and Andrew passed him one of the brass powder flasks.

Now, point it down and this allows the powder to fall into the measuring tube, hold it over the muzzle and use your thumb to press in the lever and that simultaneously opens the end of the tube, allowing the powder to fall into the barrel and shuts of the end of the measuring tube"

Paul did as he was bid, "You now have now poured a measured amount of powder down the barrel," finished Andrew.

Paul had followed his instructions as a bemused June looked on with mixed feelings. Andrew now opened the wooden box and passed Paul a small square of greased cloth and a round lead ball.

"Place the cloth over the end of the muzzle and push the ball in on top as far as you can. That's it, now withdraw the ramrod, keeping a tight grip on the rifle with your knees, and using both hands, ram the ball and patch down the barrel as far as they will go."

Seeing the questions etched on Paul's face he continued, "In order for the ball to take the rifling and spin when fired, it should really be slightly larger than the diameter of the barrel's interior, but that would make it very difficult to load, so the idea is to use a slightly smaller ball wrapped in a greased patch, and then the greased patch makes it a tight fit in the barrel so that the internal grooves can impart spin to the ball. Using a patch in this way makes it easier to load and also helps to clean the inside of the barrel and keep fouling to a minimum.

"I see," said Paul, confident now that he had rammed the ball all the way down.

"Now lift the gun with your right hand just behind the trigger guard and the barrel pointing slightly up. Using your thumb, pull the cock back to the half-cock safety position." Andrew then passed Paul a small powder horn and continued, "Now push the steel of the frizzen forward to open the priming pan and pour some priming powder into the pan from the powder horn. That's it, that's enough, now close the pan by pulling the steel back, and apart from the fact that you are only half-cocked, you're ready to fire."

Andrew now led Paul back over to the firing range and gave him a pair of protective goggles and ear defenders, "Put these on Inspector, we wouldn't want a spark from the pan to go in your eye."

June looked on apprehensively as Andrew continued to instruct Paul, "Stand sideway to the target and sight down the top on the barrel,"

Andrew made a few adjustments to Paul's stance and the way the butt of the rifle nestled against his shoulder and said, "OK, you're good to go, aim high and slightly left of the target centre, and pull the hammer back to full cock when you're ready to fire. Hold nice and steady and squeeze the trigger."

He turned to June and indicated that she might want to put her fingers in her ears, just in time.

Paul aimed as he was told, pulled the cock back, took a deep breath and squeezed the trigger. There was a bright flash from the pan and a moment later a load bang and Paul felt the kick of the recoil.

"Wow! He exclaimed, lowering the weapon, how did I do?"

Andrew raised a small pair of binoculars and looked at the target, "Well, you've hit the target about half way in from the outer edge, not a good score, but it's an achievement just to hit the target first time, so well-done Inspector.

"Thank you Andrew, that was quite an experience, but I don't think I'd like to have to go through that process of loading in the middle of a battle, it certainly does take some time, doesn't it?"

"It's swings and roundabouts, Inspector, the advantage of a rifle is that it's far more accurate than a smoothbore, the disadvantage is that a trained infantryman could load and fire a smoothbore four times in the time it takes to load and fire a rifle once. That's where the Baker rifle excels, it can be loaded and fired the first time with a patched round, and then in the heat of battle the bullet can be loaded without the patch, in the same as a smoothbore. Do you think you would you like to join our little club then, Inspector?"

Paul looked over at June, but she rolled her eyes and turned away to leave.

Paul and Andrew both smiled at June's reaction and Andrew said, "Well now Inspector, would you like me to hang up a pig carcass?...I could show you how the bayonet performs."

June looked back with an expression of pure horror on her face and both men burst out laughing.

"Well damn the two of you.....especially you Guv." she declared, but had to turn way quickly in case they saw her begin to laugh.

Paul shook Andrew's hand as they parted, "Look," said Andrew, "I've just thought, Ray has a builder's yard somewhere, I don't know how big it is...."

"That's OK Andrew, we've already searched it. Thank you for all your help, and allowing me to fire your pride and joy, it was an interesting experience."

"No trouble, Paul, isn't it, look feel free to come back and have another go whenever you want."

"Thank you, would you mind if I brought a friend?" asked Paul, thinking of Richard.

"Not at all, Paul. The more the merrier."

"So, it looks as we have to hope Travis fired his gun at the yard, Guv." said June as they drove back to the station.

Looks that way, June. Andrew's a nice chap, don't you think?"

Chapter Fourteen

Reg. entered Paul's inner office with a grim expression on his face, "Take a seat Reg, you look like you've got bad news to impart."

"I've been doing background checks on Jack Williams, Guv. and it turns out he has a brother, Daniel Williams, his sheet is clean, but what concerns me is the fact that he owns and runs a car breakers yard, and often disposes of scrap cars for his brother. So, if Jack needed to get rid of his wife's car in a hurry, I'd say his brother could be very useful.

"Get down there straight away and see what you can find."

"John and Phillip are already on their way there Guv. and I've just received a search warrant for the site."

"Good work Reg. I'm at a loose end until forensics finish searching Travis's yard so I'll come with you."

On the way out of the office Paul called to June, "Give me a call as soon as forensics get in touch will you June, I'm just off to Williams's brother's breaker's yard with Reg."

Daniel Williams's breaker's yard turned out to be no small affair. As they drove in, Reg and Paul found themselves driving along an avenue of scrap cars piled three, and in some places four high on either side of them. Three hundred yards in the pile of cars on the right gave way to some single storey buildings. They stopped the car and got out to take a look. Venturing into the first building they found themselves in a large warehouse structure with floor to ceiling shelves on all four walls filled with various car parts.

"Where is everyone?" asked Reg.

"I've no idea Reg, the place seems empty, but John and Phillip should be here already, let's take a look around."

As they turned to leave, they noticed that under the shelves to their left there was a large metal cage, and their presence in the warehouse had just woken the occupant. A large German Shepherd was staring at them with obvious suspicion, and began to alternate between growling and barking in an extremely unfriendly manner. Both men were grateful the cage was shut.

"Well I guess someone will show up now that we've set off the alarm," said Paul as the two men left the building.

Indeed, as they exited, two men dressed in boiler suits with, **Williams's Breakers,** emblazoned across the back, approached at a fast walking pace from the far end of the yard, "Can we help you?" the larger of the two inquired, in a manner not unlike that of the German Shepherd they'd just met.

"I guess he's the dog owner," Paul whispered to Reg. and then in a louder voice, "We're looking for the owner, Daniel Williams, and two of our colleagues who should be here by now."

"Oh, more police is it? Mr Williams is up the other end of the yard operating the crane and your two have just driven up there to see him, I told them we don't usually allow private vehicles up that end."

"Quite right too," acknowledged Paul, as he and Reg. got back into their car and drove past the two men to join John and Phillip.

Looking back Paul said, "I think that big chap wants to set his dog on us Reg, what's the betting it's out of its cage when we come back down?"

"If it is and we have to get out of the car I'll let you deal with it Guv. June tells me you're good with animals."

"Thanks Reg but I'm not sure that thing back there qualifies."

"Are you talking about the dog or its owner, Guv?"

"Take your pick, Reg"

At the far end of the yard there was a sharp turn to the right and as they rounded the corner they could see Phillip, standing in front of a large crane, frantically waving his hands in the air, trying to attract the attention of the operator, who was just about to lower the Ford Fiesta that he had attached to an enormous magnet, into the gaping jaws of the large crusher before him.

John, who had just reached the top of the ladder at the side of the crane, began to bang on the door, also trying frantically to get the operator to stop. Finally, after much banging and waving that seemed to go on for ever, the crane operator became aware of them and stopped what he was doing. He climbed out of the crane's cab and proceeded to follow John back down the ladder.

"What's going on, why have stopped me working?" he demanded.

"We're looking for Daniel Williams, is that you?" asked Paul as he and Reg joined them.

"Yes, I'm Daniel Williams, what do you want with me?"

"That car you've got up there, we believe it belongs to Sandra William your sister-in-law."

"So, Jack brought it in and asked me to scrap it for him, there's nothing illegal in that, we'll sort out all the paperwork later, why are the police interested?"

"We've been unable to contact Sandra William, and we're concerned for her safety, will you bring her car down please, we wish to examine it."

"Look, the reason you can't find Sandra is because she and Jack have had a row and she's gone off somewhere with another man."

"Just bring the car down here, now, please."

"Have it your own way, but you're just wasting your time and mine. What do you expect to get out of searching her car anyway?"

Daniel Williams climbed back into the cab of the crane and Paul and the rest stepped back to make room for Sandra's car as it was deftly lowered at their feet beside the crusher. With the Ford Fiesta sitting on the ground in front of them, Reg. and Phillip opened doors to look inside. Daniel had, in the meantime, climbed from his cab and now joined them.

"Well, what is it you hope to find in there, anyway, you already know it's Sandra's car?"

John was standing by the car's boot and said, "Guv. the boot's locked and it looks as if the key has been broken off in the lock."

"Worried now, Paul turned to Daniel Williams and said, "Get that boot open now....did you break the key off?"

No, it was like that when we got it."

"Are you going to tell me you'd crush a car without checking the contents of the boot!"

"Well not normally, no, but I took it for granted Jack would have removed anything valuable or dangerous, he knows the routine."

Danial called to one of his employees who had appeared on the scene, "Harry, get me a crowbar will you and get this boot open."

"What time did Jack drop the car off?" asked Reg.

"It must have been sometime late last night or early this morning, he has his own keys to the yard, he rang me at seven this morning to say it was here and that he wanted it crushed straight away."

"Did you ask him why? It doesn't look like a scrapper to me."

"Sandra's gone off with this other bloke, like I just told you. Jack's really pissed off about it, and he said he wanted to punish her by scrapping her pride and joy,"

"It didn't occur to you to enquire how she'd gone off, if she didn't have her car?"

"I never gave it a thought, perhaps her boyfriend picked her up in his, I don't know."

Harry returned with a crowbar and prised open the boot. As soon as it was open, he gasped and stepped back.

John was standing nearest and got there first, to see Sandra's body stuffed inside and taking up almost the entire boot space. He leaned in to feel for a pulse as the others gathered around anxiously.

Daniel stared in horror at his sister-in-law's body, "Jesus Christ, Jack, what have you done?"

John stood up and declared excitedly, "I think there's a pulse, but it's very faint."

Paul looked over towards Reg to confirm that he was already phoning for an ambulance and used his own mobile to call June at the station. "June we've just found Sandra Williams, we're at Daniel Williams' yard. I need SOCO down here now."

"Will do Guv. How's Sandra, is she alive?"

"Only just, she's unconscious, and with very little pulse, she was in the boot of her own car that was just about to go in the crusher. We need to locate Jack Williams and arrest him for attempted murder. Ring around and see if you can find out where he is...but don't tell him we've found his wife, just say we need another word with him, a few details about her car or where he thinks she might have gone, that sort of thing...we need to know where he is but I don't want him spooked and doing a runner."

"I understand Guv, leave it with me."

The wait for the ambulance seemed to take an age but eventually it arrived and the team of one man and one woman transferred Sandra into the back of their vehicle so they could work on her.

Paul looked around for Daniel Williams and found him sitting on an oil drum with his head in his hands weeping.

"You really had no idea?" Paul asked as he approach the obviously distressed man.

"Christ! No....I like Sandra, she's alright, too good for Jack. He's my brother, and I love him, but I've always known he has a nasty temper and a short fuse, but my God! To put Sandra in the boot and then ask me to crush it, that's insane....evil, I can never forgive him for that.....never...how is she?"

"They're working on her in the back of the ambulance, I'll check in a minute or two and let you know."

"Thank you....if she dies.....I'll..." Danial broke down weeping again and Paul went to check on Sandra.

Leaning in through the open ambulance door Paul asked, "How is she?"

"We're going to get her to hospital now we've stabilised her," said the young female paramedic, "but she's sustained a nasty blow to the left side of her head and she's still unconscious, so she'll need a brain scan as soon as possible. We're just off now."

"Where will you take her?"

"Southmead."

Paul closed the ambulance door and walked over to update Daniel on his sister-in law's condition, as he had said he would. "Do you know where Jack is now?" Paul asked.

"No, I've no idea, he could be anywhere."

"I'd like you to ring him, just to tell him you've crushed the car, nothing else, and ask him where he is. Can you do that for me, do you think? Without giving the game away that we've found Sandra."

"Give me a minute to compose myself, the way I feel at the moment, he's sure to smell a rat. Why don't I text him instead?"

"OK, that's a good idea, do that for me then."

Paul briefly thought about borrowing Daniel's phone and sending the text himself, but decided that the text would read more genuine if Daniel sent it himself.

"What do you want me to put exactly?" asked Daniel.

"Just say that you've crushed.....no wait a minute....say that you're just about to crush the car and ask him if he's sure he wants it done, end by saying, where are you anyway?"

Daniel typed the message into his phone and pressed send.

Two minutes later he received a reply from Jack, "Yes, go ahead and crush it, I'm not feeling too well so, I'm going to have a day at home, J.

"Christ!" roared Daniel, "Even now that he's had time to calm down he still wants me to crush the car, perhaps he doesn't know Sandra's in there."

Paul put a hand on Daniel's shoulder, "I'm sorry Daniel, but he knows. She went back to him last night and hasn't been seen again until we opened that boot, but maybe it was an accident and he thought she was dead."

"Which hospital have they taken Sandra to?"

"Southmead, one of my men can drop you there if you like."

"No, I'll be fine Inspector, I can drive myself there.

"Phillip, you and John stay here until SOCO turn up. Reg you come with me, let's go and arrest Jack Williams, get Peter and Derrick to meet us there.

Paul and Reg pulled into the driveway of Jack and Sandra's house closely followed by Peter Cook and Derrick Price, "You two go around the back," ordered Paul, "Reg and I will take the front."

Paul banged on the door, which was opened almost immediately by Jack Williams, "You again!" he declared in dismay, "What's in going to be this time? Not more drugs I hope."

"Will you do the honours Reg, this is your collar?"

"Thank you, Guv. it will be a pleasure. Jack Williams, I'm arresting you for the attempted murder of Sandra Williams."

Jack just stared at them in amazement, "Attempted murder....did you say attempted murder....are you telling me Sandra is still alive!...Oh my god...well that's wonderful news, I never meant to hurt her, it was an accident, how is she, is she alright?"

"Fat lot you care," said Reg as he led him away.

****

"That was good work, Paul. getting to Sandra before she died," said Jillian Simmons, "have you managed to locate the whereabouts of Jack Williams?"

"Oh yes, I know exactly where our Mr Williams is, he's in one of our cells, waiting to be interviewed."

"Well that is good news, have you arrested him for the attempted murder of his wife?"

"On his own doorstep, as soon as he opened the door."

"That's excellent, do you think his brother knew Sandra was in the boot when he was going to crush the car?"

"I don't believe so, he seemed genuinely shocked when we opened the boot and found her, and he was so angry with his brother for putting him in that position. Plus of course, he effectively gave his brother up with the text message he sent, so we have no intention of bringing any charges against him, not as things stand at the moment anyway."

"In that case Jack was taking a chance wasn't he, I mean what if Sandra had come around and started making noises when she was in there?"

"John said her pulse was so faint that he could only just detect it and she hadn't regained consciousness on the way to the hospital even, so I think Jack thought she was dead when he put her in the boot."

"June put her head around the door and said, "I've just spoken to the doctor treating Sandra Williams, Guv, they're going to operate on Sandra to relieve pressure on her brain, then he said they'd probably put her into an induced coma to let her heal. He said he thought she has a good chance of surviving, but they won't know how much damage has been done until she regains consciousness."

"Thanks, June, have you told the others?"

"Not yet Guv. I thought I'd let you two know first."

"I'll tell them then," said Paul rising from his chair and entering the main room with Jillian. "Listen up everyone, June has just been on the phone to the hospital, and Sandra Williams is going to have an operation to relieve pressure on her brain. The doctor says the chances of her surviving are looking good.

However, they won't know if there is any permanent damage until she comes around. The one thing that is certain however, is that, the fact that she is alive at all today, is down to Reg and John and Phillip, so well done guys, that was a very good day's work."

There was a buzz in the room as everyone took their turn congratulating the three on saving Sandra's life and most of them missed the fact that Paul had now been joined in his office by Steven Wyatt from forensics.

"Tell me you've got some good news for me Steven," said Paul anxiously.

"Well I think you might be a little bit pleased, Sir, we retrieved one hundred and seven various shapes and sizes of lead projectiles from the earth embankment at the yard, six of which are of the type we were looking for."

"That's good, but can you prove they were fired from the gun that killed Newbridge?"

"Absolutely no doubt whatsoever."

"**Yes**!" shouted Paul so that everyone could here.

He then stood up, walked over to his filing cabinet, and removed a large bottle of Talisker 18 year old scotch whiskey and handed it to Steven, "I'm told you're a bit of a whiskey connoisseur, Steven, so I took some advice from someone who knows a thing or two about whiskey himself, and I got you this, I hope it's acceptable."

Steven took the bottle from Paul's hands, and studied the Label, "Wow! Thank you Sir.....crikey, that must have set you back sixty quid, at least, you must really want to nail this guy."

Paul led Steven into the main room, "More good news everyone, Steven here, has managed to match some bullets retrieved from Raymond Travis's builder's yard to the gun used to kill Peter Newbridge, and that was found in the car with John Winchester. So quite how our Mr Travis is going to explain that I don't know, especially as we know he himself owned such a gun. Anyway, I think I shall round off, a not too shabby day by arresting him along with Mary Newbridge."

"Reg June, would you care to join me?"

"Before you go, Guv," said John, who had just taken a call, "there's a Nathanial Clark at the front desk, said you know him and he wants a word."

Paul and June had met Nathanial while working on a previous case and he had proved to be a valuable contact. June was convinced he was some kind of secret agent for the British Government, and he did seem to have access to all sorts of top-level information.

"You two go on to the car," said Paul, "I'll catch up with you in a minute."

As Reg and June made their way to the car, Paul looked across the entrance lobby to see Nathanial indicating that they should talk outside.

After exiting the building together Paul asked, "What's the matter Nathanial, not afraid we've got the lobby bugged are you? I take it you're still working in the murky corridors of power."

"Nothing murky about my corridors Paul I can assure you and my new office is extremely well lit thank you."

"I'm sorry to rush you Nathaniel but I'm just off to arrest someone for murder, can what you want me for wait a bit?"

"I'd just as soon say my bit now, I won't take long. I understand that you have arrested a certain Jack Williams, is that right?"

"How the hell would you know about that so soon after the event, I wonder?"

"How and what I know is irrelevant Paul. We, I think, have a certain mutual respect and even liking for one another, otherwise I wouldn't be risking my career by telling you what I'm about to."

Paul frowned, "Go on, I'm all ears."

"Jack Williams hasn't always been Jack Williams."

"Yes he has, I've seen his birth certificate.....oh....don't tell me he's one of your lot, or on witness protection or something?"

"Not witness protection exactly, but he was very useful to us towards the end of the troubles, so we helped him go into hiding after the troubles."

"What troubles are you talking abo....Christ! you're talking about Northern Ireland.....Was Jack Williams IRA, is that it?"

"Jack Williams couldn't care less about politics or religion Paul, all he cares about is money. Well he had a certain talent that the IRA and other groups needed so he made money out of the troubles, both from them and us, which is why it was wise for him to disappear. Fortunately, for reasons best known only to Jack, he was going by a different name back then, which is why I said he hasn't always been Jack Williams, for a while he was someone else."

"So the easiest way for whoever he was back then to disappear was for him to resume his real identity."

"Got it in one Paul."

"But none of what you've told me prevents me from arresting and charging Jack Williams with attempted murder."

"No, and he very much deserves to be locked away for a considerable time, but you need to know and understand that he is a much more dangerous man than you think. He has a good lawyer and I suspect will be out on bail soon and he very much holds a grudge. You need to watch your back and look out for those you care about Paul. I'm convinced that if he gets out, he'll try to find a way to get to you. That's all I wanted to say Paul, I need you to understand that while that man is free, you and yours are at risk."

"Well thanks for the warning Nathaniel," said Paul as the two men shook hands and Nathaniel departed.

Paul turned to where June and Reg where waiting for him at the car and walked over to join them with just a brief look back over his shoulder at a departing omen.

Chapter Fifteen

As Raymond Travis turned his car into Eastfield Road his eye was instantly drawn to the activity outside Mary Newbridge's house. Mary was being escorted out of the house by two men and a woman, who helped her into the back of their car.

It was obvious that Mary was being arrested and just as obvious that the police had somehow gathered enough evidence to charge them both with at least the murder of Peter Newbridge. He pulled in and parked at the end of the road to think. They would have an alert out to look for his car for sure, so he took what he needed and left it where it was, he needed to get away, and his car was now a liability.

There were things he needed from his house in Henleaze Walk, so he walked to the bus station and caught the bus to Bristol, wondering how he was going to gain access to his house if the police were watching it.

****

Mary Newbridge looked defiantly at Paul and June across the interview room table, as Paul asked, "Where's Raymond Travis?"

"I don't know, why am I here?"

"You're here to answer the questions you and Raymond failed to answer the last time we spoke to you. The difference being, that now we have evidence to prove that your husband Peter was shot inside the static caravan that you and he own in Minehead."

"I'm not going to answer any questions until I have a lawyer here."

As if on cue, there was a knock at the door and Phillip announced, "The duty solicitor is here for Mrs Newbridge Guv. shall I show him in?"

"Yes please, Phillip," then turning to Mary, "I'll give you some time to talk to the duty solicitor, but when I come back, I shall be back requiring answers."

****

Raymond Travis had taken more buses in the last two hours than he had since he used them to get to school and back, and he was now, both scared and short of funds. He'd tried using his card to withdraw money at the bus station but his account appeared to be frozen. As he turned onto Henleaze Walk, he could see his house some one hundred and fifty yards further up on the opposite side of the road. As he walked cautiously along, he looked closely at every car. Just four houses down from his own on the oppose side of the road was a one-year old Ford Mondeo with the driver sitting behind the wheel, apparently reading a magazine.

241

There were no doctor's surgeries or clinics of any kind in the road, and it was too far from the shops to be someone waiting for a returning shopper, so it could only be a police officer, watching his house.

He wondered if they were also watching the back, but thought it unlikely. The houses in his road and in the road behind were all of the same design. Built in the 1930s the semi-detached properties had small driveways in front of a lean-to single garage at the side of the house and beside the garage a narrow gate giving access, along the side of the garage, to the back of the house, the garden of which backed onto the garden of the house behind.

The property directly behind his was 150 Lake View Road and the owners, Mr and Mrs Collins, would be at work at this time of day and their children had all grown up and left home so the house would be empty.

He turned back and made his way into Lake View Road. Happily, there was no sign of any police officer sitting in an unmarked car in this road, so with a brief check that no curtains were twitching he slipped through the front gates that were always left open for the owners return and with fingers crossed, tried the gate beside the garage. His luck was in, the gate was unlocked and he slipped through it and into his neighbour's back garden.

Hopping easily over the low fence that separated his garden from his neighbour's he made his way up to his back door. Half expecting police to swoop in from all sides he nervously fumbled in his pocket for his keys and let himself in.

Once inside his property he had two minutes to make his way to the front of the house and punch in the code that would turn off the alarm. Concerned that the police may have changed the alarm code, the relief he felt when he heard the bleep and saw the little red light change to green was palpable.

He turned and rested his back against the front door until he felt his heart return to something like a normal rhythm. Upstairs, he entered the front bedroom where he kept his collection of firearms and was pleased to see that the police hadn't removed it. Crawling on all fours to keep under the front window, he made his way across the room to the cabinet where he keeps his important documents. Opening the doors he removed his passport, driving licence and insurance documents, together with his one thousand pound cash float.

With those items now in his jacket pocket he reached to the back of the cabinet and slid aside the secret central panel revealing a hidden space behind. Reaching into the space he took out a second world war German Luger pistol with six rounds still in the clip and a Browning semi-automatic of similar vintage with a full clip and seven extra rounds. He replaced the Luger, closed the secret panel and put the Browning in his pocket along with the extra rounds.

He risked a peep out of the window and saw the unmarked police car was still in the same position.

Figuring that the police had no reason to revisit his house unless they thought he was there, he decided to have a lie down and rest. His next move would have to wait until morning. In the meantime he felt relatively safe, surely his house would be the last place the police would think of looking for him, especially as they had the place under surveillance and it meant that he had access to what small amount of food there was in the house, tinned food mostly, he had water and a toilet, and he had a bed to sleep on. It seemed the ideal temporary hiding place.

****

"Have you had enough time with your client," Paul asked of Karl Clarke, the duty solicitor."

"Yes, that's fine Inspector, I've advised Mary Newbridge to cooperate fully with the police into your investigation of her husband's death."

"Now Mary, let me tell you what we know. We know that you and Peter left Eastfield Road together on Sunday the 17th and that you were travelling south. We have ample evidence to prove that Peter was shot inside your static caravan, and we have his car caught on a speed camera returning the next day, with you driving."

"So, Mary, tell us what happened on Sunday 17th June, when you and Peter visited your static van that day?"

Mary seemed to resign herself to the fact that the police could prove she and Raymond had murdered her husband, "OK Inspector, it was Ray's idea to persuade him to go there."

"Go on."

"Ray was already there waiting. I told Peter that I wanted to leave him and that Ray wanted to speak to him, so the three of us sat and talked in the van. We told Peter that I wanted a divorce plus two thirds of the savings, but he refused."

"I'm not surprised, what made you think he'd give you two thirds... what made you even think you'd be entitled to two thirds of the money?"

"Everyone thinks that Peter is the one who has moved on since our son died, but they're wrong. He sees no point in spending any of our money now, even though he earns really well, he's got well over a million in savings that I know of, and maybe even more that I don't know about. We could be living well....we could have a big house with grounds and a big kitchen, we could be enjoying holidays abroad, we could afford to go out for nice meals or the theatre. I should be entitled to enjoy the rest of my life....But no, we live in a small terraced house, we never go on holiday or have a night on the town, and he expects me to run the house and feed us both on the pittance he gives me for housekeeping....he won't even let me have a car of my own....Well, he's kept me in virtual poverty for too long.....I've had enough."

"You could have walked away at any time Mary, you didn't have to kill him."

"I wanted the life I'm entitled to, if I'd have divorced him, I wouldn't have got even half of what I'm owed for all those years."

"So, was it you or Ray that shot him?"

"I've never handled a gun, I'd have probably ended up shooting Ray."

"So, Ray shot Peter, what happened after that? Didn't anyone hear the shot?"

"Ray used a cushion to muffle the sound, but it was still quite loud, I was worried someone had heard it, but nobody came to investigate, I suppose if anyone did hear, they thought it was a car back-firing, or something, because no one came."

"What did you do then?"

"Ray had it all figured out, we cleaned the inside of the van, then wrapped Peter's body in a blanket and put him in the back of Ray's car."

"Why Ray's car?"

"I couldn't face the prospect of driving all the way back to Bristol with Peter's body in the boot, so we agreed that Ray would have it in his and follow me back. Ray had planned everything, we knew you were looking at Winchester for the murder of Thomas Carter, Peter had told me that much, and that he intended investigating the case and getting the evidence to convict Winchester before the police. He said it was going to be the scoop of his career.

Well, Ray figured that we could make it look as if Peter was also murdered by Winchester, and then we could kill Winchester and make it look like suicide."

"And you were happy to go along with all that?"

"I wasn't happy about killing anyone, no, but Peter was never going to give me what I was owed. As for Winchester, again I wasn't happy about it, but as Ray pointed out, he had killed an innocent man after cheating him out of a small fortune, so it wasn't like killing an innocent man was it?"

"So, what happened after you'd cleaned up the place, you drove to Leigh Woods?"

"That's right, Ray knew about some clearing there, I don't know how, but he said it was the perfect place. We drove the car there and left it after transferring Peter into the boot."

"When did you drop the cartridge case in Winchester's office?"

"Ray did that a couple of days after Carter's body was found, he'd been planning it ever since I told him what Peter had said, about Winchester being responsible for Carter's death. In the end, your lot must have found it almost straight after Ray dropped it."

"How did he manage to get into Winchester's office to plant it?"

"He went there to see him on some pretext or other, I don't know exactly what, but I do know he was only there a minute, that was all it took."

"Tell me about Winchester's apparent suicide, how did the pair of you stage that?"

Everything just kept pouring out of Mary now, she wanted it all out in the open, it was as if she had un unconscious need to confess, "Ray rang Winchester, pretending to be Peter, and arranged to meet him at the house. Winchester thought that Peter was going to try and blackmail him, and when Ray turned up pretending to be him, he was taking a risk, Winchester might have been planning to kill him for all he knew."

"What actually happened?"

"I don't know the details because I wasn't there, but I know there was a fight and Ray said he'd been able to render Winchester unconscious with a choke hold or something, I've no idea how. As I say, I don't know the ins and outs of what transpired at the house, only that Ray managed to stage a suicide."

"OK, Mary, that's all for now, the constable will take you back to your cell. We'll get your statement typed up so you can read and sign it."

Everyone stood up and Karl Clarke held out his hand for Mary to shake, but she declined, instead, saying sarcastically, "Well thank you Mr Clarke, you were a big help, I must say, I really don't know what I would have done if you hadn't been there for me," and walked out, leaving Karl speechless, his hand out in front of him.

****

Raymond Travis awoke from a troubled sleep and rolled onto his side to look at his bedside clock. It was almost four thirty in the morning, a day avoiding the police must have really taken it out of him. Rising from his bed he ventured to the front bedroom and peered carefully out of the window. The police car that had been parked up the road earlier had gone, but another appeared to have taken its place, this time a Vauxhall Astra. Raymond had to watch for a while before he was able to make out the fact that somebody was sitting in it.

Realising that he would have to leave by the back door, the same as he had come in, he decided not to turn on the alarm. He had work to do later in the morning, and as the police just appeared to be watching the outside of his property, he would make his house his hideout for another night, they would never suspect that he was back staying in his own house, at least, that was his hope.

He splashed some cold water on his face to fully wake up and then let himself out of the back door, locking it behind him and stealthily crossing his and his neighbour's gardens before exiting onto Lake View Road again.

He needed transport, and now he had funds he intended to hire a car. He knew there was a car hire firm operating from the top of Whiteladies Road, and he could walk that in forty minutes, there was also an all-night café nearby. He looked at his watch, it was just gone five in the morning, he would be at the café for five forty, so maybe three or four hours to kill before the car hire shop opened for business at either eight or nine.

As things turned out, he was unable to hire a car until the office staff turned up at nine, but that was fine, he had gone for a walk on the downs and that had cleared his head and given him time to think more clearly about how he was going to proceed. He needed to leave the country and he needed money. With his bank account frozen there was only one other source of money he could think of, and that was his collection of firearms. It was worth a good deal.

The young girl who turned up to open the car hire office, kept him waiting another twenty minutes, sorting out the till and getting the various forms, before she eventually said, "I'm sorry to have kept you waiting Sir, how can I help?"

"I'd like to hire a vehicle for a couple of weeks, something with a good sized boot."

She looked through the paperwork that had taken her so long to organise and said, "I could let you have a Ford Kuga for two weeks, starting today, if that's suitable?"

"Yes, that's fine."

"I just need your driving licence and insurance documents Sir, I'll photocopy them and let you have them back, and then I need you to fill in this form and sign it, it's just a declaration that you have no driving convictions or anything, you know the sort of thing, you can do that for me while I copy your documents."

It took another forty minutes to finalise everything and be shown the vehicle, but eventually Raymond drove away in an almost new Ford Kuga and made his way to an auto-parts store where he went through a not dissimilar process to obtain two new number plates for the lorry, that was parked at his yard. Then driving to a B & Q store he purchased some tools and changed the number plates on the Kuga in an isolated area of the carpark. If the police discovered he'd hired a car, at least they wouldn't be looking for one with his lorry's registration.

He knew he would have to wait until dark once again to enter his house and load his collection of firearms into the Kuga, and that the wait would be intolerable. He busied himself by getting something to eat, purchasing two large holdalls to transport the guns in and looking for a dealer he could offer the guns to.

Finding a dealer was much more difficult than he had expected, none of the big antique weapons dealers were prepared to spend the kind of money he was asking for in cash, they also insisted on proof of ownership and he had not intended to use his real name. The problems were mounting and Richard Drake Antiques, although a little too close to home for his liking, being based in Bristol, was beginning to look like his last hope.

He decided not to wait any longer, his neighbours would be at work again, so he drove the Kuga back to Lake View Road and parked outside. If he was seen entering his neighbours garden, it would still take people a while to realise that anything was wrong and a while longer to decide whether to do anything about it, like calling the police, so speed was of the essence.

He quickly made his way through the two gardens and opened his back door, he then made his way upstairs and into his gun-room where he quickly transferred his collection into the two large holdalls. Not everything would fit, he managed to get all but six of the longer muskets in the bags and carried them with some difficulty down to the back door. He then returned upstairs and brought down the remainder of the collection. In the end he could only manage one holdall at a time across the garden and over the fence, so the operation needed three journeys. Bringing out the last of the muskets he looked around before placing them on top of the holdalls in the boot. He had to lower one of the back seats to accommodate everything but he'd had the foresight to bring a blanket, which he now used to make sure all the guns were covered. It looked as if he had been panicking for no reason, the street was quiet as the grave and there wasn't a twitching curtain in sight.

He drove out of town and decided to book into a Travel Lodge for the night, he had thought of spending another night at home, but after spending so much time loading the car, the chance that he may have been seen was too great. He looked at his watch, it was gone six, he would ring the antique shop in the morning.

Richard was rearranging some silver ornaments at the front of the shop, when Margaret came out of the office and announced, "Richard, there's a man on the phone with some antique firearms for sale, a whole collection by the sound of it, are you interested, or shall I put him onto someone else?"

"I'll come and have a word with him Margaret,"

As Richard walked to the office his mind was working overtime. These days Richard's business mostly consisted of buying pieces that he knew he had clients for. He was lucky in the fact that he had a good reputation and an impressive portfolio of rich and important clients who commissioned him to find items for them. Although he often sold the odd flintlock to clients who wanted something a little out of the ordinary on the wall, he wouldn't normally be interested in purchasing a whole collection of firearms, unless he had someone in mind who would buy them all.

He was intrigued however, ever since Paul had taken on this latest case of his, it seemed that the only subjects of conversation between them were his violent next-door neighbour and firearms. He half wondered if he was going to be offered a Smith & Wesson revolver and with that thought in mind, he made a decision.

"Hello, Richard Drake speaking, how can I help?"

"Hello Mr Drake, my name's Ian Smith, and I find myself in a position, due to having to go abroad for work, of having to sell my collection of antique firearms rather quickly, and I'm trying to find somebody willing

253

to do a quick cash deal, do you think you'd be interested?"

"Well I'm always interested to purchase collections Mr Smith, would you like me to come and have a look at what you have, if so, give me your address, and if you're local I could come today."

"It's a little more complicated than that Mr Drake, I've already moved out of my accommodation you see. Do you think we could meet somewhere?"

Richard was becoming even more convinced that this could have something to do with the case Paul was working on and decided to play along. "How many pieces are there Mr Smith, could you bring the collection to my shop?"

"Are you in a position to do a cash deal, I'm going to be looking at the best part of a hundred grand."

"Wow! That's a lot of money Mr Smith, I would want to see some prove of ownership, and it'll take a day or so to arrange for that much in cash, could we not do a bank transfer?"

Raymond was getting desperate, if he was going to disappear, he was going to need money, "Look, I'll be honest with you Mr Drake, I swear the collection is mine, but I'm not travelling under my own name, so the proof of ownership will be in a different name, one that I'll give you when we do a deal. If you're interested, I'll give you a day to get the cash and I'll ring you with a place to meet, I swear, if you know anything about antique firearms at all, you'll be impressed with the collection, so what do you say?"

Richard waited for a while before answering, "I'll get the cash, but I'm only going to pay what the collection is worth to me, you understand that as a dealer I'll be looking to make a reasonable return."

"Understood Mr Drake, I'll ring you again tomorrow, and if you've got the money we can arrange to meet," and with that the phone went dead.

Chapter Sixteen

Paul had just updated his DCI on events when he took the call from Richard Drake, "Hi Richard, what can I do for you."

"Well I've just had a rather strange call from a man calling himself Ian Smith, who says he has a collection of firearms for sale. Now normally, I would have just recommended one of the London dealers, but this chap wants cash and says that he's moving abroad and has moved out of his property, the whole thing sounds really dodgy to me, and in view of our recent conversations, I was wondering if it had anything to do with your case."

"Did this Mr Smith say what was in the collection?"

"Mostly muskets he said, I'm sorry Paul, perhaps I should have asked more questions of him, but it must be a fair few pieces, he's talking about a hundred grand."

"How was it left, Richard, have you agreed to buy the collection?"

"I told him I could get the cash, and he said he'd ring me and we could arrange to meet somewhere."

"Well you're right Richard, it does all sound dodgy, ring me as soon as you've arranged to meet him and let me know where, we'll sort something out then. Whatever happens, don't meet him without my say-so, is that OK Richard, this could well be our man trying to raise some money, and if it is, he's already killed two people, so you let us handle it, OK."

"Absolutely Paul, I'll ring you as soon as I hear back from him, so you do think it's to do with your case?"

"It certainly sounds as if it could be Richard, I'm going to make some enquiries now, if it is who I think it might be, he's a dangerous man so if you arrange a meeting, one of us will go in your place."

"OK Paul, I'll speak to you soon."

As soon as Paul put down the phone, he called Reg into his office.

"You wanted me, Guv." said Reg as he poked his head round the door.

"Yes, who's watching Travis's place at the moment?"

"Clive's on watch at the moment Guv, Why?"

"Tell Clive to go into the house and check that the gun collection is still there, would you."

"Still there Guv? why wouldn't it be still there?"

"Because I think I may have missed a trick Reg get him to look now please."

"Will do." acknowledged Reg as he turned and left the office.

Clive Pascoe almost jumped out of his skin when his mobile rang, he'd almost nodded off after sitting in a car watching nothing happen for hours, "Hello Reg, tell me we've got him and I came come in now, please."

257

"Sorry Clive, but I do have a task for you, the Guvnor wants you to check the house and make sure the firearm collection is still where it should be."

"Why, does he think somebody's snuck in and nicked it?"

"Strange as it may sound Clive, I believe that is what he thinks may have happened. Be careful, if Travis has had access to his house, he may still be in there."

"Thanks for that happy thought Reg. I'll go and see if there's a killer in the house with a roomful of guns then shall I?"

"Do you want some backup?"

"No, that's OK Reg but I don't want you feeling guilty if I get shot or anything."

Clive got out of the car after retrieving a set of house keys from the glove compartment, together with a slip of paper that had the alarm codes written on it, and as an afterthought, with Reg's words in mind, retrieved a baton and a pepper spray from the boot.

Clive turned the key in the lock and pushed open the front door, expecting the bleeping sound from the alarm that would indicate it needed to be deactivated in the next two minutes, but there was no such sound.

Suitably alerted to the possibility that he wasn't alone in the house, he closed the front door behind him and made his way cautiously upstairs to the front bedroom where he'd been told the collection was located. Pushing open the bedroom door he looked around at the empty racks on the walls and the showcases that had been stripped clean of their contents.

"Bloody Hell," he said out loud as he took out his mobile to report his findings, "this is going to go down well."

Paul had been waiting anxiously for Reg's return, and could read the answer to his question on his face even before he spoke, "Clive said the collection is no longer there Guv. How the hell did he manage to get his hands on it?"

"Well I suppose it was easy when you come to think of it, Reg, I'm an idiot and I didn't think to put a man on the back door."

"But whoever was watching the house would have seen him go through the side gate, if they'd been paying attention."

"Well maybe he didn't go through his side gate, maybe he was clever and went through the gardens at the back...I feel so damn stupid I could scream."

What's going on Guv why has he taken such a risk to retrieve his guns?"

"For the money Reg Richard Drake has been on the phone to say that somebody has just offered him a collection of antique muskets for a cash sale."

"I still can't believe he took such a risk, he must have known we were watching the house."

"Well that didn't stop him...did it?" replied Paul angrily.

"What are we going to do Guv?"

"Well Richard is going to arrange a meeting to buy the guns and one of us is going to take his place and arrest the bastard, that's what we're going to do. When we have the location of the meeting one of us will take Richard's van to the meet, it's sign written on the side and should give Travis some reassurance that he's dealing with who he thinks he is. I shall want armed response there as well."

"You think Travis will be armed? Other than with the guns he's trying to sell I mean?"

"I wouldn't put it past him Reg. Christine Parks said he had some modern guns as well as old, and couldn't be certain he'd got rid of them all.

As Reg was about to leave June arrived and put a hand on his arm to stop him, "Stay a minute Reg you'll want to hear this, I've just been in touch with Southmead hospital, and the doctor says that Sandra has regained consciousness and it looks like she'll make a full recovery, at least physically."

"That's good news June…Reg, will you let the others know, I need to make some phone calls."

The meeting between Richard Drake and Raymond Travis had been arranged to take place at the Holiday Inn in Filton. It had been decided that Constable Clive Pascoe, would take the part of Richard Drake as he had never actually met Raymond Travis and wouldn't be recognised by him.

He drove Richard's van into the car park and selected an isolated spot away from the building to park. Getting out of the van he picked up the attaché case that supposedly contained the cash for the deal and headed for the main building. Once inside he looked around a little nervously as he walked to the reception desk, but he could see nothing out of the ordinary, even though he knew there were armed officers on site.

He waited patiently for the young female receptionist to finish booking in a guest before she said to him, "Good morning Sir, are you booking in today?"

"No," Clive replied, "My name is Richard Drake, I'm supposed to be meeting someone here at midday, when they arrive could you let them know that I'm in the lounge waiting?"

"Yes of course Sir, is there anything else I can do for you?"

"Yes, do you think you could keep this in your safe for me until I need it?" said Clive, indicating the attaché case.

"Yes, no trouble, Mr Drake did you say," she confirmed as she took the case from Clive, "it will be here when you need it Sir," she concluded, handing Clive a cloakroom ticket in exchange for the case.

"Thank you." said Clive, before heading for the lounge and ordering a coffee.

Raymond Travis had been sitting in his hire-car in the car park for over two hours, concerned that he might be walking into a trap. He hoped he would spot anything untoward happening before the appointed time and that he would be able to spot an antique dealer turning up. He assumed that Richard would be driving an estate car of some sort with a large flat roof-rack on top like most of the dealers he'd seen.

He looked at his watch to check the time, 11.55am. Richard was either already here or cutting it fine he thought, but then he spotted a small black van pulling in with Richard Drake Antiques emblazoned on the sides.

He watched carefully as the man got out of the van carrying a small attaché case. Was that big enough to hold a hundred grand he wondered? Of course it was, he reassured himself, it would all be in fifties probably.

He got out of his car and followed Richard at a distance and watched from outside the large glass doors as he approached the reception desk and spoke to the receptionist and handed her the case. Clever boy, taking no chances he thought.

Looking around the lounge for anyone who looked as if they might even live next door to a copper, Raymond approached the man he thought was Richard Drake, "Mr Drake is it?" he asked, "I'm Ian Smith."

Clive stood up and shook hands with Travis, "Good afternoon Mr Smith, would you like a coffee or something?"

"No, thank you I'd prefer to get on with our business if it's all the same, did you bring the cash?"

"Yes, it's in the safe here."

"Well if you'd like to get it, we can go out to my car and you can assess my collection."

"I don't mean to sound rude. Mr Smith, but it's a great deal of money and I don't know you from Adam, or indeed how much of the money I've brought will be needed to conclude our business, so I'd like to have a look at the collection now, and then we can discuss money, and if and when we come to making a deal, then I'll get you the money, how does that sound?"

"OK, I understand your position," said Raymond, beginning to feel a little more relaxed, "come with me and I'll show you the collection."

The two men rose and walked out of the lounge together, with Raymond leading the way.

He led Clive to the Ford Kuga and unlocked the doors, "The collection's in the boot he said, under the blanket, help yourself."

Clive hesitated for just a moment before saying, "Look, I've parked my van over in the corner there, why don't you drive over and park next to me, it will make it easier to transfer items after we've concluded our business, and it's out of the way of prying eyes."

Raymond considered the suggestion. He'd had plenty of time to consider all the possible scenarios of how the negotiations and transfer of goods could go, and understood why Richard Drake would be cautious doing a deal involving so much cash, at a strange location with a man he had never met before, so he was prepared to compromise to some extent on his plans.

"Alright, that makes sense, get in."

Clive had been instructed not to under any circumstances get into a vehicle alone with Raymond, but not only would his refusal to get in the car seem suspicious he saw no reason not to comply with the offer under these circumstances, so he slid into the passenger seat of the Kuga and Raymond drove around the car park and pulled up next to Richard Drake's van.

Watching on CCTV from the hotel security room, Paul almost had a heart attack, "I thought I told him not to get in a car with the man," he bellowed.

"Take it easy Guv." said Reg, "Clive knows what he's doing….there look, he's out again now."

"OK, but he's not getting a card from me this Christmas."

Out in the car park Raymond opened the hatch on the Kuga and removed the blanket that covered his collection.

They had to put down the second back seat so that Clive could go through the process of examining the collection, and when laid out the collection covered the entire area. Clive began examining individual pieces, pretending that he knew what he was doing.

Richard Drake had given Clive a crash course on what to look for when examining an antique gun, so he looked at each piece, checking the operation of each weapon in turn and looking for proof and maker's marks as instructed.

The plan was to come to an agreement about price and leave Raymond transferring the guns into the back of Richard's van while Clive went to get the money from the hotel safe. This would leave Raymond isolated in the car park where the firearms response team could move in for the arrest. If things didn't go that way, Clive was to play along, and try some other way to separate himself from Raymond in the car park. It was important for the actual arrest not to take place inside the hotel where innocent civilians could be put at risk if Raymond turned out to be armed.

Clive took a small notepad from his pocket and began adding figures.

"Well," asked Raymond, beginning to get anxious.

"I can go to £35,000 for the lot cash now," said Clive, knowing that Ray would be suspicious if he didn't start low.

"I said I was looking for £100,000 on the phone so don't mess me about, the duelling pistols alone are worth six, there's easily a hundred grands worth there, but I'll take £80,000, but no less, you'll make a bloody fortune out of that retail."

"£70,000," said Clive, getting into the swing of things and enjoying the moment.

"£75,000, then."

Clive held out his hand and the two men shook on the deal.

Clive handed Raymond the keys to the van and said, "Look, to save us both time, why don't you start transferring the guns into the van while I go and count out the money and bring it you?"

"Wait," Raymond thought about things before agreeing, "OK, just don't be long."

When Paul, June and Reg, who had been watching proceedings on camera in the hotel security room, saw Clive set out for reception, leaving Raymond Travis with the keys to Richard's van, It all looked to be going exactly to plan, so Paul picked up the police radio from the desk and said, "OK all units move in."

This announcement set several things in motion, Derrick stood in front of the main hotel doors to prevent anyone exiting into the car park until Raymond was successfully taken into custody, two unmarked cars with armed officers inside took up positions where they could easily block both the entrance and the exit to the car park, and three uniformed officers from the armed response team began making their way towards Raymond's position behind the cover of a hedge. The plan was simply to wait until Clive was at a safe distance, and for the armed officers to then rush Raymond and arrest him.

Oblivious to this secret activity, Raymond opened the back doors of Richard's van. The interior was empty except for a pile of blankets, clearly used for wrapping large items, and a couple of empty packing crates that were obviously used for transporting items of china, glass or other breakables. The crates themselves were full of old newspaper that had been used for wrapping breakable items before placing them in the crates. Raymond pulled the nearest crate towards him with the idea of putting the few handguns into it, and an article in the top screwed up paper caught his eye. The paper in question was, The Antiques Trade Gazette, and the article was entitled, "A Day in the Life of a Dealer." It was the name Richard Drake that had grabbed Raymond's attention. He pulled out the page in question and saw that the article was in fact an interview with Richard Drake. There was a picture of Richard included, and Raymond could see straight away that it was not the Richard Drake he had just done a deal with. He was being set up.

Withdrawing the Browning automatic from his pocket, he cocked it and called after Clive who was still less than half-way to the hotel reception.

"Hang on Mr Drake," he called out as he began to follow him, "There's just one more thing."

Clive stopped and turned back to see Raymond approaching, "What's wrong?"

Raymond caught up with him, and before anyone watching knew what was happening, Raymond thrust

267

the gun against the side of Clive's neck and grabbed his arm.

Paul along with everyone else stopped and watched in horror, how could things have gone so badly wrong?

The three armed officers now stood and trained their Heckler & Cock MP5s at Raymond Travis, calling out, "Armed police, put down your gun and lay on the floor with your hands behind your head."

Paul and his team stood looking on helplessly as Raymond ignored the command and asked Clive, "Whether you answer truthfully to my next question could determine whether you live or die in the next few minutes, so think carefully, what's in the case you had put in the hotel safe."

"Nothing, it's empty."

"God damn it!.....OK, move back slowly with me, we're going to get into my car," he whispered to Clive, and called out loud to everyone else, "We're leaving, and if anyone tries to stop us I swear I'll shoot this man, the gun I'm holding against his neck is loaded and cocked, so don't be tempted to do anything stupid."

"Give it up, Raymond," shouted Paul, from where he now stood just outside the main hotel entrance, "where do you think you can go, you've got no chance, it's all over."

On reaching the Ford Kuga, Raymond backed Clive alongside the driving door and told him to get into the driving seat, while he himself quickly pushed some of the guns to one side, lifted the single rear seat behind the driver and slipped into it, still holding the gun to Clive's neck.

"Start the engine and drive out but stop just outside the car park entrance." he ordered.

Clive did as he was told and when he stopped, Raymond called to the officers in the two unmarked cars, "Don't do anything stupid or this man dies, now drive across the entrance and exit, as I assume you've been ordered to do anyway, and block them."

The officers complied with Raymond's instructions and when they had done he issued more, "Now, turn off your engines and throw me the keys."

When the two cars had effectively blocked the car park one of the officers raised his hands so the Raymond could see them and got out of the car. He collected both sets of keys and lobbed them in through the rear window of the Kuga.

"Drive," shouted Raymond at Clive, "Put your foot down and get us out of here.

Pleased not to see any police cars on the main road as they exited, he directed Clive off the main road and into the side roads with instructions to make his way north. After they had travelled just a few streets, Raymond spotted a young woman, dressed in jeans and a light summer jacket, pointing her key at a Ford Focus to open it.

Thinking fast, he ordered Clive to pull up in the road just in front of her.

"What are you going to do," asked Clive."

"You just have to do as you're told," he said, and when the car had stopped, "now get out of the car."

As soon as they were out of the car, Raymond grabbed hold of the startled woman and held the gun to her neck the same as he had previously done with Clive, "Do as your told and no one will get hurt." He told them both, then, "Give him your car keys he ordered the woman."

"You don't need a second hostage," advised Clive, "I've got her keys, let's just take her car and go."

"Stop wasting time," called Raymond angrily, and transfer the guns into her car, and do it quickly, if I think you're stalling for time, I'll hurt her, I swear to God I will," he said as he nervously looked up and down the street for any sign of police.

The trembling woman was paralysed with fright as she watched Clive open her car and put down the larger of the two back seats, he then transfered a number of guns and muskets from their car to hers, after which Raymond told Clive to get back in the Kuga and park it in the next street.

"We'll follow behind, and if you try anything funny, it will be bad for this one," said Raymond, indicating the woman, who was beginning to cry.

"Why don't we just take her car and go?" insisted Clive, really not wanting to be potentially responsible for the woman's safety.

"Stop wasting time," shouted Raymond, pushing the muzzle of the gun into the woman's neck, causing her to cry out in pain.

"Alright, alright, I'm doing it," Clive responded, unsure just what Raymond had in mind.

Clive drove the now empty Kuga into the next street and parked as he had been instructed and the woman's Ford Focus followed behind, eventually pulling up alongside the parked Kuga. Raymond then instructed Clive to get into the driving seat of the Focus while he climbed in behind the woman, who now occupied the front passenger seat.

"Drive," said Raymond, "and head north to join the A38."

"OK, I'm doing as you say" said Clive, "but I don't see that we need the woman, you could let her go, it will be easier for you with only one hostage."

"Well I'll tell you shall I….what's your name by the way, I know it's not Richard Drake?"

"Clive."

"Well Clive, at the moment your colleagues have no idea what car we're in, but if I let…what's your name?"

"Sally," she sobbed.

"If I let Sally go, how long will it be before they're looking for her Focus?"

"OK, so you're stuck with the two of us, how far do you think you're going to get?"

"That's not what you should be concerned about, you should be thinking, what's to stop me just putting a bullet in both your heads, now I've got a clean car."

"Because, like you just said, as soon as they find our bodies, you'll need another car."

"As soon as they find Sally's body maybe, the discovery of yours wouldn't tell them very much, and I'm assuming somebody is going to miss Sally soon anyway. Is that right Sally, who is going to miss you first and when?"

Just as Raymond had finished talking a phone rang. The sound was coming from Sally's jacket pocket, "Give me your phone," he told her, realising that he had left his in the Kuga.

Sally took her phone out of her pocket and handed it to Raymond, who looked at the screen to see who was calling her, "It says work, is that where you were going?"

"Yes."

"What is it you do and where do you work?"

"I work at The Bristol Royal Infirmary, I'm a Physiotherapist there."

"Are you married, is there anyone else that will be looking for you?"

Sally began to cry, "No, I'm not married and no, nobody else is going to miss me until my rent is due again."

"Don't you have a boyfriend?"

"I did, but we just broke up."

"What about parents?"

"My dad's dead and mum lives in Surrey, I speak to her once a week,"

"When did you speak to her last?"

"Yesterday."

Raymond opened the rear window and threw Sally's phone out of the car. "I've been silly and overlooked something haven't I, where's your phone Clive?"

"Back at the station, I didn't bring it with me."

"Don't give me that, do you think I'm stupid, where is it?" Raymond demanded, once again pushing the muzzle of his gun into Sally's neck, causing her to cry out.

"It's true, they thought there was a possibility that you might want to search me, and that if you checked my phone you would know that I wasn't Richard Drake, search me if you like, I don't have a phone with me."

Raymond released the pressure on Sally's neck, "OK, but if I discover that you've lied to me, it will go badly for you...for both of you."

Clive had lied, and was now wondering if he had done the right thing, but only time would tell. He had his phone with him, set on silent, when he had met with Raymond in the hotel car park. He had, however, taken the opportunity to remove it from his person when he had transferred the guns from the Kuga to Sally's Focus. It was now sharing the space inside a gun box with a pair of eighteenth-century duelling pistols.

Chapter Seventeen

Soon after Raymond had left the car park of the Filton Holiday Inn, Paul and his team returned to the station to coordinate the search for Travis and his hostage, and as they arrived, John Campbell, who was one of two that had stayed behind, had news for them.

"They've found the Ford Kuga, Guv just a mile or so away from the Holiday Inn, it's empty, not a sign of the occupants or the gun collection."

"OK, so they've transferred to a different vehicle, check any reports of cars being stolen in the area in the last half hour, and see if you can rustle up a helicopter from somewhere, John. Did Clive have his mobile with him."

"Yes, he did Guv and we should be able to locate it using its International Mobile Equipment Identity number or EMEI, I've already set the wheels in motion, we just have to hope it's still with him and that it's still switched on.

"Good man John, let me know the second they locate it." Then turning to Reg he continued, "I want every one of Raymond's work force interviewed quickly, get the team onto it, see if any of them have any idea where Raymond could be heading for, he might have a bolt-hole somewhere that one of them knows about."

Ten minutes later, John was back, they seem to be heading north Guv, probably on the Motorway or the A38, we should get a better idea after they've passed a few more masts."

"How do you mean John? tell me how it works."

"As long as Clive's phone is turned on it sends out a signal to the nearest telecommunication mast and as he travels his phone is effectively passed from mast to mast, so we can determine which mast he is closest to."

"That's good, let's hope Raymond hasn't thought about it and dropped Clive's phone in the back of a passing truck, for all we know at the moment we could be tracing the progress of a cement lorry."

The next two hours were spent anxiously waiting for some development, and it eventually came when Phillip Strange announced, "We've just had a report of a missing woman Guv a Sally Tailor, she's just split up with her boyfriend and he called in to return some of her stuff but she wasn't there and he was worried so he rang her work and apparently she didn't turn up for her shift today. The thing is Guv. she only lives two roads away from where Travis abandoned the Kuga."

"OK, we assumed Travis had stolen a car, but perhaps he hijacked one instead and now has two hostages. Have you got the details of this Sally's car?"

"Yes Guv it's a Ford Focus."

"Well, at least we now know what car we're looking for, have we still got an idea of which way they're heading, Reg?"

"Yes Gov but they've changed tack, they now seem to be heading into Wales."

****

"Where almost out of petrol," announced Clive.

"OK, pull in at the next filling station, how much have we got left?"

"It's telling we have enough for another forty-five miles."

"Right, if the next filling station has the facility to pay at the pump, that's fine, if not, go on to the next one after that, we don't need you going into the shop to pay do we."

The next filling station they saw was only six miles further on, and when Clive turned into the station, he could see straight away that it had been modernised fairly recently, so he pulled up at the furthest pump from the shop as Raymond had instructed.

There was only one other car on the forecourt at the time and that was just leaving.

"Have you got your cards with you Sally, I don't think it would be fair to ask Clive to pay for your petrol, do you?"

Sally nervously fumbled in her jacket pocket and produced a small purse from which she took out a credit card and held it up for Clive to take.

"OK Clive, I need you to take Sally's card and fill the tank to the top, use the pay at pump facility and don't

276

forget that Sally's wellbeing is in your hands, so no funny business, understood? Turn your collar up and keep facing away from the CCTV camera that I know you just clocked. Remember it's Sally that will pay for any mistakes you make."

As Clive got out of the car, he looked over towards the little glass fronted shop. He could see the top of the till through the window on the far right but there was no sign of the cashier, who must have been either sitting, and therefore below window height, or off filling shelves.

Clive filled Sally's car and payed for the petrol at the pump as he had been instructed.

After hanging the filler nozzle back in its slot on the pump Clive turned back to the car and held Sally's card up in his right hand as he reached for and opened the door with his left in order to hand it to her.

As Sally took the card from him, she instinctively leaned forward to retrieve her bag from the foot-well, creating a space between the back of her head and Raymond's gun. Raymond's hand, that had been holding the gun against Sally's head was left protruding just forward of the door pillar and Clive quickly reached in and grabbed Raymond's wrist, pushing the hand and gun away.

At the same time he cried out, "Run Sally, run."

Sally didn't need to be told twice, keeping her head down, she ducked under Clive's arm and made a bolt for it. Raymond hit Clive on the side of his head with his left hand as he desperately tried to free his right from Clive's grip, but Clive hung on for grim death, knowing that he was now in grave danger of being shot.

Clive was at a serious disadvantage. He actions meant that he was now virtually laying across the passenger seat, and the gear leaver was sticking painfully into his neck, but he knew that he daren't let go of Raymond's gun hand. Raymond however had other ideas and after locating Clive's eye socket with his left hand began to dig in his thumb.

Clive released his hold on Raymond's wrist and cried out in pain. All then went black as Raymond brought the newly released pistol down on Clive's vulnerable head.

Raymond exited the rear of the car and quickly lifted Clive's legs inside and slammed the door shut. Running around to the driver's side he got in and lifted the top half of Clive's limp body up and pushed it sideways so that it rested against the inside of the passenger door.

As he had run around the side of the car he had briefly caught sight of Sally, running and stumbling along the road in the direction they had been travelling. She was understandably not thinking straight and had simply run away rather than running to the shop to sound the alarm.

Luckily for Raymond, the tussle did not seem to have alerted anyone to what was happening, so he was able to simply catch up with the frightened girl, pulling the car up beside her. He got out of the car and dragged her back towards it just as Clive was coming around.

Once again Raymond gave commands to Clive while holding the gun to Sally's head, "Get back in the driving seat," he demanded.

Clive staggered out of the car, holding one hand against the roof for support, "I don't think I'm in any state to drive," he said.

and when he got back in, he continued, "Look, Raymond, if you know where we're going, it would make life easier if you just told me where to head for."

"Alright Clive, head towards Wrexham for now."

The journey to Wrexham was uneventful, punctuated only by the odd bout of crying from Sally.

Back at the station, a rather breathless Reg Evans hurried into the office, "I've just spoken to Neil Roberts, one of Travis's men, and he inherited a house when his mother died, he keeps it as a holiday home now and it's situated just outside Colwyn Bay, Guv, I'll bet my life that's where Travis is heading. Neil said that Travis knows it will be vacant at the moment. Here's the address Guv." said Reg handing Paul a piece of note paper.

"Good work Reg let's get moving, John, Derrick, Chris and Peter can remain here in case needed, you, June and Phillip come with me, we'll take two cars in case we have to split up for some reason, you go with Phillip.

June can come with me…come on let's go and get Clive and Sally back."

As Paul was leaving the room he turned back, "Derrick, make sure we have an armed response team ready to go in the Colwyn Bay area if we need them, will you?"

"I'm all over it, Guv. Good luck."

As the three of them approached their destination on the A55, Raymond told Clive to look out for a turning on the right, some six miles short of Colwyn Bay, "There it is," he said excitedly, "next right, then pull into the drive of the sixth property on the right and drive straight around to the back, out of sight of the road."

Once parked, Raymond ushered them out of the car and up to the back door of a two-storey cottage that appeared to be unoccupied. Lifting the top two upturned flower pots off a stack of six, he retrieved a key and used it to open the back door.

"In you go," he ordered.

His hostages readily complied with his demand, glad to be out of the confines of the car. The back door had opened directly into the property's kitchen, a large typical farmhouse kitchen with a pine table and four chairs in the centre, a range cooker on the far left wall and a white Belfast style sink under the window, to the left of the door as they came through. The wall to the right was almost entirely taken up by an enormous Welsh Dresser stacked with blue and white china.

"Sit, both of you," Raymond ordered.

"I need the toilet," said Sally.

"So do I," said Clive.

"You'll both have to hang on a few more minutes," said Raymond, crossing to the Welsh Dresser and rummaging through the drawers until he found what he was looking for. Returning to his hostages with a roll of duct tape he proceeded to tape Clive's wrists and ankles to the chair after which he said to Sally, "Come on then, it's through here."

Sally stood up and followed by Raymond, walked out of the kitchen and into a small hallway, "Stand there," he ordered, as he opened one of two doors that were on the left, revealing a small cloakroom.

Sally walked into the room closely followed by Raymond, who looked around and checked the contents of the small over the basin medicine cabinet for any potential weapon. Seeing only plastic pill bottles, tubes of various ointments and an eyebath, he stepped back out of the room.

"Go on then, make it quick," he said.

Sally stared at him and then at the still open door, "Some privacy would be nice," she pleaded, to which request Raymond pushed the door so that it was almost closed.

After a few moments Raymond heard Sally running water into the basin to wash her hands. She pushed the door open when she'd finished and said, "There's no towel."

"Wipe em in your jeans then, and get back in the kitchen."

Once back in the kitchen Raymond secured Sally in a chair the same as he had done with Clive. Then, releasing Clive from the chair, he secured his hands together in front of him and led him to the cloakroom.

"Are you going to release my hands," asked Clive.

"I'm sure you can manage to undo a zip like that, now get on with it."

When Clive had finished, he left the room and returned to the kitchen where he was once again secured in a chair.

"We need some water," said Clive, "We've not had a drink for hours, and nor have you."

Raymond fetched three glasses from one of the dresser cupboards, filled them with water from the tap, and after drinking one himself he placed the other two on the table in front of his hostages. Clive looked at him questioningly, but Raymond simply went back to the cupboard and supplied them both with straws.

"You seem to know this place inside out Raymond, is it yours?"

"No, now shut up, I have to think."

After maybe fifteen minutes of complete silence, Raymond stood up and fetched a phone from another room. Sitting back down opposite Clive with the handset of a landline phone in his hand he asked, "What's the mobile number of your Inspector Manley?"

Paul didn't recognise the number that came up on his phone screen but answered, "Inspector Manley, who's this?"

"Hi Inspector, Paul isn't it, shall we keep it friendly?"

"Well, Raymond Travis, as I live and breathe, you're the last person I expected to ring me.... I hope my officer is unharmed?" said Paul, frantically indicating to Reg that it was Travis on the line.

"He and Sally are fine...at the moment...whether they both stay that way rather depends on you now." replied Raymond.

Paul decided to play ignorant about Sally Tailor, the less Ray knew about their knowledge of what was happening the better he thought.

"Sally?....so you've got yourself two hostages now....Oh! I see, you hi-jacked a car and driver. We assumed you'd just nicked one when we found the Kuga, we were waiting for it to be reported stolen so we'd know what you were driving. Can I speak to my officer, so I know he's alright?"

Raymond held the receiver to Clive's ear after warning, "If I even think you're trying to indicate where we are, I'll hurt Sally, do you understand?"

Clive nodded, then said. "We're both unharmed at the moment Guv," after which Raymond took the phone back.

He began, "I saw you arresting Mary Inspector, what evidence have you got against us?"

"Oh, we've got a lot Raymond, we know that you owned the gun that Peter was shot with and that was found with Winchester in his car."

Raymond racked his brains and eventually realised, "Ah, you must be talking about the insurance on my collection, I expect you've got the itemised list. Well I have to tell you that I sold that gun a few years ago, and I just forgot to inform the insurance company, so a different gun I'm afraid, Paul, no luck for you there."

"Well that's strange Raymond, because we have bullets that we can match to the murder weapon."

"Of course you have, one in Winchester's office and one in Peter's head, you can't link those to me."

"No...no, I'm not talking about those, I'm talking about the ones we dug out of the earth embankment at your yard, you know, behind where you had the target set up for your improvised shooting range."

"Ah...I see, well yes, I suppose that is going to be difficult for me to explain away, isn't it? You have been a clever little policeman haven't you"

"So you see, it really is all over, Raymond, why don't you just hand yourself in? It'll go better for you in court."

"Now listen Paul, in view of what you've just told me, I need you to lift any restriction you've had placed on my bank accounts, so that I can spend some money and buy a plane ticket, then I need you to speak to whoever you have to, to get one hundred thousand pounds, as a ransom payment for these two. My gun collection is worth that, so I don't see why it should be a problem. I'll give you an hour and ring you back, if you haven't managed to comply with my demands by then, I'll have to decide which hostage I can do without," and with last statement hanging in the air, he hung up.

Fetching a laptop from the front room Raymond connected to the internet and checked the availability of flights out of Liverpool airport, and then proceeded to book and pay for one to Rome, leaving at seven the next morning. One hour later, having given the police enough time to check his card payment and see where he was going, he rang the airline direct and changed his booking to one leaving fifteen minutes earlier to Paris. He then rang Paul for the second time.

"How are the arrangements coming along Paul?"

"I've managed to get approval to pay the money, but it's going to take a while to get it, we have to wait for the banks to open in the morning," lied Paul.

"Well that's a shame, because it will be too late for one of the hostages, have you got any preference as to which one?"

"There's no need for anyone else to be killed. Let me speak to Clive again."

Raymond held up the phone, "Reassure your boss you're both still with us Clive, there's a good buy."

"We're OK Guv." Clive shouted.

"There you are, nothing's happened to them, and nothing will if you do as you're told."

How do you propose we do the exchange?"

"That's easy, you probably already know by now that I've booked a flight out of Liverpool, so you can bring the money to me there. Then once I've landed at my destination and left there without being arrested, I'll contact you and let you know where the hostages are."

"You really can't expect us to let you leave with the money before we've secured the release of the hostages."

"Well, if you want them back alive, I don't see that you have any choice. Meet me at Liverpool airport at six tomorrow morning with the money, or the race will be on for you to find the hostages before they die of thirst and hunger, it's all up to you Paul, this is the last time we'll speak until the exchange."

"How far away from the holiday home are we now?" Paul asked June.

We're just turning into the road now Guv, there's Reg and Phillips car parked on the left. The property is the sixth one along on the right, all the houses here have some land attached so it's still a few hundred yards up the road.

Reg had left his car and now stood beside Paul's open window. "We've had a bit of luck Guv, I've let all the local authorities in on what's happening, and a very helpful Inspector Grant, has informed me that the next property along on the left from the one we're interested in, is owned by a Mr and Mrs Jones, no surprise there, but their son lives with them now, and he's ex-job, was a detective sergeant apparently. They've agreed to let us use their home as a base of operations, so to speak, we can drive up there now and just pull in, they've left the gate open. Instructions are to go just past the house and turn in through the double gates, there's room for both cars at the back of the house out of sight."

"That's wonderful Reg June and I will go first; you and Phillip give it five minutes before you come up."

June and Paul risked a quick glance at the target house as they drove past. A two storey double fronted cottage with a detached but rather ramshackle garage to the right, on the other side of the drive to the house. There appeared to be land belonging to the house all around it, but mostly to the rear, but there was no sign of any vehicle. They drove on and turned into the drive of the next property on their left as instructed. This was a similar looking property but it had been extended at the back and there were two large barns in the grounds. As they pulled up behind the house a man and a woman came out of the back door to greet them.

"Hello, I'm Roger Jones, this is my mother Irene, dad's inside putting the kettle on, I guess you could do with hot drink, is it just the two of you?"

"No, two more of us will be here in a minute."

"Well come inside and tell me how we can assist you? I used to be in the job myself, until this place became too much work for mum and dad on their own."

"Yes, so I understand, detective sergeant, I believe."

"That's right."

After Reg and Phillip turned up, everyone assembled in the Jones's kitchen and Roger's dad, Jacob, made teas and coffees for everyone as introductions continued, culminating in Roger finally shaking hands with June.

"It's lovely to meet you June," he said graciously, as he pulled out a seat for her at the kitchen table.

Phillip looked over at Reg grinning "I'm sure it was lovely for Roger to meet us as well Reg."

"Yes, it was, just not so much," replied Roger, winking at June.

"OK, girls and boys," cut in Paul, "Let's not lose sight of why we're here, we've got two people in danger and we need to stay focused."

"That was my fault," said Roger, "Tell me what you need."

"Well the situation is that we believe an armed man is holding a young woman and a fellow officer hostage in the house just down from yours on the other side of the road. We believe they're there because we've been tracking our colleague's phone, but we could really do with confirming it, in case our man found the phone and it's no longer with them. There was no sign of the Ford Focus that we think they're driving when we drove past but it could be parked at the back out of sight. Is there any way you think we could get a close look around the back without risking being seen, I don't want them to know we're here just yet."

"I could put the drone up for you if you like, it's the quietest one I could find and it's got a zoom facility on the camera."

Paul just stared at him, "You've got a drone?" he asked, incredulous.

"Yeh, we've got TV, computers, even super-markets up here now Inspector, we've also got over five hundred head of sheep on the farm, and I use the drone to keep track of them, it literally saves us hours of work. I'm pretty good at operating it as well."

"I wasn't implying that you don't have technology here Roger, just that it's a coincidence that you should have the one piece of it that we need at the moment. Can you get in close without the noise alerting them?"

"Like I say Inspector, it's the quietest on the market, I use it to keep an eye on the lambs, not spook them."

"Well yes then, Roger, that would be an enormous help."

Roger turned to June, "Well June, would you like me to show you how to fly a drone?"

"Yes Roger, that would be great."

"Give me a minute and I'll fetch it," said Roger as he left the room.

"I'd like to learn how to fly a drone as well," said Phillip, as Roger left the room, "would you like to know how to fly a drone Reg?"

"Christ! It's like being in charge of a couple kids," cried Paul, to Rogers mum and dad, who looked on smiling.

Ten minutes later Roger, June, Paul, Reg and Phillip were all clustered around Roger's laptop, eagerly watching the picture on screen, showing an aerial view of the roof of the target house.

As Roger manoeuvered the drone around to the rear of the property, using the elaborate control system that hung around his neck, Sally's car could be clearly seen, Roger even managed to zoom in on the registration plate so there could be no mistake. Paul would have liked a look through the kitchen window, but the blind had been pulled down.

Suddenly the back door opened and Roger deftly took the drone higher, but zoomed in on the person who had emerged from the back of the house.

"That's our man alright," said Paul, as they watched Raymond, make several journeys from the car to the house unloading his collection of guns.

"Blimey!" exclaimed Roger, he's got a bloody arsenal with him."

"That's his collection of antique pistols and muskets."

Confused, Roger asked, "What the hell's he doing with those?"

"Well initially he was trying to sell them to raise some money for his escape, why he's chosen to unload them here I don't know, unless he just wants the room in the car for some reason."

"What's your plan Guv." asked June. but Paul didn't have time to answer before the arrival at the back door of four officers from armed response.

Jacob made more teas and coffees as everyone sat around the table to discuss tactics.

"What have you got in mind, Guv?" asked Reg.

"Well my guess is that Travis will set off for Liverpool airport, having secured Clive and Sally in the house somehow, he won't want to take them with him," Morrice Jones, the senior armed officer asked, "What if this Travis decides it easier to just shoot the hostages before he leaves? In fact, how do you know he hasn't already done just that?"

"They were both alive when I spoke to Travis last, and I don't see any reason why he would shoot them before he leaves, he has no idea we're nearby and he has nothing to gain by shooting them."

Phillip had been the on phone, and he now announced, "Raymond Travis has booked a ticket to Rome, out of Liverpool at 7am tomorrow Guv."

"OK, let's look at a map, and see what route he'll take. Then, if we keep a watch on the house we can move in as soon as he leaves. Morrice here can arrange to intercept him before he gets back to the main road and June and I can free Clive and Sally. The only snag that I can see will be if he takes a hostage with him, but bare in mind, if he has a hostage, he'll have a gun, and there's no way he can have that with him at the airport, he'll have to get rid of it somewhere. So my feeling is that he will leave alone. Morrice?"

"That sounds as good a plan as any given what we know Inspector."

"Is there anything I can do inspector," asked Roger, anxious to help.

"You could deploy that drone of yours again in the morning, keep it up out of sight and it could give us a heads up on when he decides to leave."

"Consider it done, Sir"

Back at the house, Raymond carried in the last of his collection and placed them carefully on the furniture in the front room before returning to his guests in the kitchen.

"Why did you do it?" asked Clive.

"Do what, unload the car?"

"Kill Peter Newbridge?"

Raymond sat down, "Alright, there's no harm in telling you, your inspector has it all figured out by the sound of it anyway. I did it for Mary, Clive, she's had a miserable life with Peter over the past years, he never really got over the death of their son. After a few years of grieving, Mary wanted to have another child, but Peter refused, all he wanted to do was bury himself in his work. He earned really good money you know, Mary said that one year he published an exposé of corruption that earned him over one million pounds in terms of newspaper articles, television appearances and a book, and even on a bad year he'd rake in a couple of hundred thousand. I expect you've seen their house, haven't you, a tiny little terraced place, when they could have been living in a mansion, and he never took Mary on holiday or bought her nice things, on top of which, he expected her to run the place on a shoestring budget. Well Mary had just had enough."

"The two of you could have just set up home together, you didn't have to kill him."

"I know, and I would have settled for that, but Mary felt she was owed, owed for all the things she could have had and never did, compensation, if you like, with Peter dead she would get the lot, and she felt she deserved it, and I agreed with her."

"Who planned it?"

"We planned it together, although I suppose it was largely me, we'd actually made several plans over the

293

last year or so, and then when Carter's body turned up, everything just sort of fell into place. Peter told Mary that he believed Winchester had murdered Carter, and that he intended gathering the evidence to prove it, it was going to be his next big scoop. Well it occurred to us that if Peter decided to confront Winchester with what he knew, instead of just gathering evidence, there was always the chance that Winchester would decide kill Peter as well.

Like I say, it all fell into place, I rang Winchester pretending to be Peter and went to see him at his office, where I dropped the cartridge case. I made out that I wanted money to keep quiet, and we arranged to meet at his place. I think he was actually planning to kill me.....or rather Peter

"Well you've probably worked out the rest, Mary lured Peter to their static van, saying that there was some maintenance problem down there, and when they arrived, I was already there waiting. Mary let me in the van and I shot him, it was as simple as that."

"You'd already started to frame Winchester for Peter's murder, by planting the cartridge case, why did you decide to kill him?"

"It would all have just got too messy, let's face it, you were having trouble getting enough evidence to convict him of the murder he did commit, let alone one he didn't. It wouldn't have been long before you started looking at Mary for Peter's death, so having Winchester confess and commit suicide was the perfect solution.

You can imagine how we felt when you turned up with the speeding fine and the CCTV footage."

"Did you both kill Winchester, or was that just you?"

"Just me for that one Clive, and it almost went pear-shaped. I'd rung Winchester pretending to be Peter again, I already told him I knew he had killed Carter, and that I wanted money to keep quiet about it, this time I said I was coming to the house and I wanted the first payment. I had the gun with me, and I was just going to shoot him and make it look as if he'd shot himself."

"Why didn't you?"

"Well it turned out that Winchester had decided to get rid of Peter, rather than pay blackmail, and he tried to get in first. It's a good job I was on my guard as well, he had this long handled club and he tried to whack me over the head with it. Fortunately, I saw it coming and managed to avoid it, although I did receive a nasty blow to the shoulder instead, and we got int a tussle. Now Winchester was a big chap, but I'd done a course in unarmed combat and he was no match for me in the end, I managed to get him in a choke hold and he passed out."

"Why didn't you shoot him then?"

"I nearly did, I had the gun ready and was about to do just that, but for some reason, seeing him unconscious like that, I decided it would look better if a staged a suicide in the car. At least I wouldn't have to worry about your forensic boys analysing powder burns and blood splatter and what have you, so that's what I did. Now you know it all."

"That's quite a story, don't you feel any remorse at having killed two innocent men?"

Hardly innocent Clive, Peter had made Mary's life a misery for years, and Winchester was a cheat and a killer."

"Well there you are, you might be lucky and get a sympathetic jury, aren't you tired of running?"

"I am....but there's no way I'm going to prison, I'd rather be shot."

Chapter Eighteen

Raymond had just finished telling his story to Clive and Sally, when they all heard a distinct bleep come from where Raymond had deposited his gun collection in the front room. Clive's heart sank, he recognised the sound straight away, it was his mobile phone automatically switching off because the battery was critically low.

"What was that?" asked Raymond, "it seemed to come from the front room," he commented as he left the kitchen to investigate.

He looked carefully around the room, it had sounded a bit like an alarm, but there were no smoke detectors or burglar alarms fitted, and why just the one bleep? The only things different in the room from normal were his guns and he suddenly had a nasty thought. Walking over to his collection his eyes went to the box that was home to his pair of duelling pistols, reaching for the box, he opened it opened it and removed Clive's phone.

He carried the phone back into the kitchen, where Clive and Sally were waiting, Clive looked worried when he saw the phone in Raymond' hand.

"You're a sneaky little bastard, aren't you Clive, and a liar as well, when did you put your phone in with the duelling pistols?"

There was no point in denying anything, "When you got me to transfer the collection from your Kuga to Sally's car."

"You lied to me, and I seem to remember telling you that Sally would be the one to suffer the consequences if you tried anything, do you remember that Clive."

"Yes, I remember, but I was the one who lied to you, it's me you need to punish not Sally, come on Ray, you're not the sort of man to hurt an innocent woman, I can see that, it's not Sally's doing," pleaded Clive.

Sally was so scared she was unable to speak and just stared in horror, wondering what was going to happen to her.

"I ought to just bloody shoot the pair of you and have done with it," he raged, uplifting the gun he held in his hand and aiming a blow at Clive's head.

Clive turned his face away from the expected blow and braced himself, expecting pain, and praying there would be no permanent damage from the blow, but Raymond stayed his hand and instead walked away cursing under his breath.

Clive and Sally looked at each other wondering what was going to happen next and they could hear Raymond pacing up and down the hallway, still cursing. Clive tried his best to reassure Sally, "Listen, I don't think he's intends to hurt us, I don't think he's that kind of a man."

Sally was near tears again and replied, "But how can you say that, he's already killed two people, what makes you think he won't kill us, and why is he so angry about the phone?"

"He's angry about the phone because I left it on so that it can be traced, I'm hoping my Guvnor's not too far away. You heard him say why he was prepared to kill the others, it's different with us, Sally, or at least it is with you, and he has nothing to gain by hurting us.

Raymond came back into the room, "What do think Clive, have they managed to trace us here? Is that bloody inspector of yours outside the front door as we speak?"

"I would say the chances are pretty good that that's the case, yes. You know this is only going to end one of two ways Raymond, and that's either with you being shot or you being arrested, it's your choice, why don't you let me call my inspector and say that you're prepared to give yourself up?"

"Yeh, I could do that, but then I'd look pretty stupid if there's no one out there, wouldn't I, and didn't you believe me when I said I'd rather be shot than go to prison?"

Clive was about to speak again, but Raymond put his hand up, indicating that he should stay quiet, "Just give me a moment to think this through."

After a little more pacing, Raymond picked up the land line and rang Paul again.

"Hello Raymond," said Paul, "I thought we weren't going to speak again until the exchange, they haven't cancelled your flight or anything have they?"

"Just checking that everything is still on track, Paul, where are you at the moment?"

"In my office, why."

"You're a bigger liar than Clive, do you know that, and Clive can tell some whoppers."

"What are you talking about Raymond, you're not making any sense."

"How many people are in the office with you at the moment Paul?"

"Why?"

"Because I want you to get them all to shout out together and tell me how many people are there with you, and I want to hear a lot of voices."

"Where are you going with this Ray, I don't understand what you're doing."

"I'll tell you Paul, I've spoken to people on the phone in offices before, and there's always that office sort of sound in the background, you know what I mean. I don't think you're in your office at all, I think your outside somewhere. You see I found Clive's mobile phone just now, the crafty old sod had put it in with my duelling pistols."

"Well what can I say, I hope you're not contemplating doing anything stupid." As Paul was speaking, he gestured for one of the armed officers to come forward, "Where do we go from here Raymond, the ball's in your court?"

Paul covered the mouthpiece of his phone and whispered to the officer, "Give me your sidearm."

"I don't think I should do that Sir."

"I'm the senior officer here and I'm ordering you to give me your gun," insisted Paul.

June and Reg both started to protest but Paul put his hand up to stop them as the officer took his Glock pistol out of his holster. Indicating to Paul that it was loaded and that the safety was on he handed it to him.

Paul placed the weapon in the waistband of his trousers at the small of his back under his jacket.

"What's going on?" asked Raymond, what are you up to now?"

"It's OK Raymond, I'm going to come down and see you, so that we can discuss the situation face to face, but my colleagues don't seem to think it's a very good idea."

"I think I'd be inclined to agree with them, if I was in their shoes, but you can come if you're alone an unarmed."

Paul walked out of the kitchen and got into his car, which he then proceeded to drive to the house where Raymond was held up with his hostages. Parking his car across the entrance, he got out of the car and looked back the way he had come to see the four officers from armed response hurrying after him, closely followed by Reg, Phillip and June.

"Are you still there Raymond?"

"Yeh. I'm still here, what the hell are you up to?"

"I'm here now, it's just me, do you want me to come in the front door or the back, I'm not holding a gun, I've got one arm in the air and the other holding my mobile to my ear talking to you. What's it to be, back or front?"

"Well the front door is locked, so you'd better come in the back. If you're sure that's what you want to do?" said Raymond, grabbing hold of the back of Clive's chair, tipping it onto its back legs and dragging it around to the other side of the table so that they where now facing Sally and the back door across the top of the table. Paul began to walk around to the back of the property and approached the back door cautiously. "I'm at the back door now Raymond, I'm coming in."

"Suit yourself, but don't try anything, I'm holding a gun to Clive's head."

Paul opened the back door slowly and walked through, now holding both hands in the air. "Hello Sally, I'm Paul," he said, trying to reassure her as much as possible, and nodding to Clive.

"Nice to see you Guv."

"Good to see you too Clive."

"OK, so now you've all said how nice it is to see one another, where do we go from here?" asked Raymond.

"Well come on Raymond, you've had enough time to put this all together by now, so you must realise there are only two ways this can end……either we arrest you….or you get yourself shot. You do know the place is surrounded by armed officers?"

"Yeh, I guess, talking of which, why don't you take off your jacket for me," said Raymond, now pointing the Browning at Paul.

Paul did as requested and removed his jacket, hanging it on the back of the chair occupied by Sally.

"Now turn around for me," ordered Raymond.

Again Paul did as requested.

"Well that just goes to confirm it Sally….look at that….you should never trust a copper….now suppose you take the gun out of your waistband, hold it out to your side with two fingers and slowly walk backwards towards me."

Paul did as he'd been told and Raymond removed the gun from his hand, "Now step away and turn to face me."

When Paul turned back, he said, "What are you going to do now Raymond, you know they're not going to let you leave."

"They will if I take Sally or Clive with me…or you of course now."

"And then it all just begins over again, you running, us chasing, we'll get you in the end, and it'll probably be with a bullet."

"Well I'm not going to prison, life in there wouldn't suit me at all, I'd rather get shot than go to prison."

"Well that, at the end of the day is exactly the choice you have to make, I don't think you want to harm anyone here, I don't think you're that sort of a man, with Peter and Winchester I think you just got caught up in things, now put down the gun and give yourself up."

There was a long tense silence, during which time Raymond appeared to be wrestling with making a decision. After what seemed an eternity, he appeared to make up his mind, and announced, "I've made my decision, don't be too hard on Mary." then he lifted the gun to his own head.

Without thinking, Paul threw himself at Raymond and made a grab for the gun. As Paul crashed into Raymond, slamming him against the back wall, the gun discharged with a loud bang, the bullet smashing one of the blue and white plates adorning the Welsh Dresser, and causing Sally to scream.

Everything that followed happened in seconds, Paul and Raymond fell to the floor with Paul on top, and the gun bounced out of Raymond's hand as it hit the floor. In the same instant, two armed police officers rushed in through the back door and one of them kicked the gun away before either Raymond or Paul, who were both reaching for it, could get there.

Paul struggled to his feet, after which one man put his knee in the small of Raymond's back, and pulled his arms behind him.

"Lay still," he shouted as he handcuffed him with the dexterity of a stage magician. Between them, the two officers helped Raymond to his feet and began to lead him out of the room as Reg and Phillip entered with June.

Raymond looked at Paul as he was being led away, his face full of a mixture of anger and remorse, "Why did you stop me, you've condemned me to purgatory now?"

"Purgatory's good for the soul, I hear," said Paul as he watched Raymond being led away.

"Can somebody please get me out of this chair now," pleaded Clive, "and I'm dying for a cuppa, any chance somebody could rustle one up."

June released Sally and Clive and all five occupants of the room stared at Paul, as Reg gave voice to their thoughts, "What the hell were you thinking Guv? just coming down here on your own like that was bad enough, but why did you risk grabbing his gun?"

"I don't really know Reg. I suppose I couldn't bear the thought of yet another one not having to face prosecution, I didn't want it to end the same as with Winchester."

"We've got Mary to prosecute Guv, wouldn't that be enough?" asked June.

"Maybe.....anyway, changing the subject....I have a question for everyone."

"What's that?" asked June.

"Do any of you know a reliable place I could get my car re-sprayed?"

****

The following morning, despite a complete lack of sleep, everyone was in buoyant mood getting all the files and paperwork together for the prosecution of Raymond Travis and Mary Newbridge when June took a call on her desk phone.

"It's for you Guv." she said, handing the phone to Paul, "he won't give his name."

Paul took the receiver from her and answered, "Hello, Inspector Manley here, who's calling?"

"Hello Paul, it's nice to speak to you again, you're a difficult man to contact these days. Are you alone?"

"Paul knew the voice was familiar but couldn't place it, "Who is this?" he asked again.

"It's me, Jack....Jack Williams...don't tell me you've forgotten me already Paul.....I'm devastated."

"Ah, Jack, so have you managed to make bail have you?"

"That's right, it certainly pays to get a good lawyer these days, although I don't suppose you'd be able to afford one on your salary. By the way, have you had your car re-sprayed yet?"

"What have you rung me for Jack, I'm sure it's not to say sorry."

"No actually, it's to let you know that I bumped into an old friend of yours....Jillian....you remember Jillian, don't you Paul?..........Say hello to Paul Jillian."

Paul's blood ran cold as he heard Jillian Simmons scream. This wasn't just a regular scream, it came from the very soul her and Paul realised she was in great pain and distress."

"Christ! Jillian was just looking out for your wife….what have you got against her?"

"Well not a lot I suppose, now you come to mention it, but I thought you might want to save her from any more pain."

"OK, so what do you want me to do?"

"I want you to come and get her, alone obviously."

"Where is she?"

"She's with me at my brother's breaker's yard, he's conveniently closed it and gone away for a while, do you know, I think he's a little upset about Sandra. Now I have to tell you Paul that I have cameras set up at the yard, so I will know if you bring anyone with you and if you do, I'm afraid Jillian will suffer a great deal of pain. just so you know."

"OK I'm coming, there's no need to hurt Jillian anymore I'm on my way, just give me enough time to get there."

Everyone in the office had heard Jillian scream and were now watching Paul and waiting for an explanation, "Listen up everyone," announced Paul, "Jack Williams has taken Jillian Simmons hostage and is holding her at his brother's yard. He wants me to go and get her alone and he has cameras set up at the yard to ensure I arrive alone. Reg, I want to organise armed backup for me, I have no intention of going without it but make sure they know that if they are spotted on

307

camera, he's going to hurt or maybe even kill Jillian. I'm going to the armoury and then straight to the yard, we haven't got much time, as you all heard he's already started torturing her. Reg, I'm relying on you, I think the only way he is going to release Jillian is if he has me and I don't want him starting anything nasty on me before you get there, so if you hear me scream you come in all guns blazing, promise?"

"You've got it Guv."

After signing out some protection from the police armoury Paul drove to Daniel's breaker's yard and parked outside. The main gate had been left ajar and Paul took one of the pistols he'd been issued with from it's holster and cocked it, loading a round into the chamber.

Holding the weapon pointing in both hands he put his shoulder against the door and opened it sufficiently to enter. He put his head round the door to see the yard pretty much as he remembered it, the one exception being that there was obviously a light on in the warehouse he and Reg had first entered.

Paul was scared, so scared that he briefly thought of changing his mind and just allowing armed response to deal with everything, but then he remembered Jack's threat and realised that no matter how scared he was, Jillian would be more so, and he would be unable to live with himself if his cowardliness caused her any harm.

Steeling himself he approached the warehouse and still holding the gun at the ready he stepped inside half expecting to be attacked by the dog he had seen on his earlier visit, but much to his relief, Cujo failed to put in an appearance.

Paul now had a chance to take in the full extent of the building. In the part he now stood, the eight-foot-high metal shelving units were arranged with their backs to the walls so that there was a large area of open space in the middle but twenty feet further in the same units where arranged three units deep, at right angles to the walls and back-to-back creating lots of mini isles at right angles to the main central isle.

These isles would have been very dark if it wasn't for the fact that all had a flurescent light hanging from the ceiling between them and every other one had a window to the outside, which despite being glazed with thick opaque glass and covered with steel mesh, still managed to let in a small degree of light from outside.

It seemed that the lights could be turned on or off independent of each other, something that was apparent because although the end of the room where Paul stood and the far end, some hundred and fifty feet away, were brightly lit, the area between was in darkness.

As Paul looked towards what he thought was the far end of the building, two more sets of lights came on, illuminating the sorry looking figure tied in a chair. Paul realised that it was Jillian tied in the chair and he began to approach keeping a wary eye out for Jack.

Paul's progress was obviously being observed because every so often lights would spring into life before him as others behind were turned off. It was a tense, eerie journey.

When he was within ten metres of Jillian he could see her clearly and was shocked by what he saw. The previously attractive woman who Paul thought had a very friendly and lively character had been reduced to a pitiful figure of a human being. Her hair was tangled and her eyes half closed and swollen, whether from crying or being hit he couldn't tell. Worst of all, her skirt had been pulled up exposing two nasty third degree burns, one on each thigh.

Paul's whole being filled with anger, "Come out and show yourself, you pathetic excuse for a man," he yelled.

"Just to your left is a drum full of dirty oil Paul, you drop the gun you're holding into it and I'll come out," came Jack's chillingly calm reply.

Paul saw that he had no option but to comply and did as he'd been bid.

Jack stepped out from behind the shelving units just behind Jillian and to Paul's right. He held a gun in his hand and pointed it at her head. Paul also noticed for the first time that Jack had a laptop computer set up on a small table to Jillian's right and that he kept checking it's monitor. He suspected that it showed the images put from whatever cameras Jack had set up and hoped that his warnings had been heeded.

"Well I'm here now," said Paul, "you can let Jillian go….that was the deal after all."

"Yes that's true," Jack replied dragging another chair into view from behind the cabinets, "and as soon as I have you secured in this chair I'll untie her but first I want you to take off your jacket and turn around."

As he spoke Jack reached out and picked up a blowlamp from the shelves, it was of the type plumbers use for soldering pipes and so as to leave Paul in no doubt he pulled the trigger, causing an intense blue flame to issue noisily from the nozzle. At the sound of the flame, Jillian turned her head away and began to whimper pathetically, leaving no doubt in Paul's mind that the ugly thing had been the cause of Jillian's injuries.

Jack pointed the blowlamp towards Gillian's head,

"Do as I ask Paul, or you can have the privilege of watching Jillian's face melt."

"Ok...Ok...take it easy, I'm doing as you ask," said Paul thinking how strange it was to be going through the same ritual for a second time in as many days.

After divesting himself of his jacket Paul held it out to his side.

"In the oil-drum," said Jack, "you can always buy another one."

Paul obliged and dropped his jacket into the same drum as the gun, he then turned around so that his back was towards Jack and just as he had done the day before for Raymond Travis, he slowly removed a second weapon from the waistband of his trousers and

311

consigned it also to the depths of the oil-drum before turning back to confront his tormentor.

"Good....now come and sit here," ordered Jack smiling.

Paul, who had no intention of allowing Jack to secure him in any chair, slowly dropped to his knees turning slightly to his right, effectively hiding his right arm from Jack, who looked on amused.

"For God's sake Jack I'm begging you to stop this....I'm down on my knees pleading with you Jack, is that what you want, for me to beg for my life on bended knee, to plead for Jillian's life?"

As he spoke Paul reached back with his right hand and retrieved a small pistol from the ankle holster strapped to his right leg. He knew he had to act fast so as soon as he had the gun in his hand he stood up, pointed the pistol at Jack and fired three shots in rapid succession.

Jack hadn't known what to expect when he saw Paul stand again after his emotional plea for mercy but was enjoying the moment right up until the second he spotted the gun in Paul's hand. Realisation that he had been out manoeuvered took a moment to sink in but when it did Jack also took aim and fired at Paul.

Paul's first shot turned out to be the most decisive, hitting Jack in the flesh of the upper arm that was holding the blowlamp causing Jack to drop it and cry out in pain. Unfortunately for Paul the shot also made Jack step back and turn sideways meaning that both his other shots missed their target and ricocheted harmlessly off the wall behind.

Jack had managed to get off one shot just as Paul's bullet was tearing its way through his flesh and it passed between Paul's left arm and body cutting a groove in his side. Fortunately, possibly because of the amount of adrenalin in his system, Paul had no idea he'd been hit and was able to grab hold of the back of Jillian's chair and drag it and her to relative safety behind the cabinets.

As soon as there had been the sound of gunfire within the building the armed officers, who had been effectively hiding outside, rushed in shouting, "Armed police...put down your weapons!"

Jack had been prepared for just such an eventuality, not for one minute expecting that Paul would come without backup. On the bench against the back wall and just right of the rear door, he had prepared three petrol bombs and now, with some difficulty because of his wound he systematically lit each in turn and threw them as far as he could down the main aisle between the cabinets.

The centre of the building was immediately engulfed in flame and two of the armed officers had to retreat quickly to avoid being caught in the ensuing fire.

Paul meanwhile, took a knife from his pocket and freed Jillian from chair as black smoke began to fill their end of the storage facility. Paul and Jillian were hardly able to breath and were forced to abandon their temporary place of safety and venture out into the rear of the main aisle hoping that Jack had also had to flee the choking black smoke.

Once in the aisle and keeping low under the smoke the pair made their way to the back door only to find to their horror that Jack must have secured it after leaving by the same escape route. Paul tried to force the door open with his shoulder, discovering only then that he had been shot. In the end all they could do was stay low and shout for help in the hope that others would be in a position to provide it.

After what seemed an eternity and during which time both thought that death was the most likely outcome, the back door was opened and the pair were dragged outside into fresh air by uniformed officers.

Coughing badly, they were soon joined by Reg and June who were both adorned with helmets and flak jackets.

Jillian cried out as she lifted her skirt clear of the burns to her thighs and June seeing this and also realising that Paul was hurt as well, called for the ambulance that was on standby at the main gate to be brought up.

The ambulance, that had been driven up by an armed officer on the instructions of the officer in charge, now pulled up beside them. The rear doors opened and the driver, assault rifle in hand, now stood guard beside them as June and Reg helped the casualties inside.

Jillian laid on the bed as a paramedic gave her a much-needed painkilling injection and began treating her burns, while Paul removed his shirt so the second paramedic could dress his, thankfully not too deep, wound.

After a few minutes a uniformed Inspector looked round the ambulance door and asked, "Inspector Manly?"

"That's me," said Paul, anxious for news, "have you got him?"

"Not yet I'm afraid Sir, I'm informed he's familiar with the site and there are a million and one places he could be hiding, we have to be careful searching as we believe he's still armed. I'm Inspector Geoffrey Morgan by the way, it's a pleasure to meet you Sir"

"And you Inspector. I understand your caution, he's a nasty piece of work, were any of your men hurt in the fire?"

"No….the odd petrol bomb keeps them on their toes, it's good training for them, I was just thinking they were getting a little complacent and I was thinking about throwing the odd Molotov at them myself."

Paul grinned, "Well good luck with that Inspector," then turning to Reg, "do you think that would work with our lot Reg, the odd Molotov?"

"I'll leave you two to think that through," said Geoffrey as he walked away, "I'll let you know as soon as we find him."

Reg walked around to the side of the vehicle taking out his mobile, "I'll update the team Guv."

As Paul was having his wound dressed, he'd been marvelling at the amount of flame pouring out of the back door that had proved their salvation and wondering whether there could possibly have been enough combustible material inside to account for them. After all he reasoned, the building was mostly of metal construction, the interior shelving was metal and the vast majority of items stored were metal. The flame however quickly died off to be replaced by a plume of black smoke and just as Paul lost interest in what was emerging from the door, the figure of Jack Williams appeared from where he had been hiding in some discomfort behind the hot burning building. Gun in hand he now strode towards the back of the ambulance, firing as he came.

If anyone had asked Paul after he'd been dragged free of the fire, just what he had done with the pistol he'd used, he'd have been unable to tell them, but now, with death staring him in the face once again the weight of it is his pocket gave the answer. He quickly withdrew it, and as everyone else dived for cover, he gripped it firmly in both hands, took careful aim and fired.

Jack had managed to fire four rounds, the first two of which had been aimed at the armed officer whose back was towards him. The first round hit the officer's flak-jacket but the second pierced his upper thigh, dropping him to the ground. His third and forth shots were aimed at Paul, the third taking out the rear window of the ambulance and the fourth missing Paul's head by no more that an inch.

A fifth shot may well have found its target had not Paul's shot found the centre of Jack's chest, glancing off his sternum and tearing into his heart, stopping it and sending him to meet his maker, what or whoever that may have been.

Everyone came running at the sound of gunfire and one officer checked Jack for any signs of life and soon confirmed that he was dead. Paul dropped the gun to the ambulance floor and as all the turmoil and emotion of the past couple of days finally caught up with him, he put his head in his hands and broke down in tears.

As Inspector Geoffrey Morgan approached the rear of the vehicle June shut the ambulance doors.

"I believe there's a gun in there," Morgan enquired of her, "I now have to account for all the guns on site and for some reason Inspector Manley seems to have signed out three."

"I know you need to account for everything Sir," said June, "but please, my guvnors never shot and killed anybody before and I think he just needs a minute…..if that's alright Sir?"

Inspector Morgan seemed to understand, "Five minutes Constable."

"Thank you Sir."

Reg and the rest of the team clustered around wanting to know what was happening as the ambulance doors opened and Paul sat on the rear step.

"Is everyone alright?" asked Reg anxiously.

"Jillian's going to need a few operations and I would imagine some counselling, she's been through a horrendous ordeal, but apart from some scars I'm told she should make a full physical recovery," replied Paul.

"And what about you Guv?" asked June, "are you alright?"

"Yeh…it's just a flesh wound apparently June, though it hurts like the Devil….but I do have a question," said Paul, standing up.

"What's that Guv?"

"NOW! can I get my car sprayed?"

June and Reg exchanged a smile that said…Yeh…he's alright.

Other novels by Colin Holcombe

First Time Hard   ISBN : 978 1787233362

The Moving Finger Writes. ISBN : 978 1787233379

Murder Out of Bounds   ISBN : 978 1787233386

www.ingramcontent.com/pod-product-compliance
Lightning Source LLC
Chambersburg PA
CBHW071203100726
47908CB00002B/494